CUTTHROAT EXPRESS

BRYAN CASSIDAY

Bryan Cassiday
Los Angeles
ISBN 9781737628286
Published in the United States of America
First Edition: December 20, 2022

BOOKS BY BRYAN CASSIDAY

Knot of Fear (Scott Brody Thriller 5)
Threads (Scott Brody Thriller 4)
Electric Green Mambas (Scott Brody Thriller 3)
Horde (Zombie Apocalypse: The Chad Halverson Series Book 6)
Ice in the Blood
Crime Blotter USA
Murder LLC (Scott Brody Thriller 2)
Bolt (Scott Brody Thriller 1)
Riptide of Fear
The Payout
Force of Impact (Ethan Carr Thriller 3)
Dying to Breathe (Ethan Carr Thriller 2)
Countdown to Death (Ethan Carr Thriller 1)
The Bus Stops Here—and Other Zombie Tales
Two Moons Rising
Alien Assault
Comes a Chopper
Zombie Apocalypse: The Chad Halverson Series Books 1–5
Helter Skelter
The Anaconda Complex
The Kill Option
Blood Moon: Thrillers and Tales of Terror
Fete of Death

Chapter 1

The Mount Weather Emergency Operations Center bunker did what it was designed to do. It withstood the direct hit of an LGM-30G Minuteman III ICBM fitted with a W78 thermonuclear warhead with a yield of 350 kilotons.

The bunker's specially treated reinforced concrete deflected the EMP blast that accompanied the nuclear explosion, preventing the pulse from disrupting the electronic equipment harbored in the last redoubt of what remained of the US government.

Shaken up, Halverson and the denizens of the bunker nevertheless survived. Outside of the bunker, the radioactive fallout would kill all life in the vicinity for the next two weeks, though it wouldn't be instantaneous, depending on the amount of radiation exposure.

The radioactivity had no effect on the living dead. The millions that survived the impact of the blast continued to roam the mountainside that protected the bunker, foraging for living human flesh, having no luck, since all life had ceased in the blast range.

What remained of President Cole's body that had been obliterated by the missile he had triggered with the nuclear football lay scattered among the ghoul corpses. Halverson knew they would never be able to ID the mangled dollops of his corpse. Besides, nobody was going to search for human remains as long as zombies patrolled the area.

The president was dead, but it would take more than zombies and nukes to kill off the entire human race, decided Halverson, standing in the bunker surveillance room watching CCTV screens that were viewing the devastation of ground zero, including dead ghouls that had been torn apart by the nuclear explosion and hurled in every direction. Their mutilated bodies lay on the ground helter-skelter tossed like jackstraws as far as the eye could see.

Beyond the corpses, farther down the mountain slope, thousands of trees uprooted by the bomb blast strewed the ground, blocking the road that led to the bunker. Sporadic fires in the woods burned out of control on the scorched earth. Smoke billowed into the sky as ominous grey clouds gathered overhead.

"Looks like rain," said Halverson, CIA black ops agent, taking in the view with his grey eyes.

"The best thing for us," said Dr. Albert Morrow, President Cole's bald personal physician pushing sixty, who was standing near Halverson eying the CCTV monitor.

"How do you mean?"

"The rain will help clean the air of radiation."

"That reminds me. How long is our air gonna last here in the bunker?"

Face grim, Morrow stared at Halverson.

"We need to know," said Halverson.

"I'm not gonna sugarcoat it for you. We haven't got long to live without enough oxygen."

"Let's hear the worst."

"The vents were blocked by the ghouls before the nuclear blast, which actually helped us by keeping the nuke radiation out of the bunker. The ghouls in the air ducts helped prevent the blast from destroying the ducts. Our HEPA filters are keeping out the radiation as they are designed to do—except the ducts continue to be blocked by the ghouls, cutting off our oxygen."

"How long before there's no radiation?"

"At least two weeks."

"Do we have enough oxygen inside the bunker to last that long?"

Morrow paused a beat. "No. We'll have to reduce our intake of oxygen in order to last two weeks without fresh air."

"So?"

"If we reduce it enough, we can survive that long, but . . ."

"But what?"

"But we're all gonna feel sick because we won't get our required intake of oxygen. We'll have headaches and feel exhausted most of the time."

"We'll survive, though?"

Morrow shrugged. "Most of us should."

"Meaning?"

"Those with underlying conditions probably won't make it. Their lungs will collapse. Their hearts will give out."

"Jesus," said fortysomething Ben Strider, a SEAL senior chief petty officer, barging up to them in his imposing six-three frame. "Did I hear what I thought I just heard?"

"You wanted the truth," said Morrow.

"What if you're mistaken?"

"I hope I am. But the computers aren't—and that's where I got the information. The human body needs oxygen. We're not getting enough in this bunker with the air ducts blocked."

"What's the solution?"

"We have to reduce our oxygen intake for us to survive the next two weeks. It's gonna make us sick and tired. Unless we can get our hands on more oxygen canisters somehow."

Strider coughed. "The air's already stale."

"Our new president is following my advice. He ordered the oxygen level reduced in the ventilation system."

"So we have to feel like we're suffocating all the time?"

"Otherwise, we'll all be dead in a week."

"We'd all be better off making a run for it, I say."

"The radioactivity level is too high outside. It's enough to kill us. And don't forget the infected flesh eaters."

"Don't the president's specially equipped Suburbans have HEPA filters to keep out radioactive dust?"

"I believe they do. But you can't squeeze everyone in the bunker into those three vehicles."

"The escapees in the Suburbans could get help for the rest of us."

"Help? Help from who? Who's left out there in the nuclear badlands that can give us help?"

"You're bumming me out, Doc."

Morrow raised his eyebrows, but said nothing.

"Why'd that psycho Cole have to nuke us?" said Strider. "What the hell was he thinking? If he wanted to commit suicide, why'd he have to take all of us with him? This is what happens when you elect a nutcase for president."

"We need to move on," said Halverson. "Cole's not news anymore. He's history. We're not history yet."

"Oh yeah? How do we know we don't have another whack job as president? He might try to kill all of us, too."

"President Mims knows what he's doing," said Morrow. "I'll vouch for his sanity."

"Didn't you vouch for Cole's sanity?" said Strider.

Morrow glowered at Strider. "Are you questioning my medical skills?"

Retreating, Strider shook his head. "I don't know what I'm doing. When's this plague ever gonna end?"

"President Mims is fifty-five. He's in good health. He has all his faculties. I gave him a physical when he assumed office. He passed with flying colors."

"Somebody's coming," said Halverson, his eyes glued to the CCTV monitor, which displayed the area in front of the bunker entrance.

Chapter 2

"He must be a ghoul," said Strider, watching a figure on the monitor steering a motorcycle around the obstacle course of dead ghouls strewn on the road on his way to the bunker.

"Ghouls can't drive motorcycles," said Halverson. "They don't have the coordination."

"Well, he can't be human. The radiation would have killed him by now."

"Not necessarily," said Morrow. "He could have been outside the blast zone when the nuke hit."

"You said the radiation will kill us if we go outside."

"It will. But not right away. He could last another two weeks."

"Will he infect us with radiation poisoning if we let him inside?" said Halverson.

"Not if we decontaminate his clothing and skin," said Morrow.

"I say he's a ghoul," said Strider. "He's wearing that motorcycle helmet so we can't see his face. He doesn't want us to know he's a ghoul."

"Their brains are dead," said Halverson. "They can't think. That guy's alive."

"Not for much longer," said Strider, gripping the Brügger & Thomet MP9 strapped to his shoulder. "A couple of rounds from my little friend will make short work of him."

"He can give us news about what's going on in the rest of the country."

"Not if he's a ghoul."

Strider headed down the curved white ceramic-tiled tunnel toward the bunker entrance, which was sealed shut with a massive bombproof steel door. Halverson strode after him, the heels of his hiking boots thudding on the concrete floor.

"Don't expend a lot of energy," Morrow called after them. "You'll burn up too much oxygen. We have to conserve our oxygen if we want to live another two weeks."

"I'm not letting a ghoul in here, no matter what," said Strider over his shoulder.

"He's not a ghoul," said Halverson.

"Then how could he make it here alive? How could he live through a nuclear blast?"

"Didn't you hear what Morrow said about the blast zone?"

Strider waved him off. "He was President Cole's doctor. What does he know? Why didn't he tell us Cole was psychotic, if he knows so much?"

Strider and Halverson approached a CCTV monitor mounted on a wall in the vestibule that led to the blast door. They could see that the stranger had dismounted his motorcycle, abandoned it, and was loping toward the entrance. Wearing a helmet with a tinted visor shielding his face, he knocked on the steel door.

The steel was so thick Halverson couldn't hear the knocking.

Wandering ghouls had spotted the motorcyclist and were shambling after him over mounds of blast-victim cadavers, groping the air, tripping, and getting back up, eager to devour him.

The motorcyclist's knocking became more frantic.

He pressed the plastic button on the speakerphone.

"Let me in," he cried.

"He's not a ghoul," said Halverson. "He can talk. Those things can't talk."

"How can we be sure of that?" said Strider. "Maybe they've mutated. Maybe one of the plague variants has triggered the mutation that allows them to talk."

"At least let him in so we can question him. He deserves the benefit of the doubt."

"You'll regret it if he bites one of us."

"He's not a ghoul."

"Joon-ho, open the door so I can blast the ghoul," Strider told a twentysomething wiry Korean, who was standing near the door's control panel.

"You'll let the radiation in, sir," said Joon-ho, balking at the order.

"Close the door right after I blow him away."

"Right, sir," said Joon-ho, sounding reluctant.

"Belay that order," boomed President Mims's voice in the tunnel behind Strider and Halverson. "Nobody's blowing anybody away."

In his midfifties, clad in a bespoke dark business suit and red necktie, Walter Mims marched down the hall, the jaw on his

9

craggy face set. Just shy of six feet tall with a barrel chest, the erstwhile admiral with his military bearing cut a commanding figure. His shock of white hair jutted from his head like a crown of frost.

Chapter 3

"We need to kill the intruder, Mr. President," said Strider. "He's a ghoul trying to get in. Look at him on the CCTV."

Mims studied the CCTV screen and heard the motorcyclist yelling into the speakerphone to let him in.

"How can he be a ghoul?" said Mims. "He can talk."

"Maybe some of the ghouls can talk now."

"Not to my knowledge. Doctor?" said Mims, turning to Morrow.

"Not that I know of," said Morrow.

"Who is he? Is he one of ours sent out on a recon mission?"

"Negative, sir," said Strider. "We haven't sent anyone out since the nuke hit."

"We need to know what's going on in the rest of the country," said Mims. "Comms aren't working outside because of the EMP."

"He needs to be decontaminated, Mr. President," said Morrow.

"Let him in through the vehicle entrance. Decontaminate him when he's in the antechamber. Then let's hear what he has to say."

"Go around to the back door," Strider said into the speakerphone, watching the CCTV image of the motorcyclist.

The motorcyclist picked up his head at the sound of Strider's voice.

"Let me in," he cried. "This place is crawling with zeds."

"You have to be decontaminated first. Go to the back door."

The motorcyclist looked over his shoulder at three ghouls approaching in charred, blast-ripped clothes. Much of the flesh on their faces had melted in the intense heat of the explosion, making their faces look like plastic.

"They'll kill me," he said.

"Then get moving," said Strider. "You're not coming in this way."

"You're just gonna stand there and watch them tear me apart?"

"I suggest you shake a leg."

"Where's the back door?"

"Keep bearing right. You can't miss it."

Seeing a ghoul in tattered Bermudas dragging its feet three yards away from him, the motorcyclist bolted toward the back door. The ghoul trudged after him.

"Let him in," said Mims, heading down the ceramic-tiled tunnel to the bunker back door. "We need a firsthand report of what's happening outside since Cole fired the nuke."

Halverson, Strider, Morrow, and Joon-ho followed Mims.

"We need intel, men, and we need it bad," said Mims.

They entered the control room to the garage.

Eying the CCTV screen mounted on the wall which showed the motorcyclist pelting up to the back door, Strider pushed the green plastic button near the monitor.

The bombproof steel back door rose, allowing the motorcyclist to scramble under it and enter the sealed-off vestibule. The door lowered before any ghouls could enter.

"The decontamination room is on your right," said Strider through the loudspeaker.

"I'm not a ghoul," said the motorcyclist.

"You're covered with radioactive particles," said Dr. Morrow into the loudspeaker mic. "Enter the decontamination room, take off your clothes and your helmet, and shower down. Put on the terrycloth bathrobe hanging on the wall after you finish."

"I feel OK."

"You won't much longer," said Strider under his breath. "You're a dead man walking."

"Wash that radioactive dust off your body, and you'll be fine," said Mims into the loudspeaker mic. "Then we'll have a talk."

"What's this about radioactive dust?" said the motorcyclist, pulling a face.

"It's from a nuke that exploded here two days ago."

"I thought I saw a mushroom cloud when I was outside the other day. The ground was shaking, too. I wondered where the explosion was coming from."

"Now you know."

"I'm glad I wasn't here."

"Not that it's gonna do you any good with all that radioactive dust in your lungs," muttered Strider.

12

"Shh. Keep it down, Strider," said Mims, shutting off the mic. "If he knows he's gonna die, he might not talk. We need to know what's going on outside."

"I've never been much of a politician."

"I can see that."

The motorcyclist ducked into the decontamination room. Strider decontaminated the vestibule with the flick of a switch. Nozzles mounted in the walls sprayed decon foam into the vestibule neutralizing any radioactive dust that the motorcyclist might have brought with him.

The motorcyclist reappeared wearing a white terrycloth bathrobe, his hair still wet from his shower.

Strider raised the vestibule door electronically.

Mims, Halverson, Strider, and Morrow greeted the motorcyclist in the vestibule.

"It's hard to breathe in here," said the motorcyclist, coughing.

"I'm President Mims. What's your name?"

"Cassavetes. Mike Cassavetes. Wait a minute. Did you say 'president'? Cole is president."

In his midthirties with stubbled cheeks, standing five nine, Cassavetes had a hatchet face with brown eyes and black hair. His eyes gleaming with excitement, he was unable to stand still.

Morrow handed him an orange plastic bottle of pills. "Here. Take one of these pills every day."

"What are they?" said Cassavetes, accepting the bottle.

"Potassium iodide. They'll calm you down," Morrow lied. "You're hypertense."

Halverson cocked an eyebrow. Morrow wasn't going to tell Cassavetes the truth that potassium iodide was treatment for radiation poisoning, not hypertension, decided Halverson. Interesting. Halverson wasn't going to disabuse Cassavetes.

"Cole is dead," said Mims. "He died, valiantly defending the bunker."

Halverson rolled his eyes. Cole was the one who had fired the nuke. Cole had cracked up. There was nothing valiant about it. Political spin.

"Then you're the man to talk to," said Cassavetes. "The doctor sent me here to get help."

"What doctor?" said Mims.

"He found the vaccine for the zombie plague."

"Impossible."

Chapter 4

"It's true," said Cassavetes.

Halverson couldn't believe his ears.

Bowled over, Mims widened his eyes.

"Who's this doctor and where is he?" he said.

"Dr. Wheelhouse," said Cassavetes. "He needs help. His mountain hideout is surrounded by zeds. He's running out of food. We have to save him."

"You came from the hideout?"

Cassavetes nodded yes.

"How did you get past the ghouls?" said Halverson.

"I wasn't in the hideout when the zeds surrounded it. I was on my Harley foraging for food to bring back to our group. I couldn't get past the zeds to return to the hideout. The doc told me to drive here to get help from the government, if I ran into trouble. He told me to tell the president about the vaccine he discovered."

"There's no known vaccine for the zombie plague," said Morrow.

"The doc has found one. He wants the government to get it ASAP so they can give it to the people."

"This is fantastic," said Mims in amazement. "What do you think, Doctor?"

"If it's true, we need to get out hands on that vaccine." Morrow paused a beat. "I have my doubts. I've never heard of any Dr. Wheelhouse. If he's an expert in epidemiology, I should have heard of him."

"Do the ghouls have the entire mountain hideout surrounded?" Halverson asked Cassavetes.

Cassavetes nodded. "No way to get through them. Millions of them are squeezed together like sardines for over a mile. They're all heading for the hideout."

"Do you have comms?"

"We used to, but I haven't been able to get in touch with them since that nuclear explosion you were talking about."

"The EMP from the nuke knocked out everyone's electrical equipment."

"My cell phone doesn't work."

"All cell towers around here were wiped out by the blast and the EMP," said Mims.

"Where's that leave us?" said Cassavetes.

"In a spot. The question is, how do we get the vaccine?"

"I can take you to the mountain hideout. That's why the doc sent me. To be your guide."

"If you live that long," mumbled Strider.

"What?" said Cassavetes. "I couldn't hear you."

"Nothing."

"How long is it gonna take us to get there?" said Halverson.

"Depends on how many zeds we run into. They're blocking a lot of the roads," said Cassavetes, and suffered a coughing fit.

"You OK?" said Morrow.

"The air in here is putrid. What happened to your air purifiers?"

"We're running out of oxygen."

"Open your air vents."

"Zeds, as you call them, tried to get in here through the vents. Their corpses are blocking them."

"Can't you take them out?"

"They keep crawling back in," said Halverson.

"The nuke wasted thousands of them," said Strider, "but there were millions more where they came from."

"The only way we can get the breathable air in the bunker to last is by cutting down on the amount of oxygen we're inhaling," said Morrow. "We're inhaling just enough to stay alive."

"Then what?" said Cassavetes.

"We either find a way to clear the vents permanently, or we'll have to move out of here."

"Which is not a good option," said Mims. "All of our state-of-the-art equipment is here. And this bunker offers us the best protection from the ghouls."

"That's where you come in, Cassavetes," said Morrow. "Your vaccine would protect us and the other remnants of humanity from becoming infected with the plague."

"The only existing vaccine is in Wheelhouse's lab in the mountain hideout. We need to go back there. The reason I made it here safely is because he vaccinated me before I left."

16

There was an uneasy silence.

"It's a suicide mission," said Strider. "Everywhere is crawling with infected flesh eaters."

"When did that ever stop you?" said Mims.

Strider snorted a cynical laugh.

"Any other volunteers?" said Mims.

"You can't get there without me," said Cassavetes. "I'm the only one that knows the way."

"Didn't you write down your coordinates?" said Strider.

"I don't know anything about coordinates. I memorized my trip here."

Strider shook his head with disapproval. "Anyone else want to die? Halverson, this is a perfect fit for you. Mission impossible, and all that."

Probably true, decided Halverson. Ever since the ghouls had killed Victoria, he felt like something was missing from his life—a raison d'être. Her loss had made him feel empty inside. His life was meaningless.

Maybe his constant battle with the ghouls gave his life meaning without her. If he wasn't killing them, he didn't feel alive. He wanted to kill as many of the scumbags as possible.

"I'm in," he said.

Strider grinned. "I knew it. I read you like a book, man."

Halverson grunted.

"Anyone else," said Strider. "Let me see the hands of volunteers for our suicide mission."

"You really would make a lousy politician, Strider," said Mims.

"I told you, Mr. President."

"Does anyone else want to volunteer to save mankind?" said Mims, searching the faces of the group around him. "Raise your hand."

Nobody raised a hand.

"We're gonna need more than two people for any chance of success."

"I'm in," said Cassavetes."

"You're in for as long as you last," said Strider.

"What's that supposed to mean?"

"Let it go, Strider," said Mims.

"I don't understand," said Cassavetes.

"Don't pay any attention to Strider—except as your commanding officer during this mission."

"I don't get it. Is he calling me a pansy?"

"We need you," said Strider. "You're in."

Another coughing fit racked Cassavetes's body. "This bunker air sucks. I feel like I'm gonna be sick."

"It ain't just the bunker air."

"There you go again calling me a pansy."

"Strider, can it," said Mims.

"I'm gonna puke," said Cassavetes, turning green. "Is there a head around here?"

"Over here," said Halverson, and led him down the tunnel to a restroom.

When Halverson and Cassavetes were out of earshot, Mims called Strider over to him. "I want a word with you, Strider."

"Yes, Mr. President."

"Will you knock it off with the wisecracks?"

"He's gonna die from radiation poisoning, Mr. President. There's no way he can continue living much longer with all the radioactive dust he breathed when he was outside."

"You know that, and I know that. I don't want Cassavetes to know it. How would you like to know you're gonna drop dead any minute from radiation poisoning?"

"I wouldn't like it."

"Exactly. If he knows he's living on borrowed time, he might decide not to go on the mission with you. He's the only one who knows the directions. You need him with you."

"All right, sir. But what happens when he drops dead during the mission before we reach Wheelhouse?"

"We'll cross that bridge when we get to it. The sooner you start the mission, the better."

"Three people isn't enough for a successful mission— especially when one of them will die en route."

"Stop talking like that."

"It's a suicide mission, sir."

Mims shot him a reproachful look. "I know you need more than three people. I also know a lot of people who will want to volunteer."

"Sir?" said Strider, puzzled.

"You know perfectly well who I'm talking about."

The puzzled expression remained on Strider's face.

Chapter 5

Halverson combed his cropped hair as he stood in front of the mirror over the sinks in the restroom and listened to Cassavetes puking his guts out in one of the stalls.

The guy didn't sound good, decided Halverson. He wondered how long Cassavetes could live with all that radioactive dust in his lungs. Nobody could save the guy now. The damage was done.

Halverson heard the toilet flush.

Cassavetes staggered out of the stall, wiping his mouth.

"The air in this place is impossible to breathe," he said. "How can you guys stand it?"

"You get used to it."

"It literally makes me sick," said Cassavetes, approaching a sink.

He splashed cold water onto his face.

"We're not gonna be here much longer, anyway," said Halverson. "We need you to guide us to Wheelhouse."

"I don't know how much longer he can hold out. The zeds are surrounding him. We're gonna need a couple of battalions to get through them."

"Not gonna happen."

Cassavetes confronted Halverson. "Why not? I'm talking millions of zeds."

"We'll be lucky to get ten guys to go with us."

Cassavetes's eyes popped. "Ten guys against a million zeds. Are you kidding me?"

"Exactly why nobody wants to volunteer. They know it's a suicide mission."

"Why doesn't the president order a battalion to go with us?"

"We don't have a battalion."

"Then he should order everyone here to go—to give us half a chance."

Halverson ran his fingers through his hair, studying his reflection in the mirror.

"He's not gonna do that," he said. "Mims is a decent guy. He's not gonna order anyone to their deaths. He's only accepting volunteers for this mission."

Cassavetes stared at the image of his drawn face in the mirror. "Then we're doomed."

Halverson said nothing.

"Wheelhouse told me you had battalions here that could rescue us," said Cassavetes.

"His intel's wrong."

"I don't understand. Don't you guys want the vaccine?"

"Of course."

"Then everybody in this bunker should go to rescue Wheelhouse."

"You're not the one to make that decision."

"I just want half a chance to save Wheelhouse and get the vaccine."

"You don't understand. The president said only volunteers will go."

Cassavetes shook his head. "There are too many zeds at the hideout."

"You made it alone. We can do it with our volunteer force."

"I'm vaccinated. None of you are. If we're going back with only ten people, we're DOA."

"Can you imagine how dull life would be, if we lived forever?"

"I'm only twenty-eight. I want to live at least past this year. I'm not even married. I'd like to marry and have kids."

Halverson wasn't going to tell Cassavetes the guy wouldn't last another year. Maybe not even another week with all the radioactive dust Cassavetes had inhaled on his trek to the bunker.

"Welcome to the apocalypse," said Halverson.

The klaxon sounded.

"What's that?" said Cassavetes.

"Break-in," said Halverson, whipped a SIG P365 semiautomatic from his hip holster, and burst out of the restroom.

A red warning light flashed in the hallway, as the klaxon blared.

Chapter 6

"Section 6 is breached," announced a voice over the loudspeaker.

Halverson belted to section 6, as did other members of the bunker. Cassavetes followed him.

When Halverson reached the section, he saw an open air vent with a ghoul crawling out of it. Having entered through the air duct, two other ghouls were shambling across the floor.

Strider charged into the room and trained his MP9 on the lead ghoul, who was a roly-poly middle-aged guy with a creased, decomposing jowly face. He was wearing a Padres ball cap askew on his head. Strider squeezed off a burst from his weapon. The 9mm slugs blew the ghoul's face into a cloud of shards, sending the cap flying.

Behind Padres the thirtyish blonde ghoul whose gobs of makeup did her putrefying looks little good was wearing a cranberry tracksuit smeared with coagulated blood and staring at a cell phone in her hand like she knew what she was doing. She looked up at Halverson and snarled at him. Hanging her mouth ajar, she exposed her fragmented teeth, half of which were black and carious.

Halverson double-tapped her head with his SIG. One of her green eyes popped out of her skull and dropped to the floor, followed by the blonde, whose brain Halverson had grooved with lead.

A skinny male ghoul in his twenties tried to scrabble out of the duct, groping at the air and squirming.

Strider raked the ghoul's face with a burst from his MP9, all but splitting the ghoul's head in half.

Halverson didn't know what was holding the ghoul's skull together, as the ghoul continued to flail away in the duct.

"That zed doesn't know it's croaked," said Cassavetes.

"I guess its brain is still intact," said Halverson.

Halverson waltzed up to the ghoul and fired three slugs into its forehead. The ghoul stopped moving and became limp. Halverson latched onto the ghoul's jaw and hauled the body out of the duct.

"Watch out for that thing's teeth," said Cassavetes.

Halverson dumped the corpse on the floor without touching the creature's teeth.

He noticed flies swarming out of another air vent twenty feet away. He strode over to it.

"This duct shouldn't be open," he said, swatting at the flies.

As he reached the duct, a hand shot out of it and attempted to grab Halverson's arm. Halverson yanked his arm out of the creature's grasp. Dressed in a cop uniform, a milky-eyed redheaded female with her hair in a disheveled bun tried to squirm out of the vent, swiveling her head and growling.

Halverson put two bullets into her temple. She stopped squirming.

He snagged her arm, yanked her out of the vent, and dropped her carcass on the floor.

"We need to shut these air ducts," said Strider. "The HEPA filters have been breached. Radioactive dust is entering the bunker."

"The ghouls keep breaking through," said Joon-ho.

"Fill these vents with concrete," said Halverson. "It's the only way to stop them."

"I'm way ahead of you," said Strider. "I sent for a detail of masons to take care of it."

Halverson plugged a teenage male ghoul with long, straggly hair who was trying to writhe out of the first vent.

"Halverson, you and Joon-ho are with me," said Strider. "The president wants to see us. You too, Cassavetes."

Halverson, Joon-ho, and Cassavetes followed Strider out of section 6, as a team of cement masons wheeled in a cement mixer toward the open vents.

Chapter 7

Strider led Halverson, Cassavetes, and Joon-ho to the president.

His face haggard, Mims was sitting behind his desk in his windowless bunker office, the Stars and Stripes hanging from a flagpole behind him.

"I'm having trouble getting volunteers, Strider," he said.

"Maybe you shouldn't tell them it's a suicide mission, Mr. President," said Strider.

"I haven't used those exact words. But they should know what they're getting into. They have that right."

"I'm only going because I have to and I'm vaccinated," said Cassavetes. "I know what's waiting for us."

"Do any of you have any ideas how I can get volunteers?"

"You told me earlier you knew people who would volunteer, Mr. President."

"They let me down. Well, what about it? Any ideas?"

Nobody answered right away.

"I know guys who'd volunteer, Mr. President," said Halverson.

"They'd have to be real patriots. Do you know such men?"

"No. But what about the prisoners in section 8?"

"They're in the brig."

"Offer them a pardon if they agree to go on the mission."

"Those losers are the bottom of the barrel," said Strider. "You're talking rapists, murderers, and serial killers. The mission would never succeed with them."

"I'm not so sure," said Mims, thinking about it.

"You want me to lead a squadron of murderers and rapists on a suicide mission?" said Strider, flabbergasted.

"You need killers. And those guys are killers."

"The problem is, they would probably kill the rest of us on the mission."

Mims ignored him. "They have nothing to lose. I think they'd go for it."

"Can I give you my honest opinion, Mr. President?" said Strider.

"Go ahead."

"It's a bad idea. If the ghouls don't kill us, the convicts will."

"We don't have any other choices. If you want out, let me know. I'm not gonna force anyone on this mission, not even you, Strider."

Strider chuffed. He rubbed the back of his neck.

"Let me remind you, we need that vaccine," said Mims. "It's the only thing that will give us a chance against the ghouls."

"Living like this is no option," said Strider, grim-faced.

"I knew I could count on you. Halverson? Are you in if your team includes criminals?"

Halverson's life was a train wreck. The ghouls had killed Victoria, the only one he cared about. They had also killed his brother. He was alone with nothing to live for. He felt like he was standing around waiting for death.

"A suicide mission's right up my alley," he said.

"Good man. Cassavetes? We need you. Without you, there's no mission. You're the one who knows the way."

"Nobody said anything about teaming up with serial killers," said Cassavetes.

"It's the end of the world," said Halverson. "What do you expect?"

"This plan sounds nuts."

"Got a better one?"

"How about a drink?"

"I'm glad you're on board, Cassavetes," said Mims. "How about you, Joon-ho?"

"Can I talk to you in private, sir?" said Joon-ho.

"Why certainly," said Mims and drew him aside.

"The doc says I'm dying of pancreatic cancer," said Joon-ho, keeping his voice low. "So, I'm in. Gonna die, anyway, you know." He gave a hopeless shrug.

Nodding, Mims patted him on the back.

They returned to the group.

"The country can't thank all of you enough for your sacrifices," said Mims, eying the volunteers. "I'll give each of you a Medal of Honor when you return."

"And if we don't return?" said Strider.

"Eliminate the negative and accentuate the positive. You *will* return."

"I already got a death sentence hanging over my head, anyway, even if we return," muttered Joon-ho.

"As long as we don't return in pine boxes," said Cassavetes.

"You need to eliminate the negative, Cassavetes," said Mims.

"Yes, sir."

"Strider, you and Halverson pick the rest of the team from section 8."

"The cons will be overjoyed to see us when they hear our deal," deadpanned Halverson.

Mims removed a manila folder from a desk drawer and beckoned to Strider.

"Here are your choices for new recruits," said Mims. "This is a file of the names of the convicts in the stockade."

Strider approached the president's desk, accepted the file, and flipped through it, reading the convicts' names and their criminal records.

"We could always use a serial killer," said Strider, studying a con's rap sheet. "This guy Rafferty sounds like a prime candidate for our dream team."

"I don't think this is funny," said Cassavetes.

"How can we take a suicide mission seriously?"

"All right," said Mims, "knock it off. Strider, you and Halverson go down and handpick your recruits. I want you men to leave chop-chop to save Wheelhouse and get that vaccine."

Strider and Halverson retreated from the president's office.

"The cons are gonna want to whack us more than they want to do the ghouls," Halverson told Strider on their way out the door. "We represent the government that put them behind bars."

"It should keep us on our toes," said Strider, file in hand.

"Or put us in our graves."

Strider cracked a grin. "Not you. Aren't you immortal?"

"Not likely."

"We wrote you off for dead a long time ago, and then you show up on our doorstep nailed to a cross. Not many guys could pull that off."

"I got lucky."

Strider laughed. "We're gonna need more than luck to pull off this miracle."

Chapter 8

Clad in an orange jumpsuit, Rudolf Damon was sitting in his
jail cell watching a fly buzzing around his head. Like the rest of the
male prisoners, he had a buzz cut. All of thirty-three years old, he
was short and skinny, but exuded manic energy like a modern-day
version of Charles Manson. Damon's eyes cut quickly back and
forth as they watched the bluebottle.

Strider and Halverson appeared at the door to Damon's cell.

"This is Rudolf Damon," said Strider, reading Damon's
dossier, "aka the Cincinnati Cannibal. He murdered ten teenage
boys during a three-month killing spree. He attracted them to his
house by selling them dope, like weed and Molly. After he tortured
and knifed them to death, he butchered, boiled, and ate their body
parts."

Damon picked up a paperback thriller he had been reading,
tore off a page, and started chewing it.

"People taste better," he said, his mouth full.

"We'll make you a proposition, Damon," said Strider, looking
up from Damon's rap sheet. "How would you like to eat some
zombies?"

Damon cut his eyes back and forth following the fly buzzing
around his head.

"Why, I wouldn't hurt a fly," he said.

"Yeah, you and Norman Bates," said Strider. "It's a ticket out
of here if you say yes. A presidential pardon. Are you listening,
idiot?"

Damon kept watching the fly swooping in front of his face.

"What do I have to do?" he said.

"Join us on our suicide mission to get the vaccine for the
zombie plague."

"Why me?"

"The president wants only volunteers."

"President Cole? I didn't vote for him."

"Cole's dead. Our new president is Walter Mims."

"What happened to Cole?"

"He nuked himself."

Damon continued watching the fly soaring around the cell.

"Let me get this straight," he said. "All I do is join your mission and I get a presidential pardon?"

"Not quite," said Halverson, who had been watching Damon's antics. "You have to survive the mission to get the pardon."

"What am I supposed to do on this mission?"

"Kill ghouls," said Strider.

"Sounds like fun," said Damon, preoccupied with watching the fly.

The fly landed on his knee.

"We thought you'd say that," said Strider. "Welcome aboard our pleasure cruise."

"You see, I'm not gonna kill that fly, even though it would be a piece of cake with a swat of my hand," said Damon, staring with his eyes crossed at the fly as it crooked its leg.

"You can go back to eating your book. We'll return for you later."

Damon ignored him, entranced by the fly.

"With him onboard, our chances are looking up," said Halverson.

Strider shook his head in disgust, as he headed to the next cell.

Chapter 9

"Next up, Rafferty," said Strider, coming to a halt in front of another cell.

A tad short of five nine, Rafferty had a stocky build, and was doing pushups on his cell floor. He had thick black hair stubble on his head and sported a walrus mustache.

He paid no attention to Strider and Halverson.

"What's his claim to fame?" said Halverson.

"He's a serial killer," said Strider, reading the dossier in his hands. "He's a married man with a wife and two girls. He was a carpenter who lived in a suburban house in Glen Rock, New Jersey. He would bury his victims under the floors of the houses he helped build. He murdered ninety women over a period of seven years. His wife and children had no idea of his second life. He was captured at the age of thirty-five after a German shepherd at one of the houses he built dug up the corpse he had buried there. He's now thirty-eight."

"Ninety-one," said Rafferty, continuing his pushups.

"Are you talking about your pushups?" said Halverson.

"I'm talking about my victims, wise guy. Get your facts straight."

"Your rap sheet says ninety," said Strider.

"It's wrong. Our corrupt government wrote it, right? They lie about everything. What do you expect?"

"You sound proud of butchering women."

"They were hookers, runaways, and skanks. Nobody cried at their funerals. Nobody cared."

"You're a piece of work."

"Want my autograph? Is that what this is about?" said Rafferty, finishing his pushups and getting to his feet, his face flushed and sweaty.

"I'd like to waste you, honestly."

"Is this visit about the lethal injection I'm supposed to get?" said Rafferty, wiping sweat off his brow with the back of his wrist.

"In a way."

Rafferty looked puzzled.

"We're authorized to make you a deal," said Strider.

"Authorized by who?"

"The president of the United States."

"What's the offer? A choice between lethal injection and a firing squad?" said Rafferty.

"That's what I would offer you."

"Very funny. I bet you're running short on lethal injections in this dump," said Rafferty, surveying his cramped cell with disdain. "The air sucks in here, by the way."

"That's not the offer," said Halverson.

"OK. What is it?"

"Do I have to?" Strider asked Halverson.

"You heard the president," answered Halverson.

"I'd rather just walk away."

"He didn't give you that option."

"Are you finished with the Abbott and Costello routine?" said Rafferty.

His expression sour, Strider faced Rafferty. "The president is prepared to offer you a full pardon if you take part in our mission to obtain the vaccine for the zombie plague."

"What's the catch?" said Rafferty.

"It's a suicide mission," said Halverson.

"In place of lethal injection?"

"Do you accept or not?" said Strider.

"Why am I being given a choice?" said Rafferty, confused.

"The president wants all volunteers. If you don't volunteer, you don't go with us."

"A choice between this dump and a suicide mission, huh? I gotta think about it."

"Now who's the one cracking jokes?" said Halverson.

"The clock is ticking," said Strider. "We're getting ready to go."

"I get a full pardon when we come back?"

"That's the deal."

"Like I said, the air sucks in here. I'll take the offer."

"Surprise, surprise," said Halverson.

"Are you two goons going, too?"

"Uh-huh."

"What? You don't like living either?"

Strider and Halverson walked away.

"I want it in writing," Rafferty called after them, grabbing his cell bars. "I don't trust politicians. Know how to tell a politician's lying? When he opens his mouth. Where's my lawyer?"

"You can bring him along on the mission," said Strider.

Rafferty gave the bird to the back of Strider's head.

Chapter 10

Strider and Halverson proceeded to the next cell.

"What do we have here?" said Halverson.

Strider consulted his dossier. "An armed robber. Stefan Purl."

A thirtyish muscular black man sat on his bunk reading a dog-eared paperback copy of *Soul on Ice* by Eldridge Cleaver. Purl ignored his company and continued reading.

"Purl robbed a Wells Fargo bank in Chicago and shot and killed two cops on the premises," said Strider, reading Purl's rap sheet out loud.

"Why'd you have to kill them?" Halverson asked Purl.

"Because they were in my way," answered Purl, not looking up from his book.

"Why'd you rob the bank in the first place?" asked Strider.

"Because I needed money," answered Purl. "Why does anyone rob a bank?" Purl continued staring at the book in his hands. "My girlfriend was in the hospital on account of a car accident, and I needed to pay for her surgery."

"And that gives you the right to whack out people?"

"I have the right to live, and so did my girlfriend—when she was alive."

"What about the two cops you took out?"

"What about them?"

"Don't they have rights?"

"Collateral damage. My girlfriend needed surgery. I couldn't afford it. So I went to the bank to make a withdrawal."

"My heart bleeds for you, cop killer."

"Then get the hell out of here," said Purl, flinging his book at Strider. "I didn't ask for your company."

Strider flinched as the book bounced off the cell's steel bars and fell to the floor.

"It wasn't my idea to come here," said Strider, glaring at Purl.

Purl eyed his book on the floor, reading the title. "*Soul on Ice.* That's a good title for a book. The story of my life."

"I could care less about your life. You're a cold-blooded murderer."

"I ought to write a book. The things I could tell you would make your hair stand on end."

"Let's cut to the chase," said Strider, irritated.

"Fine with me. Good-bye."

"Listen up. The president sent me. He wants to offer you a pardon."

Purl guffawed, slapping his large hands on his knees. "Of course, he does. And I'm a millionaire in disguise."

"All you have to do is go on our suicide mission," said Halverson, his face wooden.

"You guys crack me up. Tweedledum and Tweedledee."

"He's not kidding," said Strider.

"What did I do to deserve this presidential pardon?" said Purl.

"It's what you're gonna do."

"From my cozy jail cell?"

"You're coming with us to get the vaccine for the zombie plague." Strider paused for effect. "If you agree to volunteer."

"The president's not forcing anyone to go," said Halverson.

"All I have to do is volunteer, and I'm out of here?"

"Easy-peasy, huh?"

"Except for one little thing. It's a suicide mission," said Strider. "Which means, you're not coming back."

"I get it. I'm volunteering to suicide myself to save the taxpayers money on a lethal injection. Is that it? It's all about money with the government, isn't it?"

"Look, I don't enjoy talking to you. It wasn't my idea. It's the president's. Do you volunteer or not?"

Strider sounded more pissed off than usual, decided Halverson. He wondered why.

"Sounds like my kind of deal," said Purl. "The same kind of deal I been getting all my life. A raw deal," said Purl with amusement. "Nobody's better than the Man at making raw deals."

"You wanna just sit here and feel sorry for yourself?"

"It sounds like you're in charge of the mission."

"What of it?"

"Isn't the president coming with us?"

"He has to lead the country."

"What's left of it," said Halverson.

"That figures," said Purl. "The president gets this bright idea of a suicide mission and picks the guys who go on it. Easy for him. Is there some way I can become president? Fat chance, huh?"

"Are you done flapping your gums?" said Strider. "Do you accept the offer or not?"

"I been getting suckered all my life by the Man. I might as well get suckered again. I'm in."

"There's a special hell for cop killers."

"I guess you're gonna be my guide there."

Purl stood up, well over six-feet tall, strutted over to Strider, and stared at him.

"My pleasure," snarled Strider.

Chapter 11

"Next victim," said Halverson, walking with Strider to the last cell on Strider's list.

Clad in her orange prison garb, a five-ten slender blonde sporting a pageboy cut was standing in her cell staring at them, as if she expected them.

Strider took up position in front of the cell door and read the woman's rap sheet.

"I knew you'd be coming any minute," she said.

"Why?" said Halverson.

"I had a premonition that something evil was coming my way."

"I get the feeling I'm gonna like you, Laci Vostok," said Strider without looking up from his rap sheet in his hands.

"I doubt it," she said.

"Laci Vostok, age twenty-eight, from Murfreesboro, Tennessee, left a dysfunctional family of alcoholics and joined the army. Father a foreman in a steel factory."

"When he wasn't out of work—which was most of the time."

"You two didn't get along, I take it."

"My father didn't like himself so he took it out on me when he got drunk."

"It says here you killed your CO," said Strider, looking up from her rap sheet at her. "You don't like COs?"

"Not if they try to rape me."

Strider read further. "He was never able to tell his side of the story, and there weren't any witnesses to corroborate your testimony."

"Well, he wouldn't assault me while other people were present, would he?"

"We have to take your word for it."

"You think I made it up?"

"You were found guilty of murder."

"I was railroaded by another CO who testified against me. He said I had a history of disobeying orders. He was another asshole who wanted to get inside my pants."

"How did you kill him?" said Halverson.

"I kneed him in the groin. When he buckled over, I shot him in the head with his service revolver."

"Am I gonna have to watch my back when I'm around you?" said Strider.

"Not much I can do to you behind bars, is there?"

"I have a proposition for you. The president has, actually."

"You COs are all alike with your propositioning women," said Laci.

"You're right that I will be your CO. Let me rephrase this. The president is offering to grant you a full pardon if you join our mission."

"What kind of mission?"

"A suicide mission," said Halverson.

"I sort of like the décor here," said Laci, "*and* my friends the rats that snuggle with me at night and keep me company."

"You'd rather face a firing squad?" said Strider.

"Get executed here or get executed on a suicide mission. Some choice."

"I don't have to remind you you're not in a good bargaining position."

"You guys really know how to attract a girl," said Laci, her lips dripping with sarcasm, prinking her hair.

"You have a problem with authority figures. Is that it?"

"Does anyone like being told what to do?"

"A lot of people do. Otherwise, they wouldn't know what to do with themselves."

"I don't have any problem figuring out what to do with myself. I don't need somebody ordering me around."

"Somebody's got to be in charge. It's the way of the world."

"The world is a hellhole."

"It is now," said Halverson, thinking about the hordes of ghouls shambling amok across the nuke-devastated wasteland.

"It always has been," said Laci. "As long as the lying assholes are in charge, it always will be."

"Is this your way of saying yes?" said Strider.

"What if I told you to take your offer and shove it?"

Strider shrugged. "Your choice. We can only take volunteers. If you don't volunteer, you're staying put."

He adjusted his folder containing the dossiers and walked away, Halverson in tow.

"I'm in," she said. "What have I got to lose? I'm dead whether I stay or go. But if you put the moves on me, CO, I will kill you. You know I will."

"This is starting out well," Halverson told Strider.

Strider gave him a look.

Chapter 12

Strider and Halverson met Marta Costello walking toward them in the ceramic tunnel, as they headed to the president's office. She was wearing jeans and a white blouse.

In her twenties, her body toned, Marta had survived the psychotic cult leader Zodiac as had Halverson before they had made their way to the safety of the Mount Weather bunker. She was a coder before the apocalypse who had also survived a rapist and the resulting Stockholm Syndrome before she had teamed up with Halverson.

She had a trusting face, which never ceased being disillusioned by people.

"I want to volunteer for the mission," she said.

The three of them came to a halt in the tunnel.

Strider searched her face with puzzlement. "You do realize it's a suicide mission?"

"I do. I feel cooped up here. I feel sick all of the time because of the noxious air. And I'm claustrophobic. This bunker freaks me out. I want out."

"Even if it means a headstone with your name on it?" said Halverson.

"I'm positive I'm gonna die here if I stay. This bunker is a coffin," she said, pulling at her blouse collar so she could breathe, her face smeared with sweat.

"The other members of this suicide team are homicidal maniacs. Are you OK with that?"

"I survived a rapist and that Zodiac psycho. All I know is, I have to get out of here."

"We got a serial killer/rapist, a cannibal, a CO killer, and a cop killer in this gang of cutthroats," said Strider. "Any one of them could decide to murder the whole team."

"I want out of here. I don't care who's coming with us."

"You might come to regret your decision—too late."

"It's my decision."

Strider turned to Halverson. "I'm thinking of scrubbing the mission."

"The president won't like it."

"What's to stop this gang of psycho killers from killing us?"

"We'll have to keep our eyes peeled."

"I don't like the idea of giving psychos guns."

"Don't arm them till we get into a fight with the ghouls."

"Even then, I don't like the idea," said Strider, shaking his head.

"Then give them knives."

"So they can shove them in our backs?"

"We can't let our guard down."

"These guys aren't choirboys," said Strider, exasperated. "Especially Rafferty. He's dangerous because he appears normal. He's anything but. He was married with a family and was normal to all appearances, going to church on Sundays and raising his two daughters. Even while he was raping and murdering ninety-one women, nobody thought there was anything odd about him. Even his own wife and kids didn't suspect him."

"We know he's a serial killer, so we'll be on our guard."

"Are you guys trying to get me to change my mind?" said Marta. "If you are, you're failing."

"As long as you're volunteering, we'll take you," said Strider. "The president told me to accept any and all volunteers. The problem is, the other volunteers are homicidal maniacs—except for you, Halverson, and Joon-ho, that is."

"You forgot Cassavetes," said Halverson.

"Who's living on borrowed time."

"What are we waiting for?" said Marta.

"You can't back out, once we leave," said Strider. "We're not gonna double back for anybody. You better be damn sure about your decision to go with us."

"The sooner we get out of this crypt, the better," said Marta, coughing on the fetid air.

"If you stay here, you'll probably live a little longer," said Halverson.

"If you call this living. I can't even breathe."

"We don't have time to dick around," said Strider. "Let's see Mims."

He strode down the tunnel. Halverson and Marta followed him.

"Do we have enough people?" said Marta.

"It makes no difference how many we have," said Halverson. "This mission can't succeed."

"Maybe it can," said Strider.

Halverson did a double take. "Why the about-face? You don't want to scrub the mission anymore?"

"I thought it over."

"What are you talking about?"

"If Cassavetes could make it here by himself, why can't our team of determined and well-armed folks make it back to his starting point?"

"I prefer you when you're not cracking jokes."

"I'm serious. Cassavetes did it. Why can't we?"

"He didn't have a bunch of murdering psychopaths with him."

"What's to prevent them from scramming once they get their hands on guns?" said Marta.

"Where are they gonna scram to?" said Strider. "The infected ghouls are everywhere. No place is safe."

"I can't believe there aren't safer places than this bunker somewhere out there where you can breathe," said Marta, screwing up her face, her complexion ashen.

"Let's tell the president we're ready to rock and roll," said Strider, his gait determined.

"Is this what they call DEFCON 3?"

"We're way beyond DEFCON 3," said Halverson. "We're at DEFCON 1. This is all-out war on the infected ghouls."

"What are we calling this operation?"

"Operation Death Guaranteed."

"Let me remind you, we need that vaccine," said Strider.

Chapter 13

When Halverson, Strider, and Marta entered the president's office, Cassavetes was standing with Mims waiting for them. Cassavetes had exchanged his terrycloth bathrobe for jeans and an olive drab T-shirt.

"Did you get enough volunteers?" said Mims, wheezing on the inadequate oxygen in the room.

"Cassavetes made it here by himself," said Strider. "I guess we can make it to his hideout with our group of nine."

"Nine is all you could round up?" said Mims, the disappointment obvious on his face.

"The only volunteers we got from the convicts were the ones on death row."

"Half of our crew will be serial killers and the like," said Halverson.

Holding his head down in thought, Mims paced in a small circle behind his desk.

"Is that enough people?" said Mims, holding his head up.

"How many is enough to commit suicide?"

"We're not talking about a circular firing squad," rapped out Mims. "We're talking about a mission to get the vaccine that's our only hope of survival."

"We're surrounded by millions of zombies—more like billions. They're gonna do everything they can to stop us."

"You sound like a defeatist, Halverson. If you want out, say so. I want only volunteers on this mission."

"If anyone can do it, we can," said Halverson, his face unreadable.

"That's more like it."

"I second that," said Strider, standing to attention.

Mims cleared his throat.

"Cassavetes told me something you're all entitled to know," he said, eyes sincere as he searched everyone's face.

"It's about time we got some good news," said Strider.

Mims ignored him. "Cassavetes told me Dr. Wheelhouse vaccinated him before he came here."

"I guess it must work," said Marta, cheering up.

"The point is, all of you *aren't* gonna have that same protection when you leave."

"Did any of the ghouls bite you?" Halverson asked Cassavetes.

"No," answered Cassavetes.

"Then how can we be sure it works?"

"None of them bit me because they knew I was vaccinated. They have a sixth sense about it. It prevented them from biting me."

"So it works like garlic keeping away vampires?"

"Why not?"

"Or maybe you just beat the odds and didn't get bit."

"I'm telling you, the doc vaccinated me. The vaccine works."

"We need to get our hands on it," said Mims, rubbing his hands together. "We can save our country with the vaccine." He became thoughtful. "We'll call it Operation Save America." His eyes beamed. "Yes, I like the sound of that. Operation Save America," he said, pumping his right fist.

Total silence.

"I'm glad all of you agree," he said. He turned to Strider. "Where's the rest of your team?"

"In the joint, Mr. President. It's not safe to let them out till we're ready to leave."

"Of course. I hope they understand the importance of their mission."

Nobody said anything.

"I'm sure they do," said Mims. "This is the most important mission ever undertaken in this country. Our very survival as a nation depends on the mission's success."

"Want me to bring them here so you can give them their orders, Mr. President?" said Strider. "I can have prison guards bring them. They're in sore need of a pep talk."

"They won't all fit in here. Take them to the situation room."

"Yes, sir," said Strider, saluting Mims.

"I'll be there shortly."

Everyone filed out of the office, leaving Mims alone with his thoughts.

Chapter 14

Their wrists handcuffed, their ankles shackled, Rafferty, Rudolf Damon, Stefan Purl, and Laci Vostok made their way down the tunnel, escorted by four prison guards.

"How are we supposed to kill the infected in these things?" said Rafferty, lifting up his shackled foot and rattling his chain. "We won't stand a chance."

"I knew this 'pardon' was a put-up job," said Damon. "Instead of getting lethal injections, we're gonna get fed to infected ghouls."

"Just what you deserve."

"What do you mean by that?" said Damon, taking umbrage.

"You're a cannibal, aren't you? Time for you to pay the price and get cannibalized," said Rafferty, laughing scornfully. "What goes around comes around."

"And you're supposed to be better than me because you're a serial killer? Give me a break."

"I have no respect for cannibals. When you eat one of your own, that's the pits."

"I have no respect for serial killers. At least, when I kill, I eat my victim. Like other animals do. We kill to eat. It serves the purpose of keeping me alive. Being a serial killer serves no purpose. It's a waste."

"What do you mean, it serves no purpose? It's entertainment to me."

"Murdering a bunch of women is entertaining?"

"They deserved to die. They were hookers and sluts. Nobody wanted them around, so I got rid of them. Let me tell you, it was fun doing it, and I did the human race a favor."

"I have no respect for you. To kill for pleasure makes no sense."

"You're no better than a zombie. You kill and eat your victims just like they do."

The prisoners' chains clattered as they dragged them along the tunnel floor.

"Where are they taking us?" said Purl. "Are they gonna feed us to the infected?"

"We're going to the situation room," said Rafferty.

"What's that?" said Damon.

"It's where the president starts wars."

"Maybe he'll give us guns there," said Purl.

"I heard you rob banks and murder cops," Damon told Purl.

"I ain't braggin'."

"I got no respect for bank robbers and cop killers."

"You got no respect for nobody. What do I care?"

"I kill for food. I'm better than you."

"Why don't you write a cookbook?" said Rafferty. "I got the perfect title. *To Serve Man*."

Damon shot Rafferty a dirty look.

Purl groaned. "This is gonna be a long journey.'

"I'm hungry," said Laci.

Damon leered at her. "Me, too."

"Me, three," said Rafferty, ogling her.

"I don't respect either one of you," said Laci. "You're both so ugly, neither one of you could get a date."

"Knock it off," said the lead uniform, a bald, fortysomething fireplug.

"She's OK," said Purl. "She killed her CO."

"We're off to see the big guy," said Rafferty, smiling. "Everybody, try to look presentable."

"Ha ha," said Laci, her face expressionless.

"Politics," said Purl, shaking his head. "I never voted in my life."

"Makes no difference which liar you vote for," said Damon. "One bum takes the place of another on election day. That's what I always say."

"You sound like a genius."

Damon scowled at Purl.

"We're all geniuses here," said Rafferty. "That's why we're in chains."

"We're a threat to their authority," said Damon. "That's why they keep us locked up."

"I thought it was because we're murderers," said Purl.

"Look at you. You killed some cops so you could pay for your main squeeze's operation. That makes you a threat to their authority."

"I don't see the connection. Saving my girlfriend is a threat to them?"

"Because you killed a cop, the symbol of the Man's authority."

"I'd rather be in solitary confinement than listen to you guys," said Laci.

"I don't care what you think," said Rafferty.

Laci spat on the floor in disgust.

"I didn't volunteer for this mission to make friends," said Rafferty. "I volunteered to get out of jail."

"Then you should be happy," said Damon. "Everyone here hates you."

"Knock it off," said the screw. "We're almost there."

"I never met a president before," said Purl.

"Did you see that movie where they killed Kennedy?" said Rafferty. "Remember what Oswald did when he scoped Kennedy from the sixth floor of the School Book Depository in Dealey Plaza?"

"Are you saying that's what we should do to Mims?"

"Kind of hard in our condition," said Rafferty, lifting up his foot and rattling his shackles.

"Are you being snarky again?" said Laci. "I thought being in the slammer was the worst thing. Maybe I was wrong. Maybe joining you creeps is even worse."

"What movie are you talking about?" said Damon. "The movie I saw said Oswald was a fall guy. He didn't kill Kennedy. Some fairy did."

"I didn't ask you," said Rafferty.

"And I didn't ask you to join this mission."

"I know. The president did."

"The big guy himself," said Purl. "We all got personal invites from him."

"It just goes to show you he's got no taste," said Rafferty.

"I'm getting tired of your wisecracks," said Purl, furrowing his brow.

"What are you gonna do about it?"

46

"As soon as they take these chains off me, you're gonna find out, bright boy."

"I passed up a lethal injection for this?" said Laci.

"Here we are," said the screw, approaching a door.

Chapter 15

The screw led them into a large square room that contained a rectangular table in the middle of it. The table could seat sixteen people. The president was standing behind a lectern at the head of the table.

Strider, Halverson, Marta, Joon-ho, and Cassavetes, were sitting at the table.

"Welcome, men and women," said Mims, observing the entrance of the convicts. "I'm sure all of you want to know what this mission is about."

"It's about a pardon," said Rafferty. "That's the only part I care about."

"Don't interrupt the president," said Strider, glaring at Rafferty.

Rafferty raised his eyebrows, unimpressed. "Anything you say, teacher."

"This mission is about saving America," said Mims. "In fact, we're calling it Operation Save America. I'm sure every one of you can get on board with that. Am I right?"

The prisoners grumbled.

"Don't you want to save America?" the president said, baffled by their response.

"So we can go back to the joint?" said Rafferty.

"I thought I made myself clear in my offer. If you succeed at this mission, I will grant all of you full pardons."

"There's a rumor going around about another name for this mission."

"What name?"

"Operation Death Guaranteed."

"That's not the name of the mission. Don't believe the lies you hear."

"How are we supposed to fight the creatures if we're in chains?" said Damon.

"You won't always be in chains," said Mims. "You have my word on that."

"If this is such a great mission, why isn't anybody volunteering for it?" said Rafferty.

"I'm not gonna sugarcoat it, ladies and gentlemen. It *will* be a dangerous mission. But the sacrifices you make in the line of duty will never be forgotten by your country. I will give each of you a Medal of Honor when you return. This I promise you."

"Isn't that the job of congress?"

"Congress was disbanded for lack of members. I have plenary power, including the power to award you the Congressional Medal of Honor."

"All we have to do is get killed?" said Damon.

Purl snickered.

"Not true," said Mims. "Whoever succeeds in the mission gets the medal. Dying has nothing to do with it."

"I'd rather have the full pardon," said Laci.

"You'll get both, I promise you." Mims beamed. "I'm so proud of your patriotic spirit. It will never be forgotten, I assure you. You're all heroes. It's people like you who made this country great. Your willingness to endure hardship for the cause of liberty is admirable. What this nation needs is more people like you, people willing to sacrifice everything for our beloved country."

"This beloved country put us in jail," said Rafferty.

The other prisoners mumbled their agreement.

Mims stared at him, hacked off at the interruption.

"It's never too late to redeem yourselves," he said. "And I'm glad all of you chose the path to redemption. Nobody forced you to volunteer. You made the decision on your own to save America from the invading infected ghouls," he said, raising his fist in defiance. "We shall never bow to the invaders. We shall destroy every flesh eater that attacks us. And we shall win this war."

"Are you coming with us?" said Rafferty.

Mims cleared his throat. "Why, no. I must lead the country. My place is here."

"Aren't you the commander in chief?"

"I am indeed. And I will lead this country from its seat of power here in the bunker."

"You're too good for us, huh?" said Laci. "Figures."

"Not true. We are all equal in America. Nobody is too good for anybody. If it wasn't for my job as president, I'd go with you."

Rafferty laughed. "Yeah, right."

"Son, I have your best interests at heart," said Mims, touching his heart with his hand. "Believe me when I say I do. I will do everything in my power to make your mission a brilliant success."

"All you have to do is obey orders and we'll make it," Strider told Rafferty.

Rafferty rattled his leg irons in a disdainful gesture.

"You men and women make me proud to call myself an American," said Mims, surveying the audience and nodding with approval. "Godspeed to you."

After everyone filed out of the situation room, Mims felt lightheaded and gasped for breath.

"Dr. Morrow, I need oxygen," he called out.

A door opened and Morrow appeared, wheeling a green metal canister of oxygen to Mims. Mims collapsed in his chair, snagged the oxygen mask, and took deep breaths.

"I'd be dead without this oxygen," he said.

"Too bad we don't have enough to go around," said Morrow.

"When we get that vaccine, we'll be able to leave this suffocating bunker. The ghouls won't be able to infect us."

"They'll still be able to bite us."

"Cassavetes says the vaccine keeps the ghouls from biting him. It repels them somehow."

"I don't see how that would work," said Morrow, looking skeptical.

Somebody knocked on the door.

Mims removed the oxygen mask from his face.

"Get that oxygen out of here," he told Morrow.

Morrow rolled the oxygen canister out of the situation room.

"Come in," said Mims.

Strider and Halverson entered and closed the door behind them.

"Is that the best you could do?" said Mims, reinvigorated by his hits of oxygen.

"You said you wanted only volunteers, Mr. President," said Strider.

Mims shuffled a pile of documents on his desktop perusing them.

"A bank robber/murderer, a woman who killed her CO, a serial killer, and a cannibal," he said. "Are you kidding me?"

"They're the only ones who volunteered."

"I thought we would get a couple of decent volunteers."

"Marta Costello's coming, Mr. President," said Halverson. "I'll vouch for her."

"And so is Joon-ho," said Strider. "He's a good man."

Mims read the two top dossiers again. "A cannibal and a serial killer." Screwing up his face, he looked up. "They may do more harm than good. Can we trust them?"

"We have to. We need as many people as we can get. I doubt all of us are gonna make it alive."

"You're my last best chance, Strider. Don't fail me."

"Yes, sir," said Strider, his jaw set, saluting Mims.

"You and Halverson are my best men."

Halverson didn't salute because he wasn't in the military. He was a CIA black ops agent who used to report to the director of national intelligence until the director was killed by ghouls. Halverson now reported directly to the president.

Before the plague hit, the CIA was prohibited from working on domestic soil. The war with the ghouls changed everything. Now CIA clandestine operations could take place anywhere in the world, including within the US.

Strider and Halverson left the room.

Mims commenced gasping for breath.

"Doctor," he cried. "More oxygen."

Morrow burst into the situation room wheeling the oxygen canister to Mims's desk.

Chapter 16

In the capacious bunker garage Joon-ho was attaching a snowplow to the front of the president's black stretch limo known as "the Beast."

It wasn't called the Beast for nothing. Eighteen feet long and weighing eight tons, it had eight-inch-thick armor plating, including its floor, to protect it from bomb blasts and five-inch-thick windows strong enough to stop a .44 Magnum bullet.

The Beast resembled a Chevy Suburban more than any other vehicle, but it was actually a unique stretch limo that shared no parts with any other vehicle.

Strider and Halverson entered the garage.

"Almost finished, Joon-ho?" said Strider.

"Yes, sir," said Joon-ho, looking up from his work.

"How many vehicles are we taking?" Halverson asked Strider.

"Three. We've got two Suburbans beside the Beast."

"Are they both armored and have bulletproof glass like the president's?"

"They can all withstand a drone attack. The roof, the floor, and the two sides are armored with eight-inch-wide high-tensile steel plates."

"The snowplow's a good idea to clear the ghouls out of the road. We don't want the creatures getting caught under our wheels. They can bring the vehicle to a complete halt, once their bodies get wound around the axles and stuffed into the wheel wells."

"These things are built like tanks," said Strider, circling the Beast with a smile of approval on his face.

Two uniforms were busy attaching snowplows to the two black Suburbans.

"If anything can get through the ghouls, these can," said Halverson.

"The only problem I foresee is fuel. The EMP from the nuke knocked out the electrical grid for hundreds—maybe thousands—of miles around here. We're not gonna be able to pump fuel at the gas stations that weren't annihilated in the nuclear explosion. The fuel pumps are all electric and won't work."

"Can't we siphon fuel from the diesel pumps?" said Joon-ho, tightening a screw on the snowplow.

"The gas station fuel tanks are below the ground," said Strider. "To siphon fuel from them your empty fuel receptacle has to be below the tanks. The answer's no."

"Don't we have any fuel stockpiled here in the bunker?" said Halverson.

"We do. And I hope it's enough. But you never know. These Suburbans guzzle fuel. Each vehicle is equipped with two five-gallon jerricans of diesel fuel."

"How far away is Wheelhouse's hideout?"

"Cassavetes said it's over five hundred miles away."

"How did he make it here on a motorcycle?" said Joon-ho.

"Did I hear someone say my name in vain?" said Cassavetes, approaching the group.

"How did you get gas for your motorcycle?"

"I siphoned it from abandoned cars on the road. The roads are filled with cars abandoned by people who fled for their lives."

"Didn't they abandon their cars because they ran out of gas?"

"Sometimes. Sometimes they got stuck in traffic jams, got out of their cars, and ran like hell. I also was able to use gas station pumps because the EMP hadn't struck during the first leg of my journey. The electrical grid was on at that point."

"Done," said Joon-ho, stepping away from his handiwork, a Phillips screwdriver in his hand.

"Let's get ready to rock," said Strider. "I'll take the Beast. Halverson, you're in charge of number two. Joon-ho, you take number three. The vehicle code names are Cardinal—One, Two, and Three, respectively."

Cassavetes was standing in front of the CCTV screen near the exit watching the ghouls massing in front of the garage door.

"The zeds are all over the place," he said. "It's like they know we're getting ready to leave."

"How can they know?" said Marta, stepping up to the monitor to gaze at the ghouls milling outside.

"They don't know," said Strider. "They're just foraging for food. That's all their brains can think of. Food."

"It's creepy," said Cassavetes, enthralled by the slogging ghouls.

"Cassavetes, you and Purl are with me in the Beast. Halverson, I hate to do this to you, but you're with Rafferty and Damon. You're the only one that can handle those two."

"I never ate anybody named Halverson before," said Damon, licking his lips and eyeballing Halverson.

"And you never will," said Halverson.

"When do you take these chains off?" said Rafferty.

"Whenever we want," said Strider.

"You're gonna feed us to the ghouls. Is that it? You're taking us along as food. You didn't tell us that part, you bastards. Or nobody would've volunteered."

"You'll get weapons when we're under attack. Not until then."

"I believe you," said Rafferty, smirking.

"I got no respect for someone that kills only women," said Damon, looking askance at Rafferty. "That's what a coward does."

"Watch who you call a coward," said Rafferty, advancing on him.

Halverson held Rafferty back.

"Are you gonna be able to handle these two?" Strider asked Halverson.

"If I can't, I'll terminate them," answered Halverson.

"We don't have enough men as it is."

"They're not any good to us if they're gonna fight each other."

"As long as they don't kill each other and you don't kill them, we're good."

"I don't kill anyone unless I want to eat them," said Damon. "I don't want to eat a serial killer. I'd throw up."

"Just looking at you, you freak, makes me want to barf," said Rafferty. "Let's get out of this place. I can't breathe," he said, gagging.

"Joon-ho, you have Marta and Laci," said Strider.

"That's what I'm talking about," said Purl.

"Why's he get the babes?" said Rafferty, leering at Marta and Laci. "I want some of that action."

"You aren't man enough," said Laci.

"I'll show you."

"You're a rapist, a chicken. Every woman you attacked rejected you when you asked them out."

"Come over here and say that."

54

Laci trudged toward him in her leg irons.

Joon-ho stood in front of her, blocking her path.

"Load up," said Strider.

"Saved by the bell," Rafferty told Laci.

"You come near me, I'll cut you open like a pig," said Laci.

"You're scaring me."

"You know it."

Rafferty blew her a kiss.

"Asshole," she said. "I'll cut you, I swear I will."

"Threats are illegal. I want her busted," Rafferty told Strider. "Throw her back in her cell."

"Shut the fuck up, coward," said Laci.

Joon-ho latched onto Laci's arm and guided her toward the third vehicle.

"Get your hands off me," said Laci, jerking her arm free.

"She's a wild animal," said Rafferty. "They're the best kind. They turn me on."

"I doubt it. You go limp when you're with a real woman."

"I've had it with you. You're not coming back alive."

"Did I touch a nerve?" said Laci, feigning innocence. "You flaccid guys are all alike."

"I'm gonna cut your head off after I drill you."

"You can only get it up for corpses, I hear. You do them after you kill your victims, huh, because you're scared to death of real-life women. It's like you're screwing one of your plastic blowup dolls when you do a stiff."

"You lesbians are all alike. No wonder you can't get a man."

"Knock it off," said Strider. "Mount up."

"Do we have to leave paradise?" said Rafferty.

Chapter 17

The team entered their respective vehicles.

A cropped twentyish uniform operating the exit door pressed a button on a panel in the control room. Humming, the steel door rose electronically.

Strider drove the Beast into the antechamber, the two Suburbans in tow.

The uniform lowered the steel door behind them. He watched the vehicles on his monitor. When the door was shut, he pressed the button that opened the heavy blast door in the antechamber that led to the driveway outside.

Their clothes in tatters, a mob of ghouls trudged into the antechamber, hissing and drooling. They groped for food.

Strider hit the Beast's gas, driving straight into the vanguard of ghouls. The snowplow swept the stumbling creatures out of the way, casting them to the side of the driveway like so many tenpins.

After the two Suburbans exited the antechamber, the uniform in the control room pressed the button that closed the blast door. Trapped inside the antechamber, the ghouls stumbled around aimlessly, seeking an exit.

The uniform pressed a red button. Nozzles in the antechamber ceiling sprayed VX, short for "venomous agent X," on the creatures, whose decrepit skin absorbed the amber-colored oily liquid nerve agent, which paralyzed their nerves and destroyed their brains. Writhing in their death throes, they fell in heaps in the antechamber, as toxic VX liquid rained down on them.

On the driveway, the three vehicles made slow but steady progress as they plowed through the onslaught of ghouls, which kept coming at them in serried waves.

"This is Cardinal One," said Strider into his walkie-talkie, so the passengers in the other vehicles could hear him. "Everybody, keep your windows powered up. We don't want to let any radioactive dust into the vehicles. Over."

"Why doesn't it kill the zeds?" said Cassavetes, riding shotgun.

"I wish I knew. Blunt trauma to their brains kills them. So does VX. It eats through their skin and paralyzes their nervous systems. Other than that, nothing seems to affect them."

"Then why did the president nuke them?"

"The force of the explosion kills them. It's the radiation that cuts no ice."

"Damn plague. We must be living in the worst period in human history. It's a wonder we haven't all gone nuts."

"Maybe we will in the end," said Purl.

Strider shot a baleful glance at him in the rearview mirror. Purl was sitting in the backseat behind a bulletproof partition between him and the front seat.

"What?" said Purl.

"You're a cop killer."

"They were in my way."

"My brother was a cop."

"Sorry to hear it."

"He was shot by a bank robber."

Purl narrowed his eyes. "Don't put that on me."

"The guy that did it was just like you. All he cared about was himself."

"I needed the money for my girlfriend's operation."

"So it's OK to whack two people to get it?"

"If they get in my way, yeah."

"People like you make me wish I wasn't human."

"You make me feel like an animal putting me in chains like this with that bulletproof glass between us. It's like riding in a Black Maria."

"I don't want you strangling me from behind. This is the president's car. Every safety precaution has been taken to protect him."

"You act like you're the president, but you aren't and never will be."

"We're here on a mission to save America. Concentrate on the mission. It's all that counts."

"It's a suicide mission, and you know it."

"Nobody forced you to come. You volunteered. Remember?"

"Not much of a choice," said Purl, his face glum. "Is this a nightmare?"

"The cold hard facts of reality are we're fucked," said Cassavetes, putting in his two cents.

"Worse than a nightmare because we never wake up from this suicide mission."

"You wanna go back to the joint?" said Strider, glancing over his shoulder at Purl.

Purl sniffed the air. "At least the air smells better here."

"These vehicles have HEPA filters to keep out radioactive dust," said Strider, returning his attention to the writhing ghouls blocking the road.

"You mean, instead of dying from radiation poisoning we're gonna die from the zombie plague?"

"Let me remind you. When we get that vaccine, we're gonna save a lot of people."

"How about ourselves?"

"Including ourselves."

"If we ever make it to this genius doctor's hideout alive."

"Your negative outlook isn't helping matters," said Strider, ticked off.

"Maybe if you removed these handcuffs I'd cheer up," said Purl, pulling at his cuffs, his face grim.

"When we're under attack, we'll free you and arm you. We've got plenty of B&T MP9s and H&K MP5s with ammo."

"Are you expecting trouble?" said Purl, dryly.

"Is that supposed to be funny?"

"I feel like we're in a funeral procession," said Cassavetes. "Can't you guys lighten up?"

"Right," said Purl. "It's only a suicide mission. What's the big deal?"

"If we're too negative, this mission will end in failure for sure," said Strider. "Look at it this way. You escaped a lethal injection."

"Pavulon, potassium chloride, and pentobarbital."

"What are you?" said Cassavetes, craning around to eyeball Purl with surprise. "A chemist?"

"I boned up on lethal injections with all the leisure time I had in the joint. The Pavulon causes muscle paralysis and respiration arrest. The potassium chloride stops the heart. And the pentobarbital is used for sedation."

"How long does it take to kill you?"

"Seven minutes, usually."

"Everything I don't want to know about lethal injection," said Strider.

"Or sometimes executioners use succinylcholine chloride instead of Pavulon," said Purl, raising his voice.

"You wasted your life. You could've been a chemist instead of a bank robber."

"Right," said Purl. "And the world's not rigged against me."

"This mission is a much better way to die," said Cassavetes. "You could last a whole lot longer than seven minutes. You might even make it back alive."

"All I got to do is survive billions of flesh-eating zombies," said Purl. "Yeah, things are looking up."

"I'm kidding. Hey, I made it on a motorcycle with no protection at all. Now we got this Beast thing built like a bulletproof tank. The zeds can't get us in this thing."

"You made it here in one piece because you're vaccinated. We're not."

"The problem with you is you think only about yourself, Purl," said Strider, focusing on plowing three ghouls out of the Beast's way.

"Yeah, well if I don't, nobody else will."

"You're selfish."

Purl resented Strider's accusation.

"Thinking about my girlfriend and paying for her surgery got me busted for armed robbery," he said. "If I really was selfish, I wouldn't have lifted a finger to help her."

"There are other ways to make money besides robbing banks," said Cassavetes.

"Not when you need it right away," said Purl. "Putting off her surgery would've cost her her life."

"We're coming to the woods," said Strider, looking alert, plowing through a throng of ghouls that were swarming in the road. "Look alive. Our field of vision will be blocked by the trees."

"We could go a whole lot faster if those things weren't in our way," said Cassavetes.

Chapter 18

Primarily oaks, spruces, and red maples grew in the dense forest that stood outside the Mount Weather bunker located in the Blue Ridge Mountains of Virginia and accessible by State Route 601. The oaks and spruces tended to be higher up the mountain, while the red maples were lower.

At this time of year, the leaves on the maples shone a fiery red. The oaks sported reddish brown leaves. The forest looked for all the world like it was being consumed by flames—an ominous warning to all who would enter. The raw beauty of the place could inspire fear as well as awe, especially now that the forest was swarming with flesh-eating ghouls.

They shambled through the trees, converging on the road in search of prey.

"Looks like there are as many ghouls here as there are outside the woods," said Strider, plowing ghouls out of the road.

"They can't mass so tightly together because of all the trees," said Cassavetes. "I noticed that coming here. They're more tightly packed on the barren mountainside."

"The problem is, they're still in the road."

"And they're surrounding us," said Purl, watching the ghouls press their gruesome faces against his window as they clawed it with their moldering fingers.

Wearing a tank top and shorts a teenage male ghoul with an iPod in his ear tried to open the back door to get to Purl. The locked door wouldn't budge. Frustrated, the ghoul pounded on the window.

"Are you sure this window is bulletproof?" said Purl.

"Positive," said Strider. "The president's vehicles were built to withstand all kinds of invasive forces." He glanced in the rearview mirror at Purl. "I ought to let that thing yank you out of here."

"What the hell?" said Purl, glaring at Strider.

"Nobody was closer than me and my brother. And a cop killer like you took him from me."

"I never saw your brother in my life. I had nothing to do with it."

Strider jumped in his seat when he heard a thump on the roof of the Beast. He looked up at the headliner.

"The hell was that?" said Cassavetes, staring at the headliner, eyes popping.

Several more thumps on the roof followed in quick succession.

Something in the upper part of the windshield caught Strider's eye. A blonde ghoul's face was peering upside down through the glass at him, her hair cascading down the windshield from her scalp. The rest of her body was lying prostrate on the roof. She opened her wizened mouth, exposing broken, jagged teeth. She tried to bite through the windshield to get at him.

"They're dropping from the trees," said Strider.

A middle-aged ghoul in a ripped navy blue suit dropped onto the car hood, gripping a lawyer's briefcase. He clung to the hood with his clawlike fingers. A bare-chested twentysomething ghoul, a former porn queen wearing a black leather miniskirt, matching fishnet stockings, and white vinyl go-go boots, dropped on top of the lawyer, one of her silicone pouches leaking out of her oversized breasts. She crawled over the lawyer to reach Strider, growling at him, leaving a trail of silicone behind her, her augmented breast shrinking.

A sixtyish priest in a black cassock dropped onto her, his robe ripped in half and barely hanging onto his rotting body, his white clerical collar smudged with dirt. The porn queen tried to shake him off her, but he clung to her neck and refused to let go.

"How are we gonna get those things off?" said Cassavetes, recoiling from the ghouls that writhed on the hood.

"I can't see where I'm going," said Strider, straining to make out the road past the ghouls.

"Give me a piece," said Purl. "I'll go out there and waste those mothers."

"Are you nuts?" said Cassavetes. "The ghouls in the woods will tear you apart as soon as you open your door."

"I'll take care of them," said Strider, checking out the dash and spotting a red plastic button near the mounted walkie-talkie.

"What are you talking about?"

"I almost forgot. These vehicles are equipped with everything."

Cassavetes shook his head, not understanding.

Strider snagged the walkie-talkie from the dash. "This is Cardinal One. Halverson, do you read me?"

"This is Cardinal Two," said Halverson in the following Suburban. "I read you five-by-five."

"What about you, Cardinal Three?"

"I copy," said Joon-ho in the last Suburban.

"Are the ghouls dropping on your roofs? Over."

"At least ten of them so far," said Halverson. "Over."

"I can't see past their bodies on my windshield," said Joon-ho, his voice tense. "I'm driving blind. Over."

A fat ghoul with his dirt-streaked prominent beer belly hanging in rolls over his trouser waistband dropped onto Strider's hood with a loud thud.

"Do you both see that red plastic button on your dash?" asked Strider. "Over."

"Copy," answered Halverson.

"Copy," answered Joon-ho. "I'm gonna have to stop. I can't see where I'm going. Over."

"Push that red button," said Strider. "It'll send an electric charge through the steel frame of the car. Over." He turned to Cassavetes. "I almost forgot we had that. These babies are outfitted to repel anything."

"What about us? What's to stop us from getting fried?" said Cassavetes.

"We're insulated. So are the interior doors. No problem."

Strider hung up the walkie-talkie and pushed the red button.

The ghouls on the hood, stiffened, grimaced, and vibrated. Smoke poured out of their electrified bodies. The electric charge jolted through their bodies and fried their brains. Their dead milky eyes glowed red as their brains burned. Losing their grips on the hood, they slid off the sizzling hood to the ground.

"All right," cried Cassavetes, digging the ghouls' plight and grinning. "We're invincible in these tanks."

More ghouls kept dropping out of the overarching trees onto the Beast's hood and roof. As soon as the ghouls hit the vehicle's steel carapace, they shuddered as if inflicted with a paroxysm.

"More fun than a barrel of monkeys," said Purl, staring out his window at the ghouls sliding off the roof.

"I wish they'd stop thumping on the roof, though," said Cassavetes, eyeballing the headliner. "The noise is getting on my nerves."

After a particularly loud thud on the roof, Strider found himself face to face with former president Cole, who was missing both arms and one leg as he sprawled on the windshield on his belly. His face was scarred almost beyond recognition by a nuclear blast, but Strider was sure it was him. Cole's body convulsed as electricity coursed through it and melted his brain.

"Wasn't that President Cole?" said Cassavetes, gaping in awe.

Cole slid off the hood, flicking his tongue and grimacing at the two men in his death throes.

Strider nodded yes.

"How did he climb up a tree with only one leg?" said Purl from the backseat.

"The blast from the nuke must've hurled him up a tree," said Strider.

"The zeds keep dropping onto us even though we're frying them," said Cassavetes, shaking his head, as another ghoul landed on the roof.

"As long as I can see to drive, we can keep going."

Strider drove forward, plowing a knot of creatures out of the road and sweeping them to the side.

"I hope it's not like this the whole trip," said Cassavetes. "I'm gonna go nuts if I have to listen to zeds dropping onto our roof day and night."

"We're already nuts to even try this suicide mission," said Purl.

Chapter 19

In the driver's seat of the second vehicle of the convoy, Halverson watched a nine-year-old boy ghoul slide off the hood, his eyes ember red from the inferno consuming his brain, his head smoking.

What kind of a world was this? wondered Halverson. Ghouls dropping out of the sky like bird turds. ICBMs with atomic warheads raining down from the clouds at the behest of the president.

Halverson wanted to cut himself off from the world gone mad. Whenever he made a connection with anyone, it increased his suffering. Like Victoria. He opened up to her and got close. Then the ghouls got her. And that was that. Getting close to other people always ended by increasing your pain. Instead of feeling pain just for yourself, you felt it for yourself and the one you cared for.

In the apocalyptic world they were living in now, you were better off going it alone, decided Halverson. It was dead certain the ghouls would rob you of anybody you made an emotional connection with.

"Let me at 'em," said Rafferty from the backseat separated from the front by bulletproof Plexiglas. "I want to rip the scumbags' heads off."

"You're good at killing, huh?" said Damon, sitting beside him.

"I've had a lot of practice."

Damon acted surprised. "You don't deny you're a serial killer? Most everyone I ever met in the joint claimed they were framed by the cops."

"The losers I killed didn't deserve to be on this earth. They were all misfits with no skills or brains. They added nothing. Damn tramps selling the only thing they had—their bodies."

"They sound like you."

"What do you mean?" said Rafferty, taking offense. "I had a job and a family—a wife and two girls. I was a decent American."

"A decent American serial killer? Are you kidding me?"

"You should talk, you stinking cannibal. You're worse than those things outside. They don't know what they're doing when they eat living human flesh. You do it even though you have a brain that works."

"I didn't kill wantonly like you. I killed people because I was hungry. Wild animals kill because they're hungry. Do you call them murderers?"

"They need to eat what they kill. You could go to the store and buy fresh beef or lamb or whatever. You have a choice. Wild animals don't. Lions are gonna starve to death if they don't kill antelopes and eat them."

"I have to eat humans. It's the only kind of meat that satisfies me."

"You're setting off my built-in bullshit detector," said Rafferty, hitting his nose with his forefinger.

Their eyes burning with rage, Rafferty and Damon wanted to grapple with each other, but their cuffed hands behind their backs prevented them.

Frustrated, Damon lunged at Rafferty trying to bite Rafferty's carotid artery. Rafferty head-butted Damon in the middle of Damon's lunge. Damon dropped unconscious on Rafferty's lap.

"Get this animal off me," cried Rafferty, trying to extricate himself from under Damon's inert body. "He's gonna bite me when he comes to."

In chains, Rafferty couldn't pull free from Damon, who remained unconscious for the time being.

Halverson glanced in the rearview mirror at them and scowled. "What am I gonna do with you two?"

"Get this animal off me. Or at least put a muzzle on him. I can't believe you put him back here with me."

Halverson couldn't very well stop and go back there and separate Rafferty and Damon. The marauding ghouls would tear him apart as soon as he left the Suburban. Halverson was tempted to let Damon maul Rafferty. He felt nothing for them. They were both cold-blooded murderers.

On the other hand, they needed every man they could get to fight the ghouls when the time came. And it would come. Halverson knew it. It was a long journey. And there were millions of ghouls out there.

Halverson radioed Strider. "Cardinal One, this is Cardinal Two. I got a situation back here. Over."

"This is Cardinal One. What kind of situation? Is your electric charge not working? Over."

"It works fine. Damon attacked Rafferty. Over."

"Fuck. I thought they were chained up. Over."

"Damon tried to bite Rafferty's throat. Over."

"Shit. You gotta separate them. We can't afford to lose any men. Over."

"I'll have to pull over and leave the vehicle to reach the backseat. Over."

"Go ahead. I'll stop and wait for you. I'll tell Cardinal Three to stop, too. Over."

"Roger that."

Halverson signed off.

He brought the Suburban to a halt. Meanwhile, ghouls continued to plummet onto its roof.

Halverson made sure his B&T MP9 was loaded with a full thirty-round magazine, released the safety, and racked the slide. He had ten spare mags stuffed into the capacious pockets of his khaki cargo pants.

"Help me," cried Rafferty, his eyes popping with fear. "I think he's coming to. I can't get him off me."

Chapter 20

Halverson surveyed his surroundings. The shambling ghouls were converging on the halted Suburban, grimacing and salivating, starving for fresh meat.

He didn't have any choice. He didn't have a muzzle on him to put on Damon. The only way to save Rafferty from Damon was to separate them. Halverson would have to put Rafferty in the front seat with him.

"I hate cannibals," screamed Rafferty, his face twisted with anguish.

Halverson took in the ghouls surrounding his Suburban. Afraid of the electric charge in its metal, they were shying away from the vehicle. They were milling some six feet from the Suburban, keeping their distance.

It would give Halverson enough room to open his door and get out. However, he knew they would attack him as soon as he exited the safety of the vehicle. Ghouls in the overhanging boughs continued to drop onto the roof, which electrocuted them. The endless thudding overhead was unsettling.

It was now or never, he decided.

He pressed the red button on the dash, killing the electric charge. He wasn't going to open the back door if it was juiced.

He opened the driver's-side door. B&T MP9 in hand, he slid out of the Suburban, confronting the ghouls, who spotted him with their dead milky eyes and shambled toward him. Halverson unleashed a burst into the nearest cluster of ghouls, blasting their skulls and blowing their brains out.

He strode to the Suburban rear door and used his key fob to open it.

"Get out," he told Rafferty, who was sitting apprehensively with Damon's head on his lap.

"Where's a piece for me?" said Rafferty.

"Get in the front seat. I'll give you cover fire."

"They're right behind you."

Halverson wheeled around and fired a burst from his MP9 into the approaching ghouls, a male and a female, both elderly with

white hair. They tried to grasp Halverson with their dirty yellow
fingernails. Halverson's bullets cut them down. They crumpled on
the ground.

A short, bearded male fiftyish ghoul wearing a blood-streaked
white shirt and black trousers with red suspenders dropped from an
oak tree and thudded on the roof.

Rafferty started and looked up at the headliner.

The ghoul slid down the vehicle and hung by its gnarled
fingers from the roof, blocking the doorway, grimacing at Rafferty,
who was mere inches away from him.

"Shit," cried Rafferty, recoiling from the ghoul and trying to
slide away from it.

However, Rafferty's escape route was blocked by Damon's
unconscious body that lay sprawled in his lap.

The ghoul growled at Rafferty, strands of saliva leaking from
the creature's sere lips.

Halverson blasted the ghoul in the back of the skull,
executioner-style. The creature's face exploded, popping its
eyeballs like ivory champagne corks onto Rafferty's chest.
Rafferty squirmed with loathing, as the eyeballs rolled off him.

The lifeless ghoul lost his grip on the car roof and fell to the
tarmac in a heap that reeked of death and decaying flesh.

Sliding out from under Damon's head, Rafferty clambered out
of the backseat, his hands cuffed behind him, his ankles in leg
irons. Stepping onto the motionless ghoul he all but lost his
balance. He managed to slide/jump off the ghoul and stumble onto
the tarmac. He regained his equilibrium and shuffled in his chains
toward the front seat.

A thirtysomething construction worker wearing a silver hard
hat lurched toward Rafferty.

Halverson blasted the ghoul's hard hat and flipped it off his
head, sending it somersaulting through the air. The ghoul kept
advancing on Rafferty, who was trying to climb into the driver's
seat. The ghoul grabbed the back of Rafferty's coveralls. Rafferty
screamed.

"Get it off me," he cried.

Halverson swapped magazines and let loose another blast at
the ghoul, turning his exposed rotting head into a colander. Dust,

maggots, and skull shards erupted from the ghoul's shattered skull. Letting go of Rafferty, his knees buckling, he toppled over.

Rafferty scrambled into the driver's seat.

Halverson slammed the back door, locked it so Damon couldn't get out, and headed to the driver's seat.

"Move over, Rafferty," he said, firing at an approaching fortyish female ghoul with a missing nose and one eye gouged out, which was hanging out of its socket by a stalk that reached down her cheek.

Rafferty sat in the driver's seat eying Halverson, not moving.

"Move," said Halverson, twisting halfway around and turning an approaching ghoul head into exploding shrapnel-like fragments behind him.

"Give me a piece and I'll move," said Rafferty.

"There's no time. The weapons are in the back trunk."

"Go back there and get one for me."

"Move over," snarled Halverson, brandishing his machine pistol.

"I'm not moving till you give me a piece. I have to defend myself against the ghouls."

Halverson sneered and trained his MP9 on Rafferty's head.

"Move over now or you're dead. Your choice. Make it fast," said Halverson, picking up on a ghoul trudging toward him on his right.

Rafferty scooched out of the driver's seat to the shotgun seat.

Halverson blasted a tall black ghoul with iron grey hair who was lumbering toward him in a black cop uniform. The ghoul's head jerked back, perforated by slugs. He crumpled.

Halverson clambered into the driver's seat, slamming the door behind him. A ghoul hand prevented him from closing the door all the way.

Craning backward, Halverson spotted the wizened hand. He cracked the door. The hand belonged to a blonde thirtyish ghoul in cerise hot pants who was trying to latch onto his arm. She looked as though she might have been beautiful while she was living— maybe even a movie star. Now she was unrecognizable. Tattered, suppurating strips of flesh were hanging off her once-smooth face, revealing glimpses of white skull bone.

Halverson let her have it. His bullets ripped through her mouth spitting her teeth out like orange pips. She jerked backward, pulling her hand away from the SUV door.

Halverson slammed the door shut. He pressed the dash's red button, electrifying the Suburban. Ghouls pressed against the sides of the car were in for a rude jolt. They convulsed and smoked, their hair on end.

Halverson turned on Rafferty. "You pull a stunt like that again and I'll blow your head off."

"If you want me to help you fight the ghouls, I need a piece."

"Why should I trust you after you wouldn't let me in?"

"If you want my help, you're gonna have to trust me sooner or later."

True, decided Halverson.

"When the time comes, you'll get a gun," he said.

He didn't know if he was ever going to trust Rafferty fully, especially after what had just happened. When it came time to give Rafferty a weapon, Halverson was going to have to be extra careful about watching his back.

This trip was loaded with land mines, and the most dangerous ones were within the convoy, he decided.

Chapter 21

"This is Cardinal One. What's happening back there? Over," squawked Strider's voice through the walkie-talkie mounted on the Beast's dash.

"Cardinal Two is good to go," said Halverson in the following Suburban. "Over."

"Any losses? Over."

"None. Everything is A-OK. Over."

"This is Cardinal Three. What'd I miss? I saw people getting out of Cardinal Two. Over," said Joon-ho in the last Suburban.

"Never mind," said Strider. "Let's hit the road. Over."

Another ghoul thumped on Halverson's Suburban roof.

"I wish they'd stop doing that," said Rafferty.

"Maybe they'll stop when they see their comrades frying on the roofs," said Halverson, firing the Suburban engine and pulling forward on the ghoul-clogged road, shoving serried ranks of ghouls out of the way with the snowplow.

Halverson was having misgivings about bringing Rafferty with them. Right off the bat, Rafferty had proved he was a double-dealer when he tried to blackmail Halverson into giving him a gun.

"Didn't your wife suspect you were killing all those women?" asked Halverson.

"Not at all," answered Rafferty. "Why should she? As long as I paid the rent and put food on the table for our family, she didn't ask questions. You know women. As long as you give them enough money to pay the bills, they're happy."

"What time of day did you kill these women?"

"At night."

"Didn't she wonder where you were going at night all the time?"

"I told her I was going to work."

"And she didn't suspect you of anything?" said Halverson, incredulous.

"Of course not. Like I said, I was the breadwinner and I kept providing for our family. That's all she cared about."

"You didn't bring home trophies from your kills? I heard that most serial killers take trophies."

Rafferty searched Halverson's face. "How do you know so much about serial killers?"

"I read a lot."

"Or maybe you have experience as one."

"I kill only when my life's threatened."

"I figure you've killed more people than me. Am I right?"

"There's no comparison."

"Actually, I did bring home trophies from my kills," said Rafferty, puffing out his chest with arrogance. "A finger here, a thumb there, a lock of hair."

"How did you hide them from your wife and children?"

"I hermitically sealed the body parts in mason jars and hid them under the floor in my basement," said Rafferty, his face smug.

"Did you ever feel like bragging about your kills to your wife?"

"No. What I did was for myself."

"Didn't she wonder why you had to work late all the time?"

"Not at all. In a way, I really was working. I was clearing the hookers off the streets, ridding the world of sluts and tramps."

"And raping their corpses."

"I'm surprised he doesn't want to rape the ghouls," chimed in Damon, who had regained consciousness in the backseat.

"You gotta be kidding," said Rafferty in disgust. "Just look at them," he said, staring out the windshield at a pack of ghouls squirming in the road. "Yuk."

"I thought corpses turned you on."

"I killed only good-looking sluts," said Rafferty. "I got taste."

"You're a psycho."

"Look who's talking," said Rafferty, craning around to glare at Damon. "A stinking cannibal. You guys are ranked even lower than short eyes by cons in the joint."

"Because they envy me. I had the courage to do what they were afraid to."

"I'm surprised another con didn't shiv you in the back."

"I love the sound of rattling human bones," said Damon, looking happy. "It's music to my ears."

"A con smashed the Milwaukee Cannibal's brains inside the joint. Death by bludgeoning," said Rafferty.

"He had a bad personality."

"You're lucky I'm not back there with you anymore. I'd kill you, nutbag."

"How come he gets to sit up front?" Damon asked Halverson. "I want to sit up front."

This was going to be a long trip cooped up with these two, decided Halverson.

Chapter 22

"What happened up front?" asked Marta, riding shotgun in the third vehicle.

"Not sure," said Joon-ho, driving down the road after Halverson. "It's hard to see with the ghouls swarming everywhere. I saw someone get out of Cardinal Two while they were stopped."

"Why do I have to sit alone back here?" said Laci.

"Because you killed your CO," Joon-ho said over his shoulder. "I can't concentrate on driving if I gotta worry about you strangling me."

"How am I gonna strangle anyone with my hands cuffed?"

"You might try to kneecap me with your foot. No telling what you might try. Forget it."

"Oh, man. You worry too much. I only killed my CO because he assaulted me. There's a lot of that going on in the military, if you haven't heard."

"Killing COs?"

"Assaults against women, stupid."

"Tell me about it," said Marta, remembering being raped by Hal, who had saved her from the ghouls after they had killed her mother and sister and she had fled in fear, abandoning them without coming to their aid, which she still felt guilt for.

One minute Hal was saving her, the next he was raping her, she decided with a shiver at the memory.

"Were you in the military, too, Marta?" said Laci.

"No. I was a coder. But I was assaulted by someone who saved me from the ghouls."

Laci nodded. "That's how they do you. It's a power thing. It's got nothing to do with love or even sex. I hope you wasted the bastard."

"Halverson shot him."

"I guess he's OK. I'll never let any man try that on me again, CO or no CO. I'll waste him in the blink of an eye."

"I know how you feel."

"I hate to be the bearer of bad tidings, but I gotta take a leak."

"Shit," said Joon-ho.

He didn't know what to do. He snagged the walkie-talkie from the dash and radioed Strider.

"This is Cardinal Three. I got a problem," said Joon-ho. "Over."

"Roger," said Strider. "This is Cardinal One. State the nature of your problem. Over."

"Laci needs to take a leak. Over."

"Crap." Strider paused a beat. "Can she hold it a little longer? I want to be out of the woods when we let her out. Over."

Laci overheard them. "I can't hold it. Want me to die of uremia like Tycho Brahe?"

"Tycho who?" said Joon-ho.

"He was a Danish astronomer. I learned that in high school."

"Shut up, you two," said Strider. "We're gonna have to stop and let her out. Over."

Laci's eyes bulged in fear. "Outside with the ghouls? They'll tear me apart."

"Then hold it or go in your pants. Over."

"I don't want to smell piss in here," said Joon-ho.

"No way," said Marta.

"I'm not wetting my pants, damn it," said Laci.

"Your choice," said Strider. "Over."

"Uremia or wet pants? Some choice."

"I'm waiting. Over."

Laci eyed the ghouls swarming at the sides of the road. A sneer curled her lip.

"Let me out with the ghouls," she said. "I hate COs. Did I ever tell you that?"

"This convoy is not separating," said Strider. "Everyone pull over till Laci's finished. Over and out."

"Blame everything on me because I need to take a leak," muttered Laci.

Joon-ho brought the Suburban to a halt. "Go on out."

"The door's locked. How am I supposed to get out?"

"Oh, yeah," said Joon-ho with dismay.

"Which means you gotta come back here and open it."

Joon-ho knew she was right.

Watching the Suburban park in the road, the throng of ghouls closed in on it, growling and drooling.

"You better hurry up and open this door," said Laci, riveting her apprehensive eyes on the ghouls, "before they get any closer."

Joon-ho cut the juice that electrified the car. He racked the slide on his B&T MP9. Heart pounding like crazy, he was about to open the door when a ghoul thudded on the roof, startling him. Infuriated, he felt like shooting through the roof to kill the ghoul, but he held back. Putting holes in the roof didn't seem like a good idea to him.

"I almost had a heart attack," he said, walling his eyes and gulping.

He flung open his door and darted onto the tarmac.

Enlivened by the sight of him, the ghouls flung their arms about in agitation and tried to walk faster.

Joon-ho fired a burst into the first row of ghouls blasting their heads into necrotic fragments.

With his car fob he unlocked Laci's door and yanked it open.

"Hurry up," he said, wheeling around to fire another burst at the ghouls.

"Where am I supposed to go?"

"In the road."

"There's no privacy here."

"Fuck privacy. You wanna go on living, hurry up."

"How do I take this jumpsuit off with my hands cuffed?" she said in frustration and fear, hobbling into the middle of the road.

Chapter 23

Beads of sweat popped out of Joon-ho's forehead and stippled it as he swapped magazines and discharged another burst at the assaulting ghouls. He whirled around, spotting a dwarf male ghoul with arms outstretched preparing to leap off the Suburban's roof onto him. He blew the ghoul's head apart. Half his head gone, the ghoul dropped to the tarmac and lay motionless.

Joon-ho slewed around to face the mob and cut down the nearest line of attackers. He bolted to Laci and retrieved the handcuff keys from his trouser pocket. He emptied his MP9 magazine into the nearest ghouls, put the MP9 down, and used his keys to unlock one of Laci's handcuffs.

The ghouls were now less than three feet from him. In a flash, he lifted the MP9 from the ground, ejected the spent mag, and replaced it with a fresh one. He blasted the front line of ghouls, spraying the air with skull shards and gobbets of brains.

Laci unzipped the jumpsuit at her cleavage, dropped the garment down over her bra, and dropped her panties so she could crouch and relieve herself.

Lunging toward her a geriatric male ghoul swiped at her hair. Laci flinched. Joon-ho shot the ghoul in the eye, driving the bullet through the back of his skull where it took a saucer-sized piece of occipital bone with it as it hurtled through the air into a fortysomething female ghoul's disintegrating face.

Straightening, Laci slid up her panties, slid her jumpsuit up over her bra and shoulders, and zipped it shut.

"Give me a gun and I can help kill those things," she said.

"Not yet," said Joon-ho, ejecting his spent mag and replacing it with a fresh one from his cargo pocket. "Get back in the car."

In her haste she stumbled on her shackles into the Suburban backseat and closed the door behind her.

Joon-ho pelted trudging ghouls frenzied by the proximity of living human flesh with a barrage of slugs which dropped them in their tracks.

Dashing back to the driver's-side doorway, he drew up when he spotted a fiftysomething female ghoul with a blue-rinse perm standing in his way growling at him.

In the passenger seat Marta kicked Blue-rinse in the back of the head and launched the ghoul staggering out of the doorway.

Joon-ho nodded his thanks at Marta, brought his gun to bear on Blue-rinse, and plugged her.

As Joon-ho stood on the Suburban rocker panel getting ready to occupy the driver's seat, a ghoul dropped from an overhanging oak bough onto Joon-ho's head.

"Fuck," said Joon-ho, startled and terrified.

He struggled to push the creature off him.

The ghoul was tall Navajo Indian with his ears chewed off, wearing a turquoise bolo tie. His legs had landed on Joon-ho's shoulders with Joon-ho's head between them. Facing Joon-ho the ghoul yanked on Joon-ho's ears. Hanging on the doorframe with one hand, his MP9 in his other, Joon-ho fell to pistol-whipping the ghoul's face.

Joon-ho knew he couldn't kill the ghoul that way. He was just trying to prevent the thing from biting him. He tried to squeeze off a bullet at the ghoul. His heart stopped. His magazine was empty.

How was he going to get the ghoul off him? he wondered. He needed to pop a new mag into his MP9. He couldn't load the gun while holding onto the doorframe with one hand.

With the ghoul sitting on his shoulders, Joon-ho jumped off the rocker panel onto the tarmac, freeing his hand, enabling him to snag a fresh mag from his cargo pocket, his back killing him thanks to the ghoul's weight.

The ghoul slid down Joon-ho's chest, hooking his knees on Joon-ho's shoulders, and tried to chew off Joon-ho's face. Joon-ho slammed his MP9 muzzle into the ghoul's face, knocking out half of the rancid creature's decayed teeth. The ghoul spat his loosened teeth out. Joon-ho shut his eyes to keep the teeth out of them. The ghoul still had enough teeth left in his mouth to bite and infect Joon-ho.

Joon-ho jammed the fresh magazine into the receiver and fired a burst point-blank at the flesh eater's temple. The ghoul fell off Joon-ho's shoulders and sprawled on the tarmac.

Joon-ho sprang back onto the rocker panel. He froze when he heard a loud growl reverberate across the land. He turned around to locate the source of the sound.

A massive black bear was climbing down an oak tree, swiping a giant paw at the ghouls that encompassed the oak.

"Now we got a bear after us," said Marta, transfixed by the black bear as she sat in the passenger seat.

"Maybe he's after the ghouls," said Joon-ho.

"Why would anyone want to eat a ghoul?"

"He's defending his territory."

"Let's get out of here."

Twenty ghouls plodded toward Joon-ho. He emptied his magazine at them, clambered into the driver's seat, and shut the door behind him. Ghouls thronged around the vehicle, pressing their rotting faces against the windows. Joon-ho pressed the red button on the dash, electrifying the SUV.

The ghouls quivered and smoked. They did a jig and dropped to the tarmac, their milky eyes turning scarlet and flaming in their sockets as their brains fried and melted.

"This is Cardinal One," said Strider through the walkie-talkie. "What's going on back there, Joon-ho? It sounds like you're wasting hundreds of those things. Over."

"All done," said Joon-ho, gasping after his hairbreadth escape from death. "Over."

"Is everyone OK? Over."

"We're fine. There's a bear over here fighting with the ghouls. Over."

"Good. I hope he rips every last one of them apart. Over."

The ghouls were biting the bear's paw, drawing spurts of blood, which they lapped up in bliss, their growls turning into purrs of contentment as they satiated their all-consuming hunger.

The bear roared.

Driven mad by pain, he jumped out of the oak into the mob of ghouls and clamped his jaws on the nearest ghoul, a roly-poly teenage male ghoul in a grey T-shirt with a Bluetooth earbud jutting out of his ear. In an access of rage, the bear tore the ghoul's head clear off its neck and spat it out at a ghoul that was feasting on his paw.

The juggernaut of ghouls pursued their onslaught of the bear, clamping their jagged teeth onto his entire body as they dragged him to the ground and piled onto him, tearing out clumps of his bloody flesh and devouring it greedily.

Blind with rage and pain, the bear roared, flailing away at his attackers as he breathed his last.

Joon-ho, Marta, and Laci watched the slaughter with silent dread.

"Nothing has a chance against those things," said Joon-ho.

The downed bear swiped his paw through the air one last time in a reflex movement as he lay dead.

Chapter 24

"This is Cardinal One. Listen up, everybody," said Strider at the wheel in the lead vehicle, walkie-talkie in hand. "Let's get moving. Over."

"This mission has as much chance of success as an ice cube in hell," said Purl in the backseat.

"Knock it off. We gotta think positive."

"This is Cardinal Three," said Joon-ho over the radio. "We're not gonna make it. Over."

"We *are* gonna make it, damn it," said Strider.

"There are too many of those things. Nothing can stop them. You kill one, and millions take its place—"

"Let's get moving," Strider cut in. "We're only defeated if we believe we're defeated. We are *not* defeated. Over and out."

"There are billions of those things out there," said Purl in the backseat, watching the creatures with bulging eyes.

"They can't hurt us in here. We have to keep moving."

"Open your eyes, man. There's nothing but ghouls out there as far as the eyes can see."

"The hell with those things," said Cassavetes, riding shotgun. "Run them all over."

"The president wants us to succeed, everybody," said Strider. "We don't want to let the president down, do we?"

"Nah," said Purl. "We sure don't want to do that. I didn't even vote for the guy."

Strider craned around to eye Purl. "What do you want us to do? Sit here and wait for death?"

"I'm not in charge."

"Then keep your trap shut."

"It's a free country, and I'm gonna have my say."

"We don't need you reminding us we're dead," Cassavetes told Purl. "In the end, we're all dead."

"Cheer me up, why don't you?" said Purl.

"If you want out, Purl, say the word and I'll leave you here," said Strider, gazing at Purl's image in the rearview mirror.

"You ain't getting rid of me that easy."

"Don't remind me you're a cop killer, and I might let you live."

"You're out for revenge against the wrong guy. I had nothing to do with your brother's death. I vote for a food break. All in favor?"

"This isn't a democracy. I'm in charge. I give the orders."

"I'm getting cabin fever locked up in here."

"We'll break as soon as we find a clearing. The whole country can't be crawling with ghouls like the woods here."

"I hope you're right."

"He is," said Cassavetes. "I found clearings without ghouls when I drove this way."

A female middle-aged ghoul with a ruby Prada purse hanging from her shoulder shambled to the Suburban and pounded on Purl's window with the flat of her emaciated hand. Purl started in his seat.

"Get out of here," he cried at her. "Why isn't she frying?" he asked Strider.

"She's touching the glass," answered Strider. "It doesn't conduct electricity."

"Then give me a piece so I can take her out."

"She can't get in. You worry too much."

"The thing isn't knocking on your window. She must've been a rich bitch with that fancy Prada handbag."

"Having millions doesn't protect you from the zombie plague."

"It levels the playing field," said Cassavetes. "It's an equal opportunity disease."

"This is Cardinal One," said Strider into his walkie-talkie. "Let's get the lead out. Over."

He fired the Beast's engine, put the transmission in Drive, and peeled off, plowing slogging ghouls out of the road.

"Do you read me, Halverson?" said Strider.

"I read you loud and clear," said Halverson.

"Joon-ho?" said Strider.

"Roger, sir," said Joon-ho.

Halverson and Joon-ho drove after Strider, who cleared the road of ghouls with the Beast's snowplow.

Chapter 25

That afternoon, after the convoy emerged from the forest, the land leveled off and the masses of ghouls began to peter out.

At the wheel, Strider surveyed the landscape. At length, he didn't notice any ghouls traipsing across the ground. Hazy clouds veiled the sky like gauze. The air felt humid.

"This is Cardinal One," he said into his walkie-talkie. "Let's take our lunch break. I want to inspect the vehicles for damage. Over."

The three vehicles pulled over to the side of the road.

"They're around here somewhere," said Purl, eying the surroundings with suspicion from the backseat.

"Cassavetes, pass out the MREs and bottled water," said Strider, climbing out of the Beast.

"Huh?" said Cassavetes.

"They're in the back."

Cassavetes circled to the back of the vehicle.

Strider opened the back door to let Purl out. "Time to eat."

Purl slid out of the backseat, looking around warily, expecting a ghoul to pop up any moment.

"Don't try anything," said Strider.

"Where am I gonna go in these chains?" said Purl. "I got a better chance with you guys than on my own."

Strider inspected the front of the Beast, casting around for any damage. Smeared with the rotting flesh of ghouls, bone chips, and strands of hair, the snowplow remained firmly attached to the front bumper.

The rest of the team piled out of the Suburbans, walked around on the grass, and stretched their legs.

Halverson saw Marta wandering toward him as he stood on the grass.

"What do you think?" she said. "Do we have any chance of success?"

"Half."

"Half a chance?" She paused. "I can't tell when you're joking."

Halverson had developed a cynical shell around him after all he'd been through during the apocalypse. He kept his feelings hidden. Plus he was trained to keep his feelings hidden by his employer, the Central Intelligence Agency.

"I'm not sure we can trust the president," he said.

"Why not?"

"The last president tried to drone me. At least, someone in his administration did. So I tend to be cynical."

"You really think he'd drone all of us? What would be the point?"

"I can't see him doing that. We're the only chance he has of getting the vaccine."

"Then why don't you trust the president?"

"Maybe it's my nature to be suspicious."

"You think this mission is some kind of setup?"

Halverson shook his head. "I don't see what he has to gain by sacrificing us. Let's not think about it. Let's think about accomplishing the mission."

"If they want us to be optimistic, why do they call this a suicide mission?"

"Because of all those ghouls out there waiting for us," said Rafferty, who had overheard them. "This operation has absolute zero chance of success. But we have fresh air to breathe—uh, the air *is* safe to breathe, isn't it?"

"If we're far enough away from ground zero," said Halverson.

"Are we?"

Halverson said nothing.

"I'm sick of living in fear all the time," said Marta. "Fear of ghouls, fear of breathing toxic air, fear of a mission that could be a setup."

"A setup?" said Rafferty. "Wasn't it understood in the beginning that we're all gonna die on this mission? Didn't you get the message?"

"I didn't care. I couldn't go on living in that bunker, breathing contaminated air. I'm claustrophobic."

"How come?"

"The bunker reminded me of being locked in the bedroom closet when the ghouls attacked my mom and sister—"

She cut herself off. She couldn't stand reliving the memory, reliving her fear of trying to help her mom and sister escape the clutches of the ghouls. In fact, she had fled her hiding place in the closet to save herself, abandoning them to their grisly fate. She hated herself for doing it. Why couldn't she have made some attempt to save them?

"What closet?" said Rafferty.

"Never mind," said Marta, turning ashen.

"How can it be worse than being on this suicide mission?"

"Knock it off," said Strider, approaching them. "This isn't a suicide mission."

"Yeah? And nobody ever dies."

"The only thing that can sink this mission is negative thinking."

"What about this air? Is it safe to breathe?" said Rafferty, sniffing suspiciously.

Strider produced his cellular-sized personal radiation detector and examined its screen.

"The air is fine," he said, "so stop spreading panic."

"Yeah, just another day in paradise."

"Take a break. Eat your MREs and relax a few minutes. Everything's fine."

Until it wasn't.

Chapter 26

A score of armed strangers on horses rode across the clearing toward the convoy.

"We got company," said Rafferty.

Halverson checked out the lead rider who sat astride a black stallion.

Pushing forty, his face tanned and withered from outdoor living, the stranger had long black hair. He was wearing a black Stetson, a white button-down shirt, black jeans, and shiny white snakeskin cowboy boots. Bandoliers crisscrossed his chest. In his right hand he brandished a large revolver, a Smith & Wesson 500 .50 Magnum with a stainless steel barrel that extended over eight inches. On his belt hung a bowie knife inserted in a sheath. On the calf of one of his pant legs was strapped a hatchet.

On closer inspection, Halverson could see the man had a bootless peg leg nestled in the saddle's right stirrup.

The stranger brought his horse to a halt in front of the convoy.

"What do we have here?" he said.

"We mean you no harm," said Strider. "We're on a mission for the president."

"A mission for the president," mocked the newcomer. "Well, I'm Richmond Gatling, and me and my militia are looking for President Cole. We plan on executing him for treason for committing high crimes and misdemeanors against the United States of America."

"Strong words, Gatling."

"What you see in my hand is a .50 Magnum, the most powerful handgun in the world."

"What you see slung on my shoulder is a B&T MP9 with a thirty-round magazine."

"Now that we've introduced ourselves, who do I have the pleasure of talking to?"

"The name's Strider."

"You're working for Cole?"

"Cole's dead."

"Dead?" said Gatling, bowled over.

"A nuke blew him up."

Gatling let out a belly laugh. "Poetic justice if I ever heard of it." He paused a beat. "Nevertheless, it saddens me to hear such news. I wanted to execute him myself for treason," he said, pointing his revolver at Strider.

"Don't point that piece at me," said Strider.

"I was demonstrating what I would have done to the traitor Cole," said Gatling, lowering his weapon. "No offense meant."

"Why do you want to assassinate the president?"

"He nuked half the country. What do you want us to do? Give him a medal?"

"He did it to save the country from the infected ghouls."

"The ghouls are still here and half the country's a nuclear wasteland."

"He's gone."

"Who's the new president?"

"Walter Mims."

"Is he planning on nuking the other half of the country?"

"I don't know his plans."

"Where is he? We just came back from DC. The White House is overrun with zeds."

"He's safe."

Arms crossed, revolver in hand, Gatling leaned down toward Strider from his horse. "I want to talk to him about his future plans for this great country. You see, I'm from Dallas, Texas, and I care about this country."

"We all do. We're trying to save it."

"What is your mission?" said Gatling, squinting his right eye.

Strider bridled. "I'm not at liberty to tell you."

"According to who?"

"According to the president, this is a top secret mission, eyes only."

Gatling's horse snorted and stepped back and forth restlessly. Gatling pulled on the horse's reins, controlling him.

"I don't think the president should have secrets from his fellow countrymen," he said. "It's unconstitutional."

"With all due respect, the president doesn't give a damn what you think."

"That's the same kind of thinking that got this country blown half to hell. I'm a voter. I have a right to know what's going on."

Halverson trained his B&T MP9 on Gatling. "Maybe you should move on."

Gatling narrowed his eyes into slits. "Who are you?"

"Halverson."

"Listen up, Halverson. I don't cotton to guns being pointed at me. Just tell me your mission, and we'll be on our way."

"Our mission is secret," said Strider. "TS/SCI. Top secret/sensitive compartmented information."

"I don't like the sound of that. How do I know you're not gonna launch another ICBM at us? You could be on your way to a secret nuclear silo in Nebraska, for all I know, with the intent to nuke the rest of this great country."

"Our mission is none of your business," said Strider, reaching for his B&T MP9 slung over his shoulder.

The members of Gatling's gang reached for their pieces.

Chapter 27

"Whoa," said Gatling. "We didn't come here to kill anyone. We want to know what direction this country's headed in because it's been going off the rails for too long, and we citizens are suffering for it. It's time to change course."

"Then vote in the next election," said Strider.

"We don't even know who's running the country for Chrissake. How can we vote when everything's kept secret?"

"I'm not here to discuss politics with you. We don't have time for it. We're in the middle of a mission that will save the country."

Steadying his horse with his reins Gatling became thoughtful. "You don't say. Hmm. Well, maybe we can help you—if you let us know what you're doing."

Strider exchanged looks with Halverson.

"We don't need help," Strider told Gatling. "We're all government workers."

"I'm not," said Rafferty. "I don't have a job. I was in the brig."

Gatling scoped out Rafferty.

"Why's he in chains if you're all government workers?" Gatling asked Strider. Gatling took in the other prisoners clad in jumpsuits. "Hell, half your team is in chains. What the hell's going on here? Secret mission, my ass. Convicts don't go on secret missions. Who are you trying to kid?"

Halverson tensed. Things could get ugly, he decided, checking out Gatling's armed gang who were glowering at Strider's team.

"We're running short on military men," said Strider.

"What kind of military man are you?" said Gatling.

"SEAL Team Six under the command of JSOC."

Gatling relaxed a bit. "I respect SEALs. My two brothers were SEALs." He got a faraway look in his eyes. "It didn't save them from the ghouls, though." He refocused his gaze on Strider. "Do you have a bone frog?"

Strider lifted the short sleeve of his camo shirt, revealing the tattoo of a bone frog on his muscular arm. "Satisfied?"

Gatling nodded yes. "You're escorting prisoners somewhere? Is that the nature of your mission?"

"I can't say."

"Transferring 'em to Leavenworth or something?"

"The mission is secret."

"There are zeds all over the place. We could help you get through."

"Let's face it," said Rafferty. "We need all the help we can get on this suicide mission."

"Suicide mission?" said Gatling, pricking up his ears.

"We need battle-hardened military men for this mission," said Strider.

"We've wasted thousands of zeds. We're a battle-hardened militia. We never back down from zeds."

Halverson could see Strider was weighing the idea of enlisting Gatling and his gang. Halverson had misgivings, since Gatling had expressed his intention to execute President Cole for treason.

"The mission is top secret," said Strider, thinking better of it.

"Look," said Gatling. "We're all on the same page here. We all want to rid the world of zeds. We can help you guys."

"What makes you think we need your help?"

"We need all the help we can get," said Rafferty.

"You're not in command here, Rafferty," said Strider.

"I don't get it," said Gatling. "A top secret mission to deliver prisoners to Leavenworth, while the zeds are taking over the world? It makes no sense. What's so important about these prisoners?"

"Don't you get it?" said Rafferty. "We're part of the mission."

"You talk too much, Rafferty," said Strider.

"What kind of help are you gonna be with your arms and legs in chains?" said Gatling, frowning in puzzlement at Rafferty.

"Our mission is time sensitive," said Strider. "We can't stand here all day chewing the fat with you."

"Tell me one thing. Where's the president hiding?"

"I'm glad you asked," said Rafferty. "He's—"

Strider trained his B&T MP9 on Rafferty's head. "Shut up or you're dead. Our mission can succeed without you."

Rafferty's eyes popped at the sight of the gun's gaping muzzle. He held his tongue.

"How many men does he have guarding him?" said Gatling.

"This conversation is over," said Strider.

"What's it worth to you?" Damon asked Gatling.

Strider swung his MP9 barrel toward Damon. "Your presence on this mission is not essential, Damon."

"I wasn't gonna tell him. I just wondered how bad he wanted the info."

"What about your freedom?" said Gatling, staring at Damon. "Is the info worth your freedom?"

"I said this conversation is over," said Strider. "Time for you to leave, Gatling. We have to be on our way."

"You need to think twice about turning down our offer of help," said Gatling. "There are millions of zeds in the direction you're heading. We just came from there. I lost two men in our fight with them."

"We don't need your help."

"Are you questioning my manhood?"

"Not at all."

"Let me tell you about myself so you understand where I come from."

"It's not gonna change my mind."

Chapter 28

Gatling commenced his story, regardless.

"I lost my two brothers during a ferocious attack mounted by the zeds just south of Fort Worth. I'm only alive today out of luck, balls, and a desperate desire to go on living.

"We were defending a hill against millions of zeds. Wave after wave of them like an ocean stretching to the horizon poured toward the three of us. They were moving as a single entity with no room between them. A unified mass of death and destruction we couldn't dream of stopping.

"Protected by an outcropping, my two brothers and me were armed to the teeth and held them off for two hours, but there were too many of them. We all had AR-15s. We ran out of ammo. We had to defend ourselves in CQB from the zeds. First the zeds bit my younger brother Seth. He pleaded with me not to let him turn. But I was out of ammo. We all were. I couldn't shoot him in the head. I couldn't bring myself to strangle him. Anyway, I thought his brain might survive strangulation and he would become reanimated as a zed. The only way to kill the things is to destroy their brains.

"I was in a quandary. I didn't want to kill Seth, but I had to. He would turn any minute. I took out my bowie knife and decided to stab him in the temple. You have no idea how hard it was to bring myself to do it—even with him begging me to do it. My older brother Joe battled the advancing zeds with his knife and hatchet, while I decided what to do. The zeds were closing in on us. I couldn't put it off any longer.

"I thrust my blade into Seth's temple, destroying his brain. He fell dead. Grief-stricken, I turned around and saw a ghoul bite Joe's forearm. Joe screamed.

"Now I would have to kill Joe, or he would turn. He didn't want me to kill him, but he knew it was the right thing to do. He knew he would turn, otherwise. I stabbed Joe in the temple and threw up, so sickened was I of what I had done to my two brothers.

"Surrounded by zeds, I knew I had no chance against them. I could think of only one way I might survive. After I puked, I fell to the ground and lay motionless, holding my breath, playing dead. My heart was thumping like crazy. I tried to will it to stop, but I couldn't. I was sure the zeds could hear it pounding against my rib cage as they converged around me.

"Paralyzed with fear, desperate to go on living, I lay there with my eyes shut as the zeds moved in for the kill. They're attracted to noise and movement, you know. I made no noise, except for my heartbeat pounding in my ears. I continued to will my heart to stop, but it kept pounding away. I didn't move a muscle. I thought my heart would burst any second, as I continued to hold my breath, terrified the zeds would attack me if they saw telltale movement in my body.

"I couldn't believe it when they passed by me, leaving me alone, searching for living creatures. They won't eat dead humans. They eat only living ones. I still have nightmares of that day."

"Is that where you got that peg leg?" said Rafferty.

"No," said Gatling. "I lost my leg later on. A zed bit my leg in another skirmish I had with them."

"I hope you wasted him."

"I blew his head clean off with my .50 Mag."

"Did a doctor amputate your leg to prevent the plague from infecting you?" said Damon, licking his lips at the thought of eating Gatling's calf.

"I did it myself. I always carry a hatchet with me, as you can see," said Gatling, glancing at the hatchet strapped to his lower leg. He grimaced at the memory. "You think it's easy cutting off your leg with a hatchet? Think again. I had to whack that thing five times before it came completely off. I was sweating like a pig the whole time. I don't know how for the life of me I didn't pass out from the pain."

"How'd you stop the bleeding?"

"I had a fire going. I heated up the hatchet blade and cauterized the stub of my leg."

"What'd you do with the leg you cut off?" said Damon, his eyes glowing as he imagined eating it.

"You ask strange questions," said Gatling.

"Didn't you ever hear of the Cincinnati Cannibal?" said Rafferty.

"What?"

"That's him. Rudolf Damon," said Rafferty with disgust.

Damon flashed a lopsided smile.

Gatling shook his head. He cut his eyes toward Strider.

"Getting back to what I was saying," said Gatling.

"Yeah?" said Strider.

"You heard my story. So don't tell me I'm not battle-hardened."

"I'm sure you are," said Strider. "I never questioned it. But we don't need your help. I thank you for the offer to join our mission."

"Actually, we're on a mission, too. My mission is to destroy every zed on this planet. Hunt them down and kill them. I'm gonna whack out every last one of them, and I'm not gonna stop till I do. There's no way we can coexist with those things. They'll never be satisfied till all of us are dead. Our only chance of continuing to live as a species is to exterminate them."

"Kill or be killed," said Rafferty, nodding. "The law of nature."

"There's nothing natural about zeds. They're an abomination. They belong in hell. And that's where I'm prepared to send every single one of them," said Gatling, his eyes blazing with fervor. "I'm gonna fight them to the death. As long as I'm breathing, I'm gonna be killing zeds."

"If these guys would unchain me, I'd join your crusade to kill zeds, too," said Rafferty.

"No power on earth is gonna stop me from taking out every zed in my line of sight."

Halverson figured the guy was obsessed, a monomaniac determined to dole out death. Gatling wasn't motivated by the will to survive but by vengeance. His life had no raison d'être other than the obliteration of zeds.

Halverson could see himself taking the same route in life if he let the lust for vengeance become his sole purpose for living. He had lost people he cared about to the zeds. He had plenty of reason to seek vengeance for their deaths. He didn't want to be blinded by vengeance, though. Then again, what was his purpose in a world gone mad, a world turned upside down into a wasteland of walking corpses? He was thinking too much, he told himself. He decided to focus on the success of the mission to obtain the vaccine for the zombie plague from Dr. Wheelhouse.

"I want to join you guys," Rafferty told Gatling. "Take me with you." Rafferty grinned. "I'm a stone killer."

Gatling stared down at Rafferty from his horse. "Have you ever run away from a zed?"

"Never. Every time I see one, I fight it."

"None of my boys have ever run away from a zed. We see them, we attack them. That's it. That's what we do. That's who we are."

"I'm with you. Kill those fuckers."

Gatling thought about it. "We could always use more men."

"You're not going anywhere, Rafferty," said Strider.

"Where do I sign up?" Damon asked Gatling. "Take off my chains and I'm in."

"We have a rule in our militia," said Gatling. "No cannibals allowed."

"Bigots," screamed Damon.

"Shut up, Damon," said Strider. "We need you here."

"I wouldn't join you bums if you begged me," Damon told Gatling.

Gatling withdrew his .50 Magnum from its holster and trained the barrel on Damon's head.

Halverson's pulse raced. He prepared to shoot Gatling.

A Hispanic guy in his late twenties mounted on a bay horse yelled at Gatling from behind.

"What is it, Pedro?" said Gatling, turning around, forgetting about Damon.

"Zeds about a half mile behind us," said Pedro.

Gatling smiled, pulling his horse halfway around so he could see the zeds.

"Let's go, men," he said. "Kill all of them."

Halverson tensed and moved his hand toward his MP9, thinking Gatling meant to kill Strider's group.

Brandishing his .50 Magnum, Gatling turned his stallion all the way around and galloped toward the scores of zeds congregating in the distance. His men galloped after him, drawing their guns, cutting loose and letting out rebel war whoops.

Chapter 29

"Gatling could mean trouble," said Halverson, lowering his hand from his MP9, his face somber, watching Gatling and his gang ride off.

Guns blazing, the militia assaulted the ghouls that were gathering on the flatland.

"I agree," said Strider. "These roving militias are seeking control of the country."

"I doubt we can trust him."

"Let's beat it before he returns."

"Maybe they won't return," said Rafferty.

"Let me go with them," said Damon, watching with a wistful expression the bloodthirsty gang waging war.

"They don't want you," said Rafferty. "Nobody wants cannibals with them. Including me."

Damon turned on Rafferty. "What makes you think I want a serial killer with me?"

"Let's get moving," said Strider, and headed back to the Beast.

"I don't want to go," said Damon, refusing to budge. "I'm enlisting in the militia when they come back."

Strider changed direction and made a beeline for Damon.

"You agreed to go on this mission in exchange for the president's stay of your execution," said Strider.

"I changed my mind," said Damon. "I want to join the militia."

Strider trained his MP9 on Damon's head. "I think you should reconsider."

"Why?"

"Because your stay of execution is about to be revoked."

"You don't scare me. Only the president can revoke it."

Strider shot Damon twice in the head. Damon crumpled on the ground.

Laci gasped.

"Anyone else want to renege on their promise to the president?" said Strider.

Nobody said anything.

"Then let's beat it," said Strider.

"Good riddance," said Rafferty, leering at Damon's corpse.

"We got one less man to take on the ghouls," said Halverson.

"We're better off without him," said Strider. "He was inciting a mutiny." He raised his voice. "Anyone else got a problem with our mission?"

"You were right to whack that scumbag," said Rafferty.

"We can't afford to lose another member," said Halverson.

"I will not tolerate a mutiny," said Strider.

Halverson nodded in agreement. But inside he was wondering if his friend Strider was becoming obsessed with the power of his position as team commander when he had shot Damon in cold blood. On the other hand, Damon had yet to prove himself a worthy adversary of the ghouls. In effect, he wanted to desert by joining the militia. Strider knew the tacit rule in the military: All deserters will be shot.

"We're only a few hours into this mission, and we're already down a man," said Halverson.

"I had no choice," said Strider. "If you're not with us, you're against us. And Damon was against us. He was a thorn in our side. He had to be removed for the good of the team."

It couldn't be easy shooting a defenseless man, decided Halverson, yet Strider had done it without any qualms that he could see. Maybe the guy was good at hiding his internal emotional conflicts.

Halverson picked up on Strider's hand shaking. Or maybe not, decided Halverson.

Spotting the direction of Halverson's gaze Strider put his hand in his pocket.

"It's getting cold out here," said Strider. He paused a moment. "What would you have done?"

"Beat his brains out with my fists."

Smiling, Strider grunted.

"None of these cons are benefiting morale," said Halverson.

"As long as they don't try to desert, we can put up with it. I'm not gonna gag them."

"Maybe if we took off their chains, it would boost their morale."

"Or they might take the opportunity to desert or kill us."

"There's that."

"Do you trust these guys enough to give them guns?" said Strider, eying Halverson.

"I haven't reached that point."

"Me either." Strider paused in thought. "What concerns me is, I don't think I ever will."

"When we run into a shitstorm, we're gonna have to trust them with pieces. Otherwise, we should eighty-six them here and now."

"I'm following orders. The president ordered us to take them with us. That's what we're gonna do. I have a feeling we're gonna need every fighter we can get."

"I might be able to bring myself to trust Laci and Purl, but Rafferty . . . I dunno," said Halverson, shaking his head.

"I know what you mean, but I get the impression he could be a good fighter. Damon, on the other hand, was floating off in his own little cloud-cuckoo-land. He wasn't any good for us."

Halverson eyeballed Gatling's militia, who, astride their horses, were busy blowing away ghouls. Their horses were kicking up clods of dirt as the onslaught raged on. Nobody was looking in this direction. What with their own gun reports and their yelling Gatling's gang must not have heard Strider's gunshot, decided Halverson.

"Time to go," said Strider.

Time to go, Holman, thought Halverson, recalling the last scene at a Chinese mission in the Steve McQueen movie *The Sand Pebbles*. The movie didn't end well for Holman.

Halverson and the team members piled into their vehicles.

Laci held her hands behind her to prevent Joon-ho and the others from noticing that he had forgotten to lock her cuff after she had taken a leak. She thought about making a run for it, but her legs were still shackled. She doubted she would get far. Having free hands wasn't much of an advantage with her legs restrained.

Her only option now was to overpower Joon-ho and seize his keys so she could unlock her shackles. She saw no opportunity to take him on. He was holding his MP9 aimed at her as they walked back to their vehicle.

She clambered into the backseat, pretending her cuffs were locked behind her back, keeping turned toward him so he couldn't see the unlocked cuff. He shut the door behind her and locked it.

Halverson shoved Rafferty into the backseat of his vehicle.

"You can sit back there now because Damon can't scare you anymore," said Halverson, locking the door.

Rafferty looked daggers at him, as Halverson climbed into the driver's seat.

"One big happy family," said Rafferty.

The convoy resumed its journey.

Chapter 30

Two hours later, Halverson saw ominous thunderheads gathering, blotting out the sun.

What started out as drizzle that barely misted the windshield and didn't require wipers turned into torrents of rain.

"Cardinal One to Cardinal Two," said Strider through the walkie-talkie in the Beast. "It's coming down so hard I can hardly see. Over."

"This is Cardinal Two. I have to follow you closer to keep you in sight," said Halverson, squinting through the downpour. "Over."

"We're gonna get some," said Rafferty, watching the sheets of rain from the backseat.

The sound of rain pounding the Suburban roof increased its din.

"I can't see six feet in front of me," squawked Strider through his radio. "We're gonna have to pull over and wait it out. The roads might be flooded ahead. Over."

"Roger," said Halverson.

"I'll tell Joon-ho we're pulling over. Over and out."

Halverson followed Cardinal One as it pulled to the side of the road.

"This mission is doomed," said Rafferty. "This is nature's way of telling us to go back."

Lightning rived the gloomy cloud cover. A flashing, crackling grid of electricity screened the sky. Halverson gazed at the lowering black sky as thunder roared overhead, vibrating his SUV. He could feel the rumble in his chest.

"We're not going back," said Halverson.

Another bolt of lightning lit the sky, followed by a growling thunderclap.

"Then it's your fault if we get electrocuted in this vehicle," said Rafferty.

"The Suburban's steel shell will protect us."

"Steel conducts electricity."

"Exactly. The steel conducts it through the tires to the ground. So keep your hands away from the steel doors."

Rafferty, who was leaning against the door, shifted his position away from it.

"Are you willing to bet your life on it?" he said.

"I'm betting both our lives on it."

"Let me out of here," said Rafferty, furrowing his brow with anxiety.

"You'd be worse off in the open if lightning strikes. This is the safest place for us."

"Then let's turn back. I'm telling you, we're jinxed."

"We have a mission to complete."

"It's not gonna happen with that Strider guy in control."

"What are you talking about?" said Halverson, turning his head around to look at Rafferty behind him.

"Didn't you see how easy it was for Strider to blow away Damon in cold blood?"

"He didn't have any choice."

"Damon was in chains, for Chrissake. Strider killed a defenseless man without batting an eye. He's a stone killer. I know what I'm talking about. Take it from me, he's a sociopath."

"Takes one to know one, huh?"

"Something like that. The point is, none of us are safe with him in charge."

"He's not gonna harm anyone who obeys orders," said Halverson.

Though Halverson didn't let on, he was wondering if Rafferty was right about Strider. Strider hadn't hesitated blowing Damon's brains out, didn't even give Damon a warning. Just *pow*. Halverson was friends with Strider, but maybe the apocalypse had changed the guy. It could change anyone. Facing death every day from the plague could change anyone's personality. These weren't normal days. They were end days. Death was everywhere. People became used to seeing corpses day after day. The plague and the flesh eaters were ravaging the planet.

"Mark my words," said Rafferty. "He's gonna end up wasting all of us, if we do the slightest thing he doesn't like."

"You worry too much."

Chapter 31

In Joon-ho's vehicle Laci was sitting in the backseat debating whether to open the door and make a mad dash though the pouring rain. She doubted the others would be able to track her in the rain. The visibility couldn't have been more than six feet—if that. She could lose them easily in the storm.

But what would she do out there? she wondered. She would get soaking wet and would have no place to go. She could seek out her parents, but they could care less about her. There was a good chance they could have died from the plague.

She would probably have a better chance of survival if she stayed with the team. On the other hand, this was a suicide mission. She was beginning to regret volunteering. What did she expect? She was a three-time loser. Every decision she ever made was wrong. How was she supposed to make a living? Her grades in high school were poor.

With no prospects she had decided to join the army. Like the TV ad said, she wanted to be all she could be and see the world.

As if she was reading Laci's mind, Marta asked, "Why did you join the army, Laci?"

"Nothing interested me," answered Laci. "I didn't have any skills or talents. I was going nowhere. Soon after I enlisted, my CO assaulted me. I guess it wasn't such a good career choice for me."

"You had no idea it was gonna happen. It can happen anywhere, not just in the army."

"I guess." Laci paused a beat. "What are you gonna do after this mission is over? See your family?"

Marta withdrew inside herself. "My family's gone."

"I'm sorry."

"The ghouls killed my mother and sister in the bedroom," said Marta in a daze. "I watched from the closet as the ghouls tore them apart. They begged me for help, but I was too terrified to help them. I didn't want the ghouls to kill me. I ran for my life. Nightmares haunt me to this day about deserting them in their time of need."

"What else could you do?"

"I could've stayed and helped them fight the ghouls."

"You'd be dead like your family if you stayed with them."

"I keep telling myself that, but I still feel guilty about abandoning them."

"For all I know, my parents might be dead. They made no effort to contact me after I went to jail."

"The ghouls killed my son Johnny," said Joon-ho, listening to them. "I fought them off and tried to save him. A gang of five of them attacked us in an alley in the Bronx. I fought them off with a baseball bat, but one of the things got past me and bit Johnny. In white heat, I bashed the thing's head in. I still remember the stink of the rotting carcass of that infected creature. It was nauseating. I smashed the heads of the remaining ghouls to pulp. I cried when I saw Johnny standing behind me, his cheek torn off, blood streaming from his wound. How could I save him? I wondered. I couldn't come up with an answer. But I had to do something. I had to help him. If they bite you in the arm or leg, you can amputate them and maybe save yourself. But not if they bite your cheek. I couldn't amputate Johnny's face. The disease was already coursing through his system and entering his brain. I watched his eyes turn milky. With a sinking stomach I could tell he was gonna turn any second. My son, Johnny, a ghoul. I wanted to scream. What was I supposed to do? I had no answer. I needed a miracle, but miracles don't exist. I had no way out. I felt crushed by my impotence. There was only one way to end my and Johnny's suffering. Sick to my stomach, choked up, I took my bat and smashed Johnny's head in. I heard his skull crack under the blow of my bat. His head collapsed into mushy brains and bone fragments. Horrified at what I had done, I dropped to my knees and, weeping, cursed God. I had no answers. Why wasn't there an answer? All I heard was silence from God and blood burbling from what was left of Johnny's pulverized head."

"Jesus," said Marta.

"That's what's so horrifying. There are no answers. You just have to take your chances and do what you think is best, or . . . ," said Joon-ho, his voice trailing off.

"Or what?"

"Or kill yourself."

A gloomy silence prevailed in the vehicle.

"You did what you had to do," said Marta.

Joon-ho didn't look convinced.

"At least you did something," said Marta. "I ran. I can never forgive myself for running away when Mom and sis needed me the most," she said, her voice breaking.

"Maybe we're in hell," muttered Laci. "That's why nothing we do can turn out right."

Marta heaved a sigh. "We're better off not thinking about it."

"Yeah. What did you do before the end of the world, Marta?"

"I was a coder."

"You look like you keep in shape."

"I do. Were you in the joint when the plague hit?"

"I was in solitary confinement in the brig. I had no idea there even was a plague. Nobody told me anything. I had no contact with the outside world."

"I guess jail was one of the safer places to be during the outbreak. The ghouls couldn't get to you."

"I didn't know they existed till the guards transferred me to Mount Weather."

"Why did they transfer you of all people?"

"President Cole got interested in my case. He wanted to have sex with me. He had a reputation as a skirt-chaser."

"And?"

"He used to invite me up to his office sometimes."

"But he kept you locked up?"

"He was the freaking president. He did whatever he wanted. It was a lousy deal, let me tell you. I got sick of it. I wanted out. I'm glad he's dead."

A lightning bolt crashed into the ground the better part of a hundred yards from their vehicle. The ground shook from the bolt's impact.

Wide-eyed, everybody started in their seats.

Smoke plumed from the wet earth and mixed with the pelting rain.

Laci smelled a sulfuric odor wafting toward them on a gust of wind.

Strider's voice came through the walkie-talkie. "This is Cardinal One. You OK, Joon-ho? Over."

His hand shaking, Joon-ho picked up his radio and answered, "We're OK in Cardinal Three. Over."

"Turn off your electrical devices during the storm. Over."

"What about the charge running through the roof? Over."

"Turn off everything. We don't want to get hit by lightning. Over."

"Will do. Over."

Joon-ho killed the current that was electrifying the SUV.

"What next?" he said, knowing no one would answer, his face pallid from his traumatic recollections of his son's death at his hands.

Chapter 32

In Cardinal Two, Halverson saw blurry grey shapes lurking in the torrential rain. He couldn't make out what they were. All he could tell for sure was they were approaching his door. There appeared to be two of them.

He wondered if it was Strider and Rafferty. Why would they be approaching without letting him know they were coming? Halverson wondered. What were they doing out in the pouring rain anyway?

The two shapes lurched closer to his door.

"Who's that?" said Rafferty, peering through the curtains of rain.

One of the figures pressed their face against Halverson's window. Halverson winced. It was a ghoul.

"Friggin' zeds," said Rafferty. "I guess getting drenched means nothing to them."

"All they care about is eating."

"Turn on the juice," said Rafferty, as the two ghouls pressed their bodies against the side of the Suburban trying to get inside.

"Not with the lightning outside. You heard Strider. Anyway, they can't get in."

Hundreds of shapes emerged from the storm to descend on the Suburbans. And then hundreds more. They mounted the hoods of the vehicles and climbed onto the windshields, where they writhed and groped, trying to figure out how to enter the vehicles.

Thousands of the plodding shapes manifested themselves out of the rain and joined the attack.

"Are we gonna just sit here?" said Rafferty, becoming animated.

Jagged lightning lit up the black clouds hanging low in the sky like clusters of giant Concord grapes. Thunder rumbled.

"This is Cardinal One. Everybody, hold your ground," said Strider through his walkie-talkie. "Over."

"Cardinal Two here. Roger," said Halverson. "Over." He turned to Rafferty. "You heard him."

"I already told you, he's a sociopath," said Rafferty. "Taking orders from a psycho killer is nuts. We're all gonna die if we listen to him. He's more dangerous to us than the zeds are."

Halverson checked all of the windows. They were covered with the putrefying corpses of ghouls that were piling onto the vehicle in their futile attempts to enter.

"We can't even see outside anymore."

Halverson sniffed the air. "It smells musty in here."

"It smells like rotting stiffs."

Halverson radioed Strider. "This is Cardinal Two. We got a situation. The ghouls are clogging our air ducts. Over."

"Shit," said Strider. "All right. Let's run the scumbags over and get out of here. Over."

"I can't see out the windshield. It's wall-to-wall ghouls. Over."

"We got the same problem. Over."

"The only way to get them off is to juice the cars. Over."

"Running electricity in a thunderstorm is risking a lightning strike. Over."

"We're gonna suffocate in our vehicle if we stay here—unless . . ."

"Unless what?" said Strider. "Over."

"Unless someone goes outside and removes the ghouls from the windshield—"

Rafferty guffawed in the backseat. "Great idea. It's your idea. You go."

"There are too many of them out there," said Strider. "We won't be able to kill them fast enough if we leave our cars. They'll overwhelm us. Over."

Halverson coughed. "We're running out of air. Over."

"Our options suck."

"Opening the door is suicide," yelled Rafferty.

"Shut up, Rafferty," said Strider. "Over."

"We need air," cried Rafferty, refusing to obey Strider. "I'm suffocating. I didn't volunteer for this mission to suffocate."

"Our mission is to save the goddamn human race," said Halverson.

"As long as I'm in charge, we're gonna save this country," said Strider. "Over."

"We can't save anyone if we can't save ourselves," said Rafferty.

"I didn't ask you, Rafferty. Over."

Halverson felt nauseous from breathing the foul air. "We can't hold out much longer without getting fresh air. Over."

He stared at the ghouls crammed against the windshield. They grimaced at him, trying to chew through the bulletproof glass, rain drenching them.

"All right," said Strider. "Juice the cars for five minutes. That should get the ghouls off our cars. Don't touch any metal in your car, especially if your hands are wet. Did everybody hear me? Over."

"Roger," said Halverson. "Out."

"Joon-ho? Over."

"I heard you," said Joon-ho in Cardinal Three. "Our air is foul. Marta is not handling it well. She says she's claustrophobic. She looks like she's gonna pass out. Over."

"On the count of three, turn on your juice for five minutes then kill it. That should remove the ghouls. After the ghouls fall off the cars, we drive out of here and find a safer place to stay. Do you copy? Over."

"I copy," said Halverson. "Over."

"I copy," said Joon-ho. "Over."

Strider counted to three.

Chapter 33

In Cardinal Three Joon-ho pressed the red button on the dash that electrified the SUV during the driving rainstorm.

"I gotta get out of here," said Marta, riding shotgun, clawing at her shirt collar, gasping for breath.

"Hold on for five more minutes," said Joon-ho.

"I feel like the walls are closing in on me. The ghouls will crush us. There are too many of them. We're getting buried alive under ghouls," she said, eyeballing the twisted bodies of ghouls mantling the windshield.

The ghouls commenced jerking on the hood as the current of electricity coursed through their bodies. Their brains and heads smoked.

As the ghouls slid off the windshield, Marta felt better since she could see outside. Not that she could see much. All she could see was driving rain. But she didn't feel like she was getting buried alive under a pile of ghouls anymore. The air inside the vehicle began to smell better slowly—a little smoky at first but gradually better. She heard a deafening thunderclap.

She was starting to relax when she felt the lightning bolt strike their SUV. The vehicle lurched.

"We've been hit," said Joon-ho into his walkie-talkie, wild-eyed. "Over."

"We heard the explosion," said Strider. "Are you OK? Kill your juice. Over."

In a state of shock, her heartbeat racing, Marta smelled the rank odor of smoke mixed with sulfur.

"We were hit by lightning," said Joon-ho, rattled, his eyes popping.

"Is everyone all right in your vehicle?" said Strider. "Over."

Joon-ho checked on Marta and Laci. They both looked pale and wide-eyed, but seemed OK.

"What the hell happened?" said Laci, blinking rapidly.

"We're all right," Joon-ho told Strider. "Just shaken up. Over."

"Kill your juice," said Strider. "Over."

Joon-ho circumspectly pressed the red button. Nothing happened.

"It's not working," he said. "Over."

"The lightning must've overloaded your circuit. Can you see well enough to drive? Over."

"Yeah," said Joon-ho, unsteadily.

"Let's get out of here," said Strider. "Over."

Joon-ho fired the ignition.

Nothing happened. He tried again and again.

Nothing.

"I can't start the car," he said. "The lightning blew out all of our electrical devices. The battery's gone. Over."

Silence on the other end of the line.

"What are we supposed to do?" said Joon-ho. "Over."

"I can't believe we're alive," said Marta, looking around. "How could we survive a lightning strike?"

"We got hit by lightning," said Joon-ho into his walkie-talkie, his voice frantic. "Repeat, what are we supposed to do? Over."

"The lightning passed through your car and took out your electricity," said Strider. "Your car got hit, not you. Over."

"How do we get outa here? Over."

Silence.

"Are they gonna leave us here?" said Laci, shifting restlessly in the backseat. "The things will crawl back on our car any second," she said, eying the ghouls, who were standing in the rain a few yards from the car looking dazed.

"Is anyone there?" said Joon-ho into his walkie-talkie, sweat beading on his forehead and above his upper lip. "Over."

"You're gonna have to transfer to our vehicles," said Strider. "Over."

"The ghouls will rip us apart as soon as we open the door—"

"We're coming back there to give you cover fire. Over."

"There are a million ghouls out there. We'll never make it—"

"We're coming to help you. Over and out."

"Sir?"

Strider didn't answer.

"Sir?" repeated Joon-ho.

"We're never gonna make it," said Laci.

"We can't stay here," said Marta.

"We're following orders," said Joon-ho. "Prepare to exit the vehicle."

"It's time to give me a gun," said Laci. "I'm not going out there without a gun."

"She has a point," Marta told Joon-ho.

Joon-ho got on the radio. "Do I give a gun to Laci? Please advise. Over."

"Do it," said Strider. "She came with us to fight. It's about time she starts. Get ready to exit your vehicle. Over and out."

"Roger that, sir." He craned around to face Laci. "The guns are in the trunk."

Dazed, the ghouls were loitering in the storm without approaching the Suburban yet.

"The things look like they're in a state of shock after the lightning bolt hit the car," said Marta.

"Make sure your weapon is ready to fire," said Joon-ho, checking his B&T MP9. "We'll load up on mags when we open the trunk."

Her pulse racing, Marta inspected her MP9.

"It's now or never," said Joon-ho.

"Exit your vehicle, Joon-ho. Over," said Strider.

"Roger," said Joon-ho, trying to sound self-assured.

Chapter 34

Halverson kicked open his door, knocking three ghouls backward. MP9 blazing, he sprang out of the driver's seat of Cardinal Two. Half a dozen ghoul heads exploded as his bullets slammed into them.

To clear a path to the back door Halverson kicked ghouls out of his way. He opened the door, rain pouring down on him.

"Get out," he told Rafferty.

Rafferty recoiled. "Are you kidding? I don't have a piece."

"Time to make your bones."

"Don't let those things in here."

"We need to save Joon-ho."

"Are you crazy? They're behind you."

Halverson ejected his empty mag and replaced it with a fresh one from his cargo pocket. He squeezed off a burst at a mother and daughter ghoul shambling toward him, growling. The mother had half her jaw missing, exposing her upper row of cracked teeth. Halverson didn't know how she could chew anything without the rest of her jaw, but he wasn't going to wait and find out. His bullets tore her skull in half vertically.

Her daughter had her whole jaw, and she was opening it as she closed in on Halverson. He double-tapped her pustulating forehead. He had to make every bullet count. He didn't want to run out of them before he reached the Suburban trunk.

Halverson spun around to face Rafferty again.

"Get out of there," said Halverson.

"Not without a piece."

"I'll give you one when we reach the trunk. Now move."

"And unlock these cuffs."

"Move it."

With the short muzzle of his MP9 Halverson pistol-whipped the face of a stocky thirtyish ghoul dressed in plumber overalls. The ghoul's maggot-ridden nose fell off. Halverson fired a bullet into the creature's eye, which exploded into jelly. The bullet tore a groove through the creature's brain. The creature crumpled.

Halverson backed away from the open door to allow Rafferty to emerge from the backseat.

"I'm not going anywhere without a piece," said Rafferty.

"Get out of there now or I'll let you have it," said Halverson, training his MP9 on Rafferty.

"You maniac," said Rafferty, his eyes bugging out with fear. "I'm coming. I'm coming."

Rafferty climbed out of the backseat.

"Unlock my wrists," he said, turning his back to Halverson.

Three ghouls emerged from the rain advancing on Halverson. He scythed their wet, moldering heads with a burst from his MP9. He fished his keys out of his damp trouser pocket and unlocked Rafferty's handcuffs with wet red hands.

Rafferty whipped his handcuff into a skinny, sixtyish, white-haired male ghoul's emaciated face. The ghoul snarled as the high-tensile steel handcuff ripped his face. But the ghoul didn't die and kept advancing on Rafferty.

"Where's my piece?" said Rafferty, dodging the ghoul's outstretched hands awkwardly because his leg irons constricted his movements.

Halverson used his car fob to pop the trunk, which was filled with ordnance.

Rafferty snagged an H&K MP5, loaded it, and unleashed a burst on two middle-aged female ghouls plodding toward him through the sheets of rain, their rotting faces dripping wet. Rafferty stuffed magazines into his jumpsuit pockets.

Halverson heard gun reports near Strider's vehicle. Wheeling around he saw Strider, Cassavetes, and Purl, their guns blazing, making their way from the Beast toward him through a herd of ghouls. The creatures dropped dead, left and right. Strider and his cohorts joined Halverson and Rafferty.

The five of them carved a bloody swath through the attacking ghouls to reach Joon-ho's incapacitated vehicle, which, it turned out, had four flat tires that had been burst by the lightning bolt as it had passed through them into the ground.

Joon-ho and Marta were letting Laci out of the backseat, who emerged, revealing that one of her cuffs was unlocked.

"What the hell?" said Joon-ho. "How'd you get free?"

"You forgot to lock it," said Laci, grinning. "I could've strangled you, but I didn't," she said, shaking the dangling cuff up and down.

"Why not?"

"Hell, who am I trying to kid? I have nowhere to go. I'm better off with the team. Safety in numbers and all that," she said, shrugging.

Joon-ho fired in her direction.

Holding her breath Laci froze in astonishment, her hair standing on end.

Joon-ho's bullets took a fat ghoul's head off. The ghoul dropped dead behind Laci.

Laci blew out her cheeks with relief.

"Now how about a piece?" she said.

"Let's go to the trunk."

Marta fired a burst into three approaching ghouls, their ragged filthy clothes sopping wet, reeking of death. Their heads exploded into bone shards and gouts of brain that catapulted into the deluge of rain.

Laci latched onto an H&K MP5 that lay in the trunk among an arsenal of machine pistols and semiautomatics. She slammed a full magazine into the MP5, racked the slide, and slewed around, blasting four ghouls that had slogged through the mud to within three feet of her.

"Grab as many magazines as you can carry," said Joon-ho, stuffing magazines into his cargo pockets.

Marta followed his lead after emptying her magazine into five ghoul heads.

Laci jammed magazines into her jumpsuit pockets.

Lightning split open the sky. Thunder crashed.

"Are we gonna get hit again?" said Laci, rain splattering her face as she looked up at the sky.

"Lightning never strikes the same place twice," said Joon-ho.

"Don't believe a word of it," said Strider, walking up, MP9 in hand, accompanied by Halverson. "It's an old wives' tale. We need to move."

Joon-ho gawked at Strider. "You mean, I've been wrong all my life about that? I always tried to get as near as possible to a place already struck by lightning when I was out in a storm."

114

"Where are Purl and Rafferty?" said Strider.

"I'll get them," said Halverson, heading back toward his vehicle. "We can't leave those two alone."

"You think they'd try to escape?" said Cassavetes, picking off a teenage female ghoul with purple hair.

"Now that they have guns, yeah," said Strider.

"We're safer together, if you ask me. The more of us together, the better. Taking off on your own makes no sense."

"They're cons. You can never trust them."

"They're idiots if they sneak off with zeds all over the place."

"Cons don't end up in the joint because they're smart."

Cassavetes stepped toward two approaching ghouls, one a seventyish male with a scraggly grey beard, the other a female pushing thirty with a curvaceous figure gone to pot. Cassavetes unleashed a furious burst at them with his MP9, ripping their faces apart, puncturing eyeballs, and knocking teeth out from their shredded mouths.

"You're pretty brave against the ghouls," said Strider.

"I'm vaccinated," said Cassavetes. "They can't infect me."

"Be careful, man. We can't lose you. You're vital to our mission. Without you, we can't find Dr. Wheelhouse."

"The ghouls won't touch me."

Strider took stock of the area with dismay. "There are too damn many of those things here. They just keep coming. We need to beat it. Where's Halverson?"

Chapter 35

Halverson joined Rafferty and Purl, who were standing near Cardinal Two spraying ghouls with bullets.

"Were you worried about us?" said Rafferty, snickering as he emptied his H&K MP5 magazine into a troop of encroaching ghouls. "We can take care of ourselves now that we got pieces."

He reloaded.

"We need to stick together to defend ourselves during an attack," said Halverson.

"They just keep coming," said Purl, blasting a middle-aged Asian male ghoul's bald head, shattering the creature's face and red plastic-framed spectacles.

"We can't hold them off much longer. They got the numbers, and they could care less about getting iced."

"The only reason they're fearless is because they're fucking idiots," said Rafferty.

"Fucking kamikaze pilots," said Purl, grimacing and letting another ghoul have it with his B&T MP9.

"Kamikazes knew what they were doing. These stooges don't know nothing."

"They're getting too close," said Halverson, gritting his teeth, firing away, and swapping mags with rain-soaked hands.

The legion of ghouls had driven a wedge between Halverson's group and Strider's. Halverson blasted the ghouls marching in the wedge.

"We can't let them cut us off from each other," he said.

"Scumbags," Rafferty cried at the ghouls, the tendons in his neck sticking out as he let loose a burst at the flailing creatures.

A female creature in her late forties, wearing a tattered salmon dress smeared with mud, grabbed Purl's arm and wrenched it toward her mouth to bite it. A rat scrabbled out of her mouth and lunged at Purl.

"Oh no you don't," said Purl and plugged her between the eyes before she could clamp her jaws on his hand.

The ghoul's head jerked back. She fell backward into the mud on the roadside.

The rat sank its claws into Purl's shoulder for purchase. Grimacing, Purl swore, grabbed the rat, and flung it with revulsion at the attacking ghouls.

"You know how to handle yourself," said Rafferty.

"I'm good at killing," said Purl, rain pouring into his open mouth as he tilted his face upward and laughed.

"It makes you feel powerful, don't it?"

"I can kill with the best of them," said Purl, closing his mouth and becoming stone-faced. He noticed Rafferty was pointing his MP5 toward him. "Don't get any ideas."

"Why would I waste you? You're not the enemy."

"Experience in life has taught me otherwise."

"What? You *are* the enemy?"

"That's the way people see me."

"You're paranoid, you mean?"

"The only one who ever helped me was my mother. And you're not her."

"You trust nobody but your mother."

"Got a problem with that?"

"You're a mama's boy."

Purl trained his MP9 on Rafferty. "You think I won't pull this trigger?"

"Why would I whack you?" said Rafferty, smiling and lowering his H&K. "Hell, you're another con. We cons gotta stick together." He lowered his voice so Halverson couldn't overhear him. "If I'm gonna whack anybody, it'll be a screw. They're the ones holding us hostage."

Purl lowered his piece, but didn't look convinced.

"What say you and me make a run for it?" said Rafferty, his voice all but drowned out by the incessant hissing of the rain impinging on the ground.

"I don't like our chances if we scram," said Purl, plugging a twentysomething rangy male ghoul with bow legs. The left one had a compound fracture in the tibia. The ghoul was coming at him wearing a cream bucket hat, fluorescent lime shorts, and espadrilles. He stopped coming and dropped to the ground with a bullet in his head. "They're surrounding us."

"We jack a car," said Rafferty.

"Might work."

Rafferty pivoted and laid a ghoul low with a short burst from his MP5.

Chapter 36

Halverson could hear Strider's group firing on the wedge, trying to cut a path through the serried ghouls to link up with him, Rafferty, and Purl.

"Strider's heading our way," said Halverson.

Rafferty leaned toward Purl. "We take out Halverson, jack the lead car, and we're outa here."

Purl eyeballed the Beast, which he could barely make out in the constant rain. At that moment, a dozen ghouls plodded between him and the Beast.

"Too many ghouls in our way," he said.

"Mow 'em down with slugs," said Rafferty.

"Over here," Halverson told Rafferty, beckoning to him. "Strider needs our help."

"They're coming at us from behind," said Rafferty.

"Let Purl take care of them. You're with me."

Rafferty balked at the request.

"I'm not asking you," said Halverson, his face drenched, drawing a bead on Rafferty's head.

Rafferty took the hint and approached Halverson.

"Let's take out some ghouls," said Halverson, as Rafferty reached his side spitting raindrops out of his mouth.

"There are too many of them. We need to beat it."

"We're not leaving Strider and the others."

"I don't want to commit suicide with you," said Rafferty, turning to go.

"He's part of the team. We don't leave anybody behind."

"Oh yeah? What about Damon?"

"Damon mutinied and tried to leave us. You do that, your life is forfeit."

"I hate following rules. And I don't like taking orders."

"Would you rather be dead?" said Halverson, looking at Rafferty like he meant it. "The motto of the US military is to leave no one behind. We're not leaving without Strider."

"I'm not in the US military."

"When you volunteered for this mission, you enlisted."

Halverson pricked up his ears when he heard what sounded like gun reports in the near distance.

"Did you hear that?" he said.

"Thunder."

"It sounded like gunshots."

"One of Strider's guys shooting?"

"It's coming from the opposite direction," said Halverson, peering into the rain without being able to see anyone other than rows of packed ghouls advancing toward the convoy.

"Howdy," said Gatling, riding out of the rain on his whinnying black stallion, biting the horse's leather reins between his teeth, gripping a Smith & Wesson .50 Magnum in each hand, a mad grin on his face.

He blasted the nearest ghoul head clear off its body with one shot.

"Looks like you guys could do with a wee bit of help," said Gatling, barely able to talk with the reins in his mouth, picking off ghouls from his horse's saddle. "What say ye, fellow travelers?"

Gatling didn't wait for an answer. He shot ghouls right and left.

The rest of his gang rode into the milling mob of ghouls and commenced firing at them. One of his gang screamed as a black six-six ghoul in a Lakers glossy purple and yellow uniform yanked him out of his saddle and tore out his jugular.

Gatling holstered one empty S&W and reloaded the other with a speed loader. He holstered the loaded one, reloaded the empty, and grabbed ahold of each in his hands. He discharged a bullet into the Laker's large head. The Laker's brain blew out of the back of his skull, taking a saucer-sized, jagged fragment of parietal bone with it.

Strider and his group managed to cut a swath through the wedge of ghouls that had come between him and Halverson.

"Let's load up and move," said Strider.

"How's Joon-ho's vehicle?" said Halverson.

"The lightning totaled it. We have to leave it."

"Nothing's more fun than slaughtering zeds," cried Gatling, as he rode his horse through the zombies, blasting their heads to smithereens.

"Why can't we stay and fight the zeds?" said Rafferty, watching Gatling with approval and something like yearning on his face.

Strider gave Rafferty a look. "Waste of our time. We got a mission to complete. Remember?"

"Gatling helped us," said Cassavetes.

"And we thank him, but our mission takes priority," said Strider. "Our mission isn't to wipe out the flesh eaters. Let's vamoose."

"Which vehicle do I go in?" said Joon-ho, downing a hunchbacked male fiftyish ghoul with his MP9.

"You come with me. Laci and Marta, go with Halverson."

Laci took umbrage.

"I don't want to ride with a serial killer," she said, eying Rafferty.

"Are you bigoted?" said Rafferty.

"I'll put his handcuffs back on," said Halverson.

"No way."

"We don't have time to argue, people," said Strider, nailing a female ghoul with a cockroach-infested beehive hairdo slouching toward him, green snot dripping out of her nose. The bullet to her brain felled her. "Shake a leg."

Chapter 37

When Halverson reached Cardinal Two he trained his MP9 on Rafferty and Laci and told them to drop their weapons.

Marta provided cover fire, protecting them from attacking ghouls.

"The zeds will get me," said Rafferty, outraged. "Do you want my blood on your hands?"

"I need to put your handcuffs on."

"How can I defend myself from the zeds?"

"You're going in the backseat. They can't get you there."

"Shove your handcuffs."

"Drop your piece."

"You won't shoot me. We already lost Damon to the psycho SEAL," said Rafferty, nodding at Strider. "We can't afford to lose any more men."

"Want to bet your life on it?"

Rafferty couldn't read Halverson's face, which looked like a stone slab.

Halverson pressed his MP9's muzzle against Rafferty's rain-slick forehead. "I can't miss from this range. Drop your piece."

Rafferty's fingers twitched. "Do you want to give me a heart attack?"

"I want you to drop your piece."

Sweat beaded above Rafferty's upper lip.

"I knew I should've shot you in the back when I had the chance," he said, releasing his H&K MP5.

"I'm not sitting in the back with Ted Bundy without a gun," said Laci, holding onto her machine pistol.

"The feeling's mutual, bitch," said Rafferty. "As soon as I get the chance, I'll take you out."

"I'm cuffing him," Halverson told Laci. "He can't hurt you."

"How can you cuff him with that gun in your hands?" she said.

"I'm gonna put it down as soon as you drop yours. Then I'll cuff him and you."

"The ghouls will tear us apart," said Rafferty.

"Marta's covering us."

Gatling's stallion reared, whinnying, as Gatling blasted nearby ghoul heads with his .50 Magnum.

Marta took out a thirtyish female ghoul dressed in a nurse's white uniform that was drenched with rain and streaked with mud.

Laci thought about making a run for it.

"You'll never make it on your own," said Halverson, reading her mind.

Grudgingly, she dropped her H&K MP5.

Halverson wasted an advancing ghoul of indeterminate age whose face was ripped away with half of the skull exposed.

Halverson dropped his MP9 and cuffed Rafferty and Laci in that order. "Get in the backseat."

Halverson picked up his weapon.

"I don't like being told what to do," said Rafferty, resisting after Laci clumsily managed to clamber into the backseat.

"You already said that," said Halverson, shoving Rafferty in the small of his back.

Rafferty cursed and stumbled toward the seat.

"I'm gonna kill you for that," he said. "You're a big man with me in handcuffs and you with a piece in your hand. Just you wait."

"Get in there. We gotta move."

Rafferty had difficulty getting into the seat thanks to his hands cuffed behind his back.

"I guess you don't like living," he said, glaring at Halverson.

Unceremoniously, Halverson helped Rafferty get completely into the seat then shut the door behind him.

"We need to go," Halverson told Marta, who was emptying her magazine into a scrawny female middle-aged ghoul wearing a mustard scrunchie in her filthy black hair.

Marta darted around the front of the Suburban to the passenger's-side door and got in, as Halverson covered her with his MP9.

After she was safe inside, he slid into the driver's seat and shut the door, trapping a ghoul hand between the door and its frame. He couldn't close the door. He cracked it enough to shoot the offending ghoul in the head. The ghoul dropped dead, removing his hand from the door as he fell into the mud with a squelch.

Halverson shut the door.

One of Gatling's men screamed in horror as two bald, bare-chested ghouls who looked like twins yanked him off his horse and commenced devouring his face.

Lightning flashed in the sky, turning it fluorescent purple.

Gatling plugged two more ghouls with his .50 Magnums, his eyes glittering with wild abandon. The lightning enlivened him, charging him with manic energy. He howled at the sky, his face savage with glee, rain pouring into his open mouth. He burst into laughter.

"At least someone's having fun," said Marta, from Cardinal Two's shotgun seat, watching Gatling.

"There's a guy who knows what he's doing," said Rafferty with admiration.

"Cardinal Two," squawked Strider over the radio, "this is Cardinal One. Are you good to go? Over."

"All set," said Halverson. "What about Gatling? Over."

"What about him? Over."

"There's no way he and his gang can kill all those ghouls. Over."

"We didn't ask for his help. We're on a time-sensitive mission. We're outa here. Over."

Ghouls swarmed around Halverson's vehicle, pressing against its sides and climbing onto the hood.

"Roger," said Halverson. "Over."

"The ghouls are congesting the road. Time to move. Over and out."

Halverson watched the Beast plow shambling ghouls out of the way. Halverson fired his vehicle's engine, threw the shifter into Drive, and peeled off after him.

Gatling kept laughing as he picked off ghouls on his rearing horse.

Chapter 38

Halverson turned on the windshield wipers to their fastest mode to sweep away the sheets of rain so he could keep Strider's vehicle in sight.

Lighting flashed.

Marta froze in her seat, staring out the windshield as if paralyzed.

"What's wrong?" said Halverson, picking up on her reaction out of the corner of his eye as he drove.

Marta said nothing.

"Are you OK?" said Halverson.

She rubbed her forehead. "I saw that lightning. I thought we were gonna get hit again. I swear my heart stopped beating when that lightning struck our car. I thought I was gonna have a heart attack. I thought it hit me."

"I'm still shaking from it," said Laci from the backseat. "I don't ever want to go through that again."

Marta held up her shaking hand. "It messed up my nervous system."

"Maybe you're in shock," said Halverson.

"Maybe I had a heart attack."

"Are you sure we didn't get hit?" said Laci.

"You're still alive," said Rafferty. "If you got hit, you'd be dead meat."

"You're an expert? Can't people survive a lightning strike?"

"The car protected you," said Halverson. "The lightning went through the steel shell of the car out through the tires into the ground. That's why all your tires are flat."

"I can't even remember what happened," said Laci. "My mind is like blank. I don't remember the lightning hitting. I smelled sulfur, and then we were all piling out of the car getting guns."

"I swear it hit me," said Marta. "And my heart stopped."

"Then why aren't you dead?" said Rafferty. "You're exaggerating. You women . . . ," he said disdainfully.

"I hear you guys," said Strider over the radio. "Actually, 90 percent of people struck by lightning survive. Very few of those strikes are direct hits. A direct hit would probably kill you. Over."

"How do you know so much? Just because you're a SEAL you think you know everything?"

"My dad was a meteorologist. I learned from him before . . . the . . . plague got him," said Strider, his voice trailing off. "He was a smart guy. He knew everything. I looked up to him."

"It doesn't take much to impress guys like you."

"What's that supposed to mean?"

"My dad was a moron. Most dads are. You find out when you get older."

"He did right by me. I didn't grow up to be a serial killer."

"You're a SEAL. Not a whole lot of difference. Don't they train you guys to kill people?"

"Be thankful I'm not back there with you."

Rafferty pshawed.

"I know I got hit," said Marta. "My body feels weird. I feel wired."

"Who cares whether you got hit or not?" said Rafferty. "Are we gonna have to listen to this bullshit for the rest of the ride?"

"I ought to throw you to the ghouls," said Halverson, glancing in the rearview mirror at Rafferty.

"You won't. You need me on this doomsday mission."

"You think we want to listen to you?" said Laci in disgust.

"At least I'm not crying about getting hit by lightning."

"I wish you were in our car when it happened."

"The only car I want to be in with you is a hearse with your corpse in it so I can fuck your stiff in the coffin."

"You sick creep. Why hasn't someone killed you by now?"

"You know you want me," said Rafferty, blowing Laci a kiss.

"Like I want a ghoul to bite me."

"I'm gonna waste you before this mission is over so I can jump your bones."

"Did you forget this is a suicide mission?" said Marta. "Nobody gets out of here alive."

"I don't know about that. I'm hard to kill."

"So are cockroaches," said Halverson. "But if you stamp on them hard, their guts splatter all over the place."

"I got your number, too, buddy. Don't think you're getting out of this alive."

"Nobody is," said Marta, staring ahead in a daze. "The lightning hitting our car was an omen."

"I don't believe in that superstitious nonsense. Omen. Duh, it's a sign from heaven. Give me a break. There's no heaven and no hell. There's just this—the eternal nightmare of the apocalypse. What you see is what you get."

"You don't know nothing," said Laci. "That's what my aunt with a club foot used to tell me when I was a kid—*you don't know nothing*. She used to scare me with that big black boot with a steel brace on it for her deformed foot that she wore as she limped around. Now I know what she meant. She was talking about you."

"Spare us. We don't want to hear about your dysfunctional family. You got a captive audience here. Remember?"

"We got a problem up ahead," squawked Strider through the walkie-talkie. "Over."

"When don't we have one?" said Rafferty.

Nobody argued the point.

Chapter 39

Strider stopped his vehicle in front of a narrow suspension bridge that spanned a river that was riding high thanks to the deluge of rain from the thunderstorm. From the driver's seat he took stock of the bridge.

It was cluttered with cars abandoned by people who had fled the ghouls.

"Why'd they leave their cars on the bridge?" said Cassavetes, sitting beside Strider.

"Maybe they ran out of gas," said Joon-ho from the backseat, where he now sat in the Beast. "What happened? I can't see anything from back here. The rain's too heavy."

"Cars are all over the bridge," said Strider. "We can't get past them to get over it."

"Come to think of it, I remember this bridge when I crossed it," said Cassavetes. "I had a motorcycle so it didn't concern me. I just drove past all the parked cars and trucks."

"The advantage of having a motorcycle," said Joon-ho.

"Yep."

"They must've run out of gas," said Strider. "Or they had to ditch their cars because of cars parked in front of them that they couldn't pass. Then they walked across. Or ran for their lives from ghouls attacking them."

"Are you saying you want us to walk across?" said Purl, sitting beside Joon-ho in the back. "The zeds would get us."

"I didn't say that." Strider paused. "Maybe we can find a way past the cars."

"I don't see any zeds around here," said Cassavetes, scoping out the surroundings.

"We'd have to push those cars out of the way somehow to drive past them," said Joon-ho.

"I *do* have a snowplow on the front of my car," said Strider. "We could use it to push cars out of our way."

"Not if they're crammed too tight together."

"Do you have a better way to move them?"

"We could release their brakes and push them out of the way."

"Some of the cars might even have keys in them," said Cassavetes.

"All right," said Strider. "You two go onto the bridge and start moving cars."

"What about zeds?" said Cassavetes.

"I don't see any around here."

"For now, anyway," said Cassavetes, inspecting the bridge warily.

Halverson parked his vehicle behind Strider's and clambered out of the driver's seat.

"What's up?" he said, approaching Strider.

"Take a gander at the bridge," said Strider. "We need to clear a path before we can cross. We need to do it chop-chop because the ghouls could show up any second."

"What about the prisoners? We could use their help."

"I was thinking the same thing. Release them and set them to work." Strider gazed at the bridge. "Where can they escape to? The bridge has a chain-link fence on each side to prevent people from falling off or committing suicide. And that's a long way down to the river below," he said, checking out the river.

"They could run to the other side of the bridge and escape."

"We'll just have to watch them to make sure they don't. They're safer with us than on their own out there."

"'Safer' on a suicide mission?"

"We need to cross that bridge ASAP. You and your crew start moving cars out of the way on the bridge."

Halverson retrieved Marta, Laci, and Rafferty from his vehicle.

"Our job is to clear a path on the bridge," said Halverson.

"How do I do that? With my teeth?" said Rafferty, grinning humorlessly.

"Do you promise not to run away if I take your handcuffs off?"

"I promise, boss," simpered Rafferty.

"Sure," said Laci. "Why not? Anything to get these things off my wrists."

"If you attempt to escape, you will be shot," said Strider, walking up to Halverson's side with Purl and addressing Rafferty and Laci. "That goes for you, too, Purl."

"Why would I want to escape a suicide mission?" said Purl.

Rafferty laughed. "Spoken like a true patriot."

"'Patriotism is the last refuge of the scoundrel,' according to Samuel Johnson."

"What does a guy that sells Band-aids know about anything?"

"We're putting our lives on the line trusting you cons," said Strider. "Don't disappoint us."

"Does that mean you're giving us pieces?" said Rafferty.

"No."

"Are you really that scared of us? Me, Purl, and Laci?"

"There aren't any ghouls around, as if you haven't noticed. You don't need guns to move cars. Let's go."

They walked onto the bridge to clear a path on the cluttered road.

The cars that weren't locked were the easiest. The team entered them, put the shifters in neutral, released the emergency brakes, and rolled the cars out of the way—if there was room for them to move. If there were too many other cars around the cars they opened, the team had to move the cars that were in the way first. Most of them were locked—in which case, they had to be broken into. Except—

"Does anyone know how to break into a car?" said Laci.

"Easy-peasy," said Purl. "Jam your elbow into the driver's-side window."

He was about to demonstrate when Strider told him to stop.

"What's the problem?" said Purl.

"You're gonna set off the car alarm if you break in."

"So what? You afraid of getting busted?"

"Do cops even exist anymore?" said Rafferty, chuckling. "This is the apocalypse, man. The end of everything."

Strider wasn't amused. "Loud noises attract the ghouls. We need to get over this bridge before they show up."

"Then how do we move the cars out of the way?" said Purl.

Rubbing his chin, deep in thought, Strider surveyed the bridge. "This is like a giant jigsaw puzzle where you have to figure out which car has to be moved and where in order to clear a path wide enough for us to drive through."

"While you're figuring it out, me and Purl will clear away cars," said Rafferty, trying the front door of a Toyota to see if it was locked. "Come on, Purl."

Purl tried a late-model fluorescent orange Camaro's door.

"The owner locked this baby up good," he said. "A carjacker would want this one. The owner probably kept the door locked even when he was driving."

"Time to make a run for it, Purl," whispered Rafferty.

"They'll shoot us," Purl whispered back.

"They can't afford to. They don't have enough men as it is. And . . ."

"And what?"

"Gunshots will attract the zeds."

"Strider will use a silencer."

"I'm telling you, they don't have enough men."

"You saw what he did to Damon."

"Damon was a psycho. He was useless as a fighter. He had to go."

"Don't you care about getting the vaccine?"

"How do we know it's any good? And you're forgetting something."

"Forgetting what?"

"This is a suicide mission. It has zero chance of success."

Pretending to ignore Strider, Rafferty kept edging away from him, trying to open different cars.

"Are you with me or not?" Rafferty asked Purl.

Purl headed in Rafferty's direction, peering into cars, searching for keys left in ignitions.

Chapter 40

"As I see it, there's not enough room on this bridge for us to move the cars out of the way," said Strider, knitting his brow.

"Let's use our snowplows and see how far we get, pushing cars out of our way," said Halverson. "We'll crush some of the cars, giving us more room to get by them."

"The plows will work as compactors," said Strider, nodding. "It might just work."

"This is the United States of America," boomed a voice from Strider's walkie-talkie strapped to his shoulder. "Everyone is ordered to shelter in place. Do not leave your premises. The zombie plague is everywhere. There is no cure. It is 100 percent fatal. Do not leave your residences for any reason whatsoever."

"Who's that?" said Halverson.

Strider shook his head, incredulous. "How did he get the frequency of my radio?"

"Those Big Tech guys can hack anything," said Cassavetes.

"Could it be the president who issued the warning?" said Marta. "He would have your radio frequency."

"Why wouldn't he identify himself as President Mims?" said Halverson.

"Who is this?" said Strider into his walkie-talkie.

"This is the United States of America," came the answer. "You are ordered to shelter in place. No one must leave their residences. This is a national emergency. The zombie plague is killing everyone. No one can survive it. Do not leave your homes."

"Can he hear you?" Halverson asked Strider.

"I dunno."

"Whoever it is doesn't know who's president. That's why he's not identifying himself. He doesn't know who took Cole's place. He may not even know Cole's dead."

"Probably some militia. They're all over the place."

"They're not telling us anything we don't know," said Marta.

"I wish they'd get off my radio frequency, though," said Strider. "If we can hear them, they might be able to hear us. I don't want anyone to find out the nature of our mission or where we're headed."

"This is the United States of America," said the voice. "You are ordered to shelter in place. Do not leave your homes till further notice."

Strider surveyed the bridge and cursed. "Where the hell is Rafferty?"

Halverson scanned the bridge. He saw Purl trying to open a Volkswagen Jetta, but no Rafferty. Halverson ran his eyes over the rooftops of the cars abandoned on the bridge. He caught sight of Rafferty jinking between cars, making for the other side of the bridge.

Strider picked up on Rafferty at the same time.

"Halt," yelled Strider.

Rafferty sped up his pace zigzagging between cars. He didn't look back.

"Halt or I'll shoot," cried Strider, fishing out a sound suppressor from his cargo pocket, and attaching it to his MP9 muzzle.

Rafferty lowered his head and kept running.

Strider trained his MP9 on Rafferty and fired a burst. Bullets ricocheted off metal car rooftops, casting off sparks.

Gasping for breath Rafferty took cover behind a rusted white van.

"I'll get him," said Halverson, breaking into a run in Rafferty's direction.

Chapter 41

His heartbeat pounding like crazy, his eyes frantic, Rafferty stood behind the van wondering what to do.

He gazed at the end of the bridge, which had scores of abandoned vehicles on it blocking his way. If he kept his head down, he might be able to make it to the other side without getting shot. Some of the parked cars were pretty low, though. It would be difficult to keep completely concealed from Strider's view, even if Rafferty bent over as he fled.

There was a stake truck up ahead, noticed Rafferty. He could use it as cover once he got past it. He looked around him. His only other alternative was scaling the chain-link fence on the side of the bridge and diving into the river below. It was a long way down.

He knew how to swim, but he was a city boy. He wasn't a survivalist who had grown up in the woods. He didn't know which side of the tree moss grew on. He didn't know which mushrooms or berries were safe to eat. The sun rose in the east and set in the west—that was the extent of his knowledge of outdoor life.

He also had to contend with his leg irons, which would circumscribe his attempts at running. What if they got hung up on the chain-link fence, as he tried to scale it?

He couldn't make up his mind what to do. Strider must have sent some of his men to capture him, even as Strider kept Rafferty pinned down with gunfire. Rafferty couldn't hide behind the van forever.

Slugs from Strider's MP9 tore into the side of the van.

Rafferty had to fish or cut bait. He had one other alternative. Surrender and head back to the suicide mission.

What was the big deal about getting wet? he wondered. He was already drenched from the rain. A little swim in the river wasn't going to kill him. The problem was, the fall might.

He hated taking orders and following rules, especially when the people giving them were such fools and assholes. Look at Strider. The guy was a stone killer. He killed people for disobeying him.

Rafferty figured his days were numbered if he continued taking orders from Strider. In the end Strider was going to lose it and waste all of them because the mission would fail—and Strider couldn't tolerate failure.

Rafferty had seen the type before. Strider was a know-it-all success story who would rather kill everyone on his team than let them go on living as witnesses to his failure of the mission. If there were no witnesses, there was no failure. If pressed on the matter, Strider would claim it wasn't his fault his team had deserted him or mutinied, sinking the mission. He would never admit failure.

Which meant Rafferty would end up dead if he continued on the mission. The only way he could survive the mission was if it was a success—which was impossible. They would never make it past the billions of ghouls that stood in their way. Even if by some miracle they did make it, they would never make it back to the bunker.

As Strider emptied his MP9 magazine firing at the van protecting Rafferty, Rafferty bolted for the chain-link fence, adrenaline coursing through him. His shackles curtailed his strides. It took him longer than he had expected to reach the fence. He couldn't afford to waste time.

He latched onto the chain-link fence, scaled it, and reached the top. Now was the tricky part—getting his shackled legs over the fence. With a sudden surge of adrenaline, he flung himself over it, hoping the river running below was deep enough to break his fall and prevent him from hitting the bottom and breaking his neck and hoping his shackles weren't so heavy that they would act like anchors and prevent him from swimming to the surface.

Strider fired a round at Rafferty as he jumped. Rafferty heard the slug whistle by his ear, or was that the roaring of adrenaline bursting through his body?

Rafferty dropped through the air, mingling with the raindrops in his descent, drawn implacably by the force of gravity.

He didn't know if Strider was still firing at him as he plummeted. He didn't care. He held his breath. The only thing on his mind was the approaching raging river, whose banks were overflowing thanks to the downpour. He slammed into the river's churning surface feet first and kept descending through the all-encompassing freezing water.

His rapid descent began to slow down. He didn't hit bottom. His lungs ached to inhale oxygen, but he held his breath underwater. He leveled out at last and swam for the surface. His shackles fought his leg kicks, but he was able to swim—barely. He couldn't swim like this very long. The shackles holding him back drained his energy. He felt the strong current sweeping him under the bridge.

Would Strider continue shooting at him after he surfaced? wondered Rafferty. How obsessed was the guy with killing all witnesses to his botched mission?

His lungs burning, feeling like he was going to pass out from lack of oxygen, Rafferty breached the river's surface and gasped for air. He didn't care if Strider took a shot at him. He had to breathe. Rain soaked his face and peppered the water like BB pellets.

Swimming with the swift current, he saw that it had carried him a good distance from the bridge. He also saw Strider on the bridge drawing a bead on him.

Rafferty gulped air and dove underwater. He had to get out of range of Strider's bullets. He put everything else out of his mind and swam down into the river's depths. Bullets zipped past him like ravenous piranhas speeding through the water to clamp their savage jaws on prey.

Chapter 42

Halverson approached Strider on the bridge. "What's the point of killing him?"

Strider fired a burst in Rafferty's direction, pelting the rain-swollen river with bullets, though he couldn't see Rafferty, who had dived underwater.

"He's a deserter," said Strider. "All mutineers and deserters will be shot dead."

"We can't waste any more ammo on him. We need it for the ghouls."

"I'm still in command here," said Strider, and unleashed another burst in Rafferty's direction. Strider swapped magazines. "I ought to send you after him to kill him."

Strider scanned the river. He saw no sign of Rafferty.

"He's not worth it," said Halverson. "We're better off without him."

Strider grunted. "I don't like seeing crooks get away with it." He paused. "I guess it's the influence of my brother, the cop, on me."

"We need to get off this bridge before the ghouls trap us here."

"Let's go to the vehicles and mount up. Time to plow a path through this graveyard of cars."

MP9 in hand, he strode toward the Beast. He saw Purl trying to open a Chevy Impala door.

"Get back here, Purl," he said. "We're leaving."

Purl looked annoyed at Strider.

"Give me an excuse to blow you away, cop killer," said Strider.

Purl grinned/sneered.

"Did you get Rafferty?" he said, making for the Suburbans.

"I got him, all right."

"He never had a chance," said Purl, shaking his head. "He wanted me to join him. I knew he wouldn't make it. The guy was loco."

"You try anything, you're dead," said Strider, brandishing his MP9.

"Where's Rafferty?" said Laci, standing near Halverson's Suburban.

"He's dead," said Strider.

"Damn. I wanted to be the one who killed him."

"I'll shoot anyone else who tries to desert. Got that?"

"Why would we try to desert this wonderful mission?" said Purl.

"Don't say we didn't tell you what you were in for. You volunteered. Remember?"

"I remember it wasn't much of a choice you gave us," said Purl, cleaning his ear out with his pinky.

"Don't think I wouldn't like icing you."

"You're not gonna be happy till you blow away everyone on this mission."

Halverson hoped Purl was wrong. However, Halverson was seeing unsettling changes in Strider's personality. Maybe the pressure of the mission was getting to him, decided Halverson. The guy was too quick to pull the trigger on his own men. Then again, it was a life-or-death mission to obtain the vaccine. If the mission didn't succeed, the government couldn't start manufacturing the plague vaccine and providing it to the public. Millions of lives—or how ever many Americans were still alive—hung in the balance.

"Joon-ho, cuff Purl and put him in the backseat," said Strider.

Sneering, Purl placed his wrists behind his back. Joon-ho snapped the cuffs on them and ushered Purl into the backseat.

"Cassavetes, you're in front with me," said Strider. "Halverson, mount up and follow my lead in the Beast."

Halverson, Marta, and Laci piled into the second vehicle.

"I'm not cuffing you because you're alone in the back," said Halverson, looking in the rearview mirror at Laci.

"Not like I'm going anywhere," she said, her face sullen.

"Your doors are locked and can't be opened from the inside."

"I already figured that out. You think I'm gonna try to kill you because you're my CO?"

"Strider's your CO."

She gave a chilling smile. "I guess you're safe then."

Maybe he should have cuffed her, decided Halverson. But he might need her to move cars out of the way on the bridge if they reached an impasse. She would need her hands free to help.

"This is Cardinal Two," said Halverson into his radio. "We're good to go. Over."

Chapter 43

Strider fired the Beast's engine and drove straight at the tangle of cars blocking the bridge.

Metal clanged and scraped against metal as his snowplow shoved the blue Ford Escort out of the middle of the road.

"You're making a racket," said Cassavetes, in the passenger seat. "I hope the zeds don't hear us."

"It can't be helped," said Strider, accelerating, forcing the Escort out of the way and compacting it since the Beast needed more room to pass it. "The only way we're getting across this bridge is by brute force."

The Escort front left fender creaked and bent under the pressure of the plow as the chain-link fence on the side of the bridge prevented the car from moving any farther. Wheezing, the Escort driver's-side door buckled. The plow powered past it.

Strider was able to drive the best part of twenty feet before encountering another roadblock of parked cars.

The rain kept coming down, but was slackening somewhat.

Strider drove his plow into a silver Ford Explorer SUV. Steel grated against steel. Gritting his teeth he hit the gas, forcing the Explorer against the chain-link fence and scraping its driver's-side door, caving it in.

Cassavetes grimaced and held his hands over his ears to block out the screeching of the steel cars brushing against each other.

"The zeds must be hearing that," he said.

"They get in our way, we'll plow them into mush."

The Beast stopped moving. Strider gave it more gas. The wheels were spinning, but they weren't gaining purchase.

"What's going on?" said Cassavetes.

"The road's slippery. Our tires are spinning."

Strider eased up on the gas. He shifted into Reverse. The tires failed to gain traction.

"This is Cardinal Two. What's up, Cardinal One?" radioed Halverson. "Over."

"We're slipping on the wet road," said Strider into his walkie-talkie. "Over."

"Why don't I give you a push? Over."

Strider nodded to himself. "That might give us enough power to shove the car blocking my path out of the way. Over."

He shifted back into Drive.

"I spotted a couple of ghouls behind us on the bridge," said Halverson. "They could be scouts of some sort. Over."

"Do they *have* scouts?" Cassavetes asked Strider. "I thought they were brain dead."

"It could be some instinctual thing like animals have," answered Strider.

"Do animals send out scouts?"

"Ants do."

"Yeah. First you see a couple. They tell their buddies, and you see a couple thousand."

"Or maybe they're stragglers," said Halverson. "They're heading in our direction. Over."

"They heard the noise we're making," said Cassavetes.

"Let's go," said Strider. "Give me a push, Halverson. Over."

Strider tried to drive forward, but cut no ice.

"Will do," said Halverson. "Over."

Strider felt Halverson's SUV nudge the Beast's tailgate. Strider dropped the hammer on his accelerator. He felt the Beast drive forward, plowing the Explorer to the side of the bridge. Sparks flew off the Explorer driver's-side door as the Beast's plow scraped along it.

"There we go," said Strider, feeling the Beast's tires find purchase on the tarmac with the assist from Halverson's Suburban.

The Beast squeezed past the collapsed Explorer, whose dented driver's-side steel door squealed in protest while its passenger's-side door pressed against the bridge's chain-link fence bellying it out over the river.

"Yes," cried Cassavetes, pumping his fist.

Breaking free from Halverson's vehicle the Beast traversed a gap in the parked cars for fifty feet. Strider saw a brand-new copper convertible Bentley blocking his way.

Picking up speed, he crashed his Suburban into it with gleeful abandon, crumpling the luxury car with his plow, telescoping the Bentley's steel carapace, which howled under duress.

"I always wanted to do that," said Strider, grinning.

"Crash into a Bentley. Yeah, we'll never be able to afford one of those things." Cassavetes roared with laughter. "Let her have it."

The Bentley yelped like a wounded animal as the plow gashed the driver's-side door and ripped open two tires, bursting them. Deflating, the tires flattened and hissed.

"Man, that felt good," said Strider, his eyes gleaming.

"Let's push that sucker all the way though the fence into the river," said Purl from the backseat. "It's halfway through the fence right now."

"You're an evil bastard, Purl," said Joon-ho, laughing.

"You want to see it go over the edge as much as I do," said Purl, smiling.

"We don't have time," said Strider. "More ghouls could be headed this way. I don't want to get trapped on this bridge with those things swarming around us."

He drove the Beast past the Bentley, leaving it a candidate for the junkyard.

"We ought to do that to all the luxury cars on this bridge," said Purl, leering at the Bentley as he rode past it.

"We got a job to do," said Strider, his face grave. "And we're gonna succeed against all odds."

"You sound like a Rambo movie."

"I'm a SEAL, a badass. I passed Hell Week in BUD/S. This is child's play compared to that."

"Goody for you," muttered Purl.

"Did you say something?" said Strider, glowering at Purl in the rearview mirror.

"Why would anyone *want* to be a SEAL? That's what I don't understand."

"It's for guys who want to amount to something in life, not a bottom feeder like you."

"If we're so different, how come we're both in this car right now on a suicide mission?"

"Maybe it escaped your attention. You're in chains. I'm in command. End of discussion."

Chapter 44

Rafferty was freezing to death in the river. He didn't want to end up with hypothermia. And his legs were exhausted from trying to swim with shackles on. Pretty soon he wasn't going to be able to hold his head above water.

He swung his arm and grabbed a log that was floating past him borne by the current. At least he wouldn't drown. But he would surely get hypothermia if he stayed in the cold water much longer.

Hitching a ride on the log, he rested his legs. He shivered, his teeth chattering. He had to get out of the water while he remained conscious. He could pass out from hypothermia any minute and drown.

The rain was tapering off.

The black clouds parted for a moment, revealing a death's head of a moon grinning down at him.

A good omen that the sky was clearing, he decided. On the other hand, seeing a skull in the sky leering at him didn't bode well. Regardless, he couldn't wait any longer. His fingers were becoming numb. His arms might be next. His face turning blue from the frigid river, he decided he had to get out of the bone-chilling water.

He pushed off the wet log and swam for the riverbank, fighting the sweeping current that kept driving him downriver.

He felt like he was losing his battle with the current, but he kept swimming using every last ounce of his energy to reach the bank. His arms were going numb. He almost passed out. He had to keep pushing himself, exhorting himself to continue swimming. He told himself if he didn't keep swimming, he would die.

His heartbeat raced. He was nearing the bank. He was approaching a slight jog in the river. He believed he would be able to reach the bank when he reached the jog, as long as he could hold steady on his course.

He felt his strength ebbing. He blacked out for a moment. He had to keep going. He couldn't give up now. He was so close to the muddy bank. The churning river roared in his ears, blotting out his thoughts.

If he could retain consciousness for one more stroke, he could reach the bank.

He lunged toward a gnarly tree root that extended from the bank like a helping hand. He latched onto the wet root and held on for dear life. Able to grab it with both hands, he yanked himself out of the water and, shivering, scrabbled onto the riverbank, more dead than alive.

Lying on his back on the muddy ground, his mouth agape, he took deep breaths, swallowing stray raindrops falling from the breaking clouds.

He thought he could hear voices coming out of the lingering rain wafted by the wind. Maybe he was hallucinating. Why would anyone be around here? he wondered. A convict on the lam, he was in the middle of nowhere, not a house in sight.

Played out, he couldn't lift a finger.

Where did he go from here? he wondered. At least he was free of the death mission. The suicide crew's days were numbered. And yet they had a team to help each other. He had no one but himself. He was used to it, though. His whole life he had felt cut off from others. There was nothing new about being on his own.

His thoughts were getting muzzy.

He felt himself drift off.

Chapter 45

President Mims sat behind his desk in his office in the Mount Weather bunker struggling to breathe. He coughed.

"I feel terrible," he said.

"You need more oxygen, Mr. President," said Dr. Morrow, wheeling the green canister of oxygen toward Mims.

Mims snagged the oxygen mask and breathed deeply.

"I don't want to be seen by the public carrying this oxygen canister around with me," he said.

"You're not getting enough oxygen because the air ducts are jammed by the ghouls."

"Carrying this canister around with me makes me look weak. We can't have the president looking weak. Nobody wants a weakling for president."

"If you don't get enough oxygen, you will feel sick."

"We need to increase the supply of oxygen to my office."

"You ordered the oxygen level to be reduced to the bare minimum for survival, so we wouldn't run out of it."

"It's obvious I need more than the bare minimum to survive," said Mims, coughing.

He affixed the oxygen mask to his face and breathed deeply.

"The average person needs air that has 19.5 percent oxygen. You ordered it cut to 15 percent in the bunker to conserve oxygen. That's why you're having so much difficulty breathing, as is everybody else."

"I'm the president. As the leader of this country, I need to be in tiptop condition. I need more oxygen."

"We all do, Mr. President."

"Not to put too fine a point on it, my health is essential to the health of this great country. I am the heartbeat of the nation. Without me in perfect health, the nation will collapse. We can't have a sickly president at the helm."

"That's why I've given you an oxygen canister."

"I told you. It makes me look weak, hauling this canister around with me and constantly reaching for the oxygen mask."

"Like I said, you need 19.5 percent oxygen to be in perfect health."

Mims got on the horn to the ventilation control room.

"This is President Mims. My doctor says I need to increase the amount of oxygen to 19.5 percent in my office."

The ventilation technician cleared his throat. "You said to reduce the oxygen to 15 percent for everyone, sir."

"There's been a change in plans. Are you questioning my authority?"

"Not at all, sir," said the technician hastily. "What about for the rest of the bunker?"

"Keep the oxygen level where it is for the rest of the bunker."

"Yes, sir." The technician paused. "If we increase the level of oxygen in your office, we will run out of oxygen faster in the bunker."

"I can do the math."

"Understood, sir."

"This is a top secret order to you alone. Do not tell a living soul about it or you will be charged with violation of the Espionage Act. Do you understand?"

"Yes, sir," said the technician, fear in his voice.

"Good man. Get it done."

Mims hung up and coughed.

He turned to Morrow. "According to you, I won't need the oxygen mask anymore. Is that correct, Doctor?"

"As long as you're in your office and the oxygen level is 19.5 percent this is true. Elsewhere in the bunker, you'll need to have the canister with you."

"I will stay in my office to avoid giving the appearance of being weak by needing an oxygen tank."

"You could increase the oxygen level for the entire bunker."

Mims shook his head no. "That will increase the speed with which the bunker runs out of breathable air. We need to have enough oxygen in the bunker so we can last until the radiation level outside becomes low enough that we can go outside and breathe the air without fear of contamination."

"Our HEPA filters will screen out the radioactive dust for our safe ventilation now."

"The problem is, the ghouls are stuffed into the air ducts, blocking all of them."

"Can't we drag them out of there?"

Mims grimaced. "Every time my men drag them out, more ghouls take their place. There are millions of ghouls out there—and they want in. They know we're in here."

"Then sooner or later we're gonna run out of air."

"That's why we need the vaccine so bad. Once we get it, we can leave the bunker without fear of being infected by the ghouls." Mims rapped his desktop with his knuckles. "Strider must succeed in his mission. Our very existence depends on it."

Chapter 46

Lying supine in the mud, Rafferty opened his eyes and saw a man staring down at him.

"Howdy," said Gatling, his horse standing behind him, the reins in his left hand, a .50 Magnum in his right.

Mounted on their horses behind Gatling's stallion, his gang looked on with curiosity.

Rafferty jackknifed up into a sitting position.

Gatling trained his .50 Magnum on Rafferty. "Did I say sit up?"

"No."

"Do you want me to blow your head off?"

"No," said Rafferty, widening his eyes with apprehension as he stared at the revolver muzzle aimed at him.

"Which prison did you escape from?" said Gatling, glancing at Rafferty's leg irons.

"None. I got a presidential pardon."

Gatling chuckled. "A presidential pardon, huh? Then why are you in leg irons? Which prison did you escape from? I don't want to have to ask you again."

"I met you earlier today," said Rafferty, his pulse racing. "I'm part of the secret mission sent by the president."

"You were part of that convoy of SUVs?"

"Yeah. Don't you remember me?"

"I remember your boss with his attitude."

"He's a jumped-up nobody."

"I don't understand why you're in shackles if you're part of a secret mission," said Gatling, knitting his brows.

"The president pardoned me from prison if I volunteered to go on this mission."

"What is the object of this secret mission, anyway?"

Rafferty weighed his alternatives. To keep his mouth shut or spill the beans.

"I'll tell you if you let me join you guys," he said.

"We could always use more men. As long as you're not afraid of the zeds."

"I'm not scared of them. Give me a piece and I'll blast their stinking heads off day and night."

Gatling kept his .50 Magnum trained on Rafferty. "Tell me about the secret mission."

Rafferty's heartbeat hammered. Staring into the barrel of a gun had a way of doing that to him. He must do what he had to do to survive. He decided to ingratiate himself with Gatling by telling him the truth. Rafferty saw no other choice. In any case, he owed no loyalty to Strider, who treated him like a dog, nor to the US government, which had thrown him in the joint.

"The president sent us to get the vaccine for the zombie plague," said Rafferty.

Gatling pricked up his ears. "You know someone who has the vaccine?"

"A doctor created the vaccine, and the president wants it."

"What's this doctor's name and where is he located?"

"His name's Wheelhouse. I don't know where he's located."

Gatling pressed his Magnum muzzle against Rafferty's wet nose. "How can you get the vaccine from him if you don't know where he is? Make sense, man. Your life depends on your answer. I don't like being lied to."

"The only guy who knows the location of Wheelhouse is Cassavetes," said Rafferty, breaking into a sweat. "He's in the lead vehicle with Strider. Cassavetes memorized the route to Wheelhouse and is giving Strider the directions."

"Me and my men could use that vaccine."

"All we have to do is follow Strider's convoy and we'll get it."

Gatling holstered his piece. "Okay. You're with us. If I find out you're lying to me, I will not hesitate to blow your head off. Can you lead us to the convoy?"

"Yeah. When I escaped from them, they were on the bridge over yonder," said Rafferty, pointing where he had come from. "Let's go."

"Not so fast."

"They'll get away if we don't get there in time."

"Uh, there's one little test I want you to take before I agree to let you join us."

"I'm listening."

"You see that pack of ghouls over there heading this way?"

"Yeah."

"I want you to waste them."

Rafferty grinned. "No problem. Give me a piece."

"Anybody could stand here and pick them off with bullets. I want this to be a test of your fighting skills."

Rafferty looked puzzled.

Gatling turned to one of his men on horseback. "Diego, give our friend here your knife."

Pushing twenty, dressed in black jeans and a black racing jacket, a black-haired lanky Hispanic with a pencil mustache rode toward Rafferty and handed him a Ka-Bar knife with a leather grip.

"Kill the zeds with that knife," said Gatling.

"By myself?" said Rafferty.

"I want to see if you're worthy of us. If you want to join my gang, you gotta know how to waste zeds."

Rafferty accepted the knife. He felt its heft in his hand.

"It would be a lot easier with a piece," he said.

"Easy's got nothing to do with it," said Gatling. "I want to assess your fighting spirit."

Rafferty counted ten of the ghouls.

"At least get these shackles off my legs to give me a fighting chance," he said.

Gatling drew his .50 Magnum from its holster, leveled the barrel at the chain linking the shackles, and fired twice, snapping the chain in half.

"Now you got no excuses," he said.

150

Chapter 47

Adrenaline coursing through his exhausted body, knife in hand, Rafferty approached the ghouls that were trudging through the mud in his direction.

All of fifty years old, the lead male ghoul wore a long white beard with maggots weaving in and out of its curls.

"You first, handsome," said Rafferty.

Holding the knife blade pointed upward, he jammed it under the ghoul's chin and up into its brain. The ghoul went limp. Rafferty yanked the Ka-Bar knife out of the ghoul's head and prepared for his next attack, flourishing the knife in front of him, taunting the ghouls.

Rafferty made short work of the next three plodding ghouls by thrusting his knife into their temples and impaling their brains. As the ghouls crumpled, he yanked the blade out of their temples.

He encountered a zaftig ghoul whose prominent breasts were spilling out of her grimy bra, which had slipped down her chest. She wore a tight black leather miniskirt and black fishnet stockings. In her hand she gripped a scarlet leather clutch. She reminded him of one of the sluts he chose as victims on his murder sprees. Her teased blonde hair stuck out of her head like the do of Frankenstein's bride in the old Universal movie.

Despite himself, knowing she was a ghoul, he felt the overwhelming desire to kill her and rape her.

She sneered at him with her pustulating face. Flies buzzed around her hairdo. She stared at him with her milky blue eyes. He ached to rip her bra off, tie it around her neck, strangle her, and rape her corpse.

Her full breasts heaving, she clawed at him with her broken fingers with dirty nails.

"Dirty slut," he hissed.

He stabbed her under her jaw, driving the blade through her tongue, her palate, and her brain.

One of Gatling's gang let loose a wolf whistle as the curvaceous ghoul collapsed. Another gang member guffawed.

Leering down at her as she lay sprawled at his feet, Rafferty was dying to fuck her. Maybe he was going nuts, he decided, appalled at his urges. Yet the urge didn't ebb. Why should he be appalled? After all, she was dead meat—like all his other victims. She was just a whole lot uglier with her putrescent flesh. They had a fancy name for it—necrophilia.

A fat fortysomething ghoul wearing blue suspenders tried a sneak attack on him. Rafferty caught sight of the ghoul out of the corner of his eye and kicked the thing in its fat gut. The ghoul bounced away, propelled by Rafferty's foot. The creature growled at him and staged another assault.

Rafferty swiped the Ka-Bar knife's deadly blade through the air like a scythe and beheaded the ghoul. The head tumbled to the ground and chewed the air, its reanimated brain still alive. The head had no mobility. Rafferty left it as it chattered its teeth at him.

The tapering rain turned to drizzle.

Four ghouls remained.

Rafferty waded into them, knife at the ready. He stabbed a middle-aged redhead in her disintegrating ear. The blade cracked through her skull, into her brain, and killed her. Her body went limp. She fell into the mud.

The next two ghouls attacked Rafferty from behind. One of them grabbed Rafferty's shoulder. Terrified, Rafferty wheeled around, shaking off the rotting hand.

He took out the two ghouls, who smelled particularly ripe, with temple stabs, careful not to let either of the two bite his hand. He felt like puking after sniffing their stench.

Bored with temple stabs, he wasted the last ghoul with a knife thrust to her milky brown eye. With her brunette hair in a ponytail secured with a green rubber band, she might have been a teenager wearing jeans and a tube top, but it was hard to be sure because her face was in an advanced state of decay, her features worm-eaten.

Rafferty returned to the stacked slutty ghoul that sprawled on the ground beckoning to him with her exposed breasts. He couldn't resist the urge any longer. He dropped his pants.

Gatling's gang hooted and whistled at him from behind. Many of them looked ill as they watched Rafferty's naked white body pronging the dead ghoul under the moonlight. Others cheered him on.

"Sometimes I think we're no better than them," said Gatling on his stallion, watching Rafferty with disgust.

"Of course, we are," said Diego on horseback beside Gatling. "We can think."

Gatling hawked and spat on the ground. "That's what I mean."

"That guy's loco if you ask me."

"We can use him. He hates those government agents as much as we do. We saved those assholes from the zeds and they upped and left us there to die fighting the zeds by ourselves. That's the gratitude we get for helping them? Bastards. I'm gonna blow away their leader Strider—after they lead us to the vaccine, that is."

Rafferty pulled up his trousers and headed back to Gatling.

"He must be crawling with germs now," Diego told Gatling.

"I'm not gonna follow his example, I can tell you that," said Gatling. "No siree Bob."

Rafferty strode up to Diego and handed him back the Ka-Bar knife.

"We don't have time for extracurricular activities in my gang," said Gatling. "We need to find your convoy and follow them to the vaccine."

"Works for me. That slut reminded me of someone I knew," said Rafferty, feeling he owed them an explanation, knowing Gatling's gang could see him when he did the corpse, hearing their wolf whistles behind him, but not caring while he fucked her dead brains out.

"You look like you're no stranger to killing. What's your name?"

"Rafferty."

"What were you in the joint for?"

"I was falsely accused of being a serial killer."

"Hmm. How many people did they say you wasted?"

"Ninety."

"You're a goddamn professional killer. We definitely need you on our side. Can you ride a horse?"

"Not really. I'm a city boy from New Jersey. But I can learn."

"That's the spirit. It's a piece of cake. Diego, do we have a spare horse for him?"

"Johnny's horse," said Diego. "The zeds got Johnny. Poor bastard."

"Fine. Give him Johnny's mount, and let's get moving. The feds got cars. They can make better time than us."

"They're trapped on the bridge," said Rafferty. "A bunch of cars are blocking their way across."

"With any luck we can catch up to them on the bridge."

Chapter 48

Halverson drove his Suburban after Strider, who plowed a Jeep Wrangler out of his way on the bridge.

"It sounded like they were laughing a couple of minutes ago when they smashed into the Bentley," said Marta, puzzled, riding shotgun.

"I guess they were bonding," said Halverson.

"Bonding?" said Laci in the backseat. "Strider doesn't get along with Purl. Purl's a cop killer, and Strider's brother was a cop who was killed by a criminal."

"How do you know that?" said Marta.

"Cassavetes told me when we were moving cars."

"Strider's not gonna let that get in the way of the mission," said Halverson. "The mission is everything to him."

"Maybe that's the problem," said Marta. "He shot Damon and Rafferty. How can our mission succeed if he keeps killing all of us?"

"If they were laughing before, everything must be OK with them."

"I say we need to watch out for our glorious leader Strider or end up laid out on slabs," said Laci.

"Strider's OK in my book," said Halverson.

However, he had noticed some disturbing traits in Strider. For instance, Strider seemed too quick to pull the trigger on his own men. But then again, half of the team were prison inmates convicted of murder and worse. Halverson couldn't blame the guy for being tough on them. That said, Strider's shooting of Damon in cold blood was hard to stomach. And then Strider had shot an unarmed Rafferty. Strider was jeopardizing the mission by reducing the team's number, making the team a weaker fighting force.

Halverson figured Strider was obsessed with the success of their mission, and maybe that was a good thing. They weren't going to succeed if all of the team tried to go AWOL like Damon and Rafferty. But was shooting them the answer?

For now Halverson decided Strider had justification for shooting them. Nevertheless, Halverson would keep an eye on Strider and would leave his mind open on the subject.

"The plague has a way of changing people," said Laci. "We need to be on our guard."

There was truth in what she said about the plague, decided Halverson. It had wiped out most of the human race. How could losing so many friends and family members not affect the survivors? He should know. He had lost his brother and Victoria to the ghouls. The point was, everyone had lost someone.

And then President Cole had nuked half the country in his desperate bid to wipe out the flesh eaters, rendering much of the country a wasteland roamed by marauding ghouls who continued to thrive on devouring live human flesh. Eventually, Cole had gone mad and nuked himself when his efforts to save the country failed.

So, yeah, the plague had a way of changing people, decided Halverson, and changing them for the worse. But not everyone became a psycho killer on account of the apocalypse. Strider was a tough guy. Anyone who had the stamina and drive to become a SEAL, the premier fighting force of the US Navy, had to be tough.

It would take a lot to send Strider over the deep end, decided Halverson.

Like the end of the world.

"Don't worry about it," said Halverson, eying Laci in the rearview mirror. "Worrying solves nothing."

"We're all gonna die," said Laci. "Don't worry about it, he says."

"If we get the vaccine, we're not all gonna die," said Marta.

"*If*," said Laci. "That's a big if. You really think we're gonna survive a billion ghouls attacking us?"

"It's better than being cooped up in that bunker. I was losing it in there. I felt like the walls were closing in on me," said Marta, blanching at the memory.

"Out of the frying pan into the fire."

"We're gonna make it if we hang on," said Halverson.

Laci scratched her throat. "Yeah, let's look at the bright side. At least we're rid of Rafferty. That sleazebag made my skin crawl," she said, shivering.

"Remember that song 'Always Look on the Bright Side of Life'?" said Marta.

"Please don't start singing that song."

Chapter 49

As Strider neared the end of the bridge in the Beast, Joon-ho commenced groaning in the backseat. Strider checked him out in the rearview mirror.

"What's wrong?" he said.

"I'm gonna be sick," said Joon-ho.

"He's turning green back here," said Purl, searching Joon-ho's face.

"Are you carsick?" said Cassavetes from the front seat.

Joon-ho groaned again. "I'm gonna be sick. I need to go outside."

"I used to get carsick when I was a kid and my mom drove me to my gramma's house. We went up this winding road on a mountain on the way to her place. All those winding roads—I couldn't take them."

"I don't want him to puke back here," said Purl. "Let him go outside. He looks like shit."

Strider watched Joon-ho's reflection in the rearview mirror with concern.

"Hold on," he said.

He scoped out the area for ghouls.

In a rush to get out, Joon-ho tried to open his door. However, a Jeep was parked too close to the Beast for him to open the door wide enough to get out.

"Close the door so we can get past that Jeep," said Strider.

Joon-ho pulled a face and closed his door. "I need to get out."

Strider drove the Suburban forward, plowing a black Tesla out of the way.

"Hurry," said Joon-ho, grimacing. "I can't hold it much longer."

"Listen to him," said Purl, scooching across the backseat as far away from Joon-ho as he could get.

Strider pulled away from the Tesla.

Joon-ho opened his door, climbed out onto the bridge, and heaved blood-streaked vomit.

"What the hell?" said Purl, watching him. "What's wrong with him? A ghoul must've bit him."

His legs wobbly, Joon-ho managed to keep standing, leaning forward, his hands on his knees.

"Good question," said Cassavetes, who was watching Joon-ho from the front seat. "I'm starting to feel sick myself."

"I figured you would," muttered Strider.

"What's that supposed to mean? Are you saying again that I'm a pussy?"

"No. Never mind."

"If Joon-ho got bit, don't let him back in the car," said Purl, his eyes bugging out with fear.

"Did anyone see him get bit?" asked Strider.

"I wasn't watching him. I was too busy trying to move cars."

"I didn't see any ghouls on the bridge," said Cassavetes. "But maybe there was one out there. There are some at the end of the bridge where we came from," he said, nodding in their direction.

"Ask him," said Strider.

Cassavetes powered down his window. "Did a zed bite you, Joon-ho?"

Dazed, Joon-ho didn't look like he comprehended the question, as he stood doubled over with pain. He threw up again, not as much this time, but it, too, was streaked with blood.

"Why is there blood in his puke—unless he's infected?" said Cassavetes.

"We can't be sure of that," said Strider. "Nobody saw him get bit."

"I don't want him sitting next to me," said Purl. "Maybe he's got blood in his barf because he's infected and he bit someone and that's their blood he's puking. Somebody, kill him for Chrissake."

"Not unless we're sure he got bit," said Strider.

"I dunno," said Cassavetes. "I feel kind of sick, too."

"Did you get bit?" said Purl.

"No way."

"Strider, you're the stone killer," said Purl. "You take Joon-ho out."

"I want to know what's wrong with him," said Strider.

Taking a deep breath Joon-ho stood up straight and took a tentative step toward the car door, his face pale.

"Don't let him back in," said Purl, cowering against the driver's-side window in the backseat.

Joon-ho approached the Beast's back door, preparing to reenter.

"Somebody, shoot him," said Purl, squirming in his seat, his face sweaty. "I don't want to turn into one of them."

"Did a ghoul bite you, Joon-ho?" said Strider.

"What?" said Joon-ho, puzzled, not sure he had heard Strider correctly, reaching for the door.

"Did a ghoul bite you?"

"No."

"Why's there blood in your puke?"

Joon-ho hesitated to answer.

"I'm sick," he said at last.

"Do you have the zombie plague?"

"He must have it," said Purl. "You saw the blood."

"Shut up," said Strider. "Let him answer."

"He must've got it from the spores," said Purl. "You don't have to get bit. You can breathe their spores and get it."

"I don't have the plague," said Joon-ho. He paused. "I guess I better tell you. I have stage four pancreatic cancer."

"He's lying. He's just saying that so we won't shoot him."

"It's the truth. That's why I volunteered for this suicide mission. I'm gonna die soon anyway," said Joon-ho, looking forlorn.

"Don't believe him. He'll say anything so we won't shoot him. Don't let him in. He'll bite me."

"I told the president before the mission that I had it," Joon-ho told Strider.

"He never told me," said Strider.

"It's bullshit," said Purl. "He's gonna turn any minute."

"Do you think you're infected?" Strider asked Joon-ho.

"No," answered Joon-ho, coughing. "No ghouls bit me. It's the cancer eating my pancreas that's causing the bleeding."

"Can we take the chance he's lying?" said Purl. "I'm the one sitting back here with him. He's gonna bite me first."

"I'm not gonna bite anyone. This is insane. I don't have the plague."

160

"How's he look to you?" Strider asked Cassavetes, who was closest to Joon-ho.

Cassavetes searched Joon-ho's face. "His eyes don't look milky. If he's turning, his eyes would be clouding up."

"I'm not turning, for Chrissake," said Joon-ho. "I'm getting into the car."

"Don't let him in," cried Purl.

"We gotta get moving," said Strider. "Get in, Joon-ho."

"If he's coming in, I want out," said Purl. "This is cruel and unusual punishment, which is outlawed in the Eighth Amendment."

Joon-ho opened the door.

"If he sits next to me, I'm gonna scream the entire trip," said Purl. "So help me."

"I ought to go back there and beat some sense into you," said Strider, glaring at the image of Purl's face in the rearview mirror. "All right. Change in plans. Joon-ho, you switch seats with Cassavetes and ride shotgun. Cassavetes, you're in back."

"Is this necessary?" said Cassavetes.

"I don't want Purl screaming the entire trip."

"Just clip Purl and be done with it. He's an anchor on this mission."

"We need every man we can get. Take a seat in back." Strider glared over his shoulder at Purl. "Is that OK with you, crybaby?"

"You're gonna be sorry when Joon-ho takes a bite out of your throat."

"I feel sick, too," said Cassavetes, his face wan. "Maybe there's something going around."

"It's called the zombie plague," said Purl.

"I didn't get bit."

"You got something else," said Strider.

"There you go again," said Cassavetes, "accusing me of being a pussy."

"If that's what I meant, I would say it. Now move into the backseat."

"Wait a minute. Are you planning on killing me like you did Damon because you think I'm a pussy? Is that it?"

"If I killed you, how would we find Wheelhouse? Why the hell would I want to kill you?" said Strider.

"He knows you're trigger-happy," said Purl.

"You shut up."

Satisfied with Strider's answer, Cassavetes slid out of the front seat and climbed into the back. Wincing, Joon-ho took Cassavetes's vacated seat and shut the door behind him.

"Are you OK?" said Strider.

"Not really," said Joon-ho. "But you know what they say. If nothing's happening to you, it means you're dead."

He attempted a smile, which turned into a grimace.

Purl shot a dirty look at his new neighbor Cassavetes. "Are you gonna start throwing up blood, too?"

"I dunno," said Cassavetes, looking uncomfortable. "I don't feel so good. Maybe all I need is rest."

"You need more than that," said Strider sotto voce in the driver's seat.

"What?"

"Nothing."

"I thought you said something."

"I didn't."

Purl continued cringing against his window, keeping away from Cassavetes.

"Just stay away from me," said Purl, staring at Cassavetes. "Stop looking at me like I'm your next meal."

Cassavetes shook his head at Purl. "I'm in no mood to eat."

"Let's get off this damn bridge," said Strider, firing the Beast's engine and plowing into a pickup truck in front of him.

Chapter 50

"What was that all about?" said Marta, who had watched with concern Joon-ho leave Cardinal One and reenter it.

"Joon-ho looked sick," said Halverson, sitting beside Marta in his parked SUV driver's seat.

"Did he get bit?"

"If he did, Strider would've shot him. He's letting Joon-ho back in, so it must be something else."

"Maybe he's carsick," said Laci from the backseat.

Halverson picked up on movement in the rearview mirror.

"Bad news," he said. "Ghouls behind us."

A constellation of four ghouls was the better part of six feet behind them.

Gunshots rang out.

Halverson checked the driver's-side mirror. He saw a man on horseback wearing a black Stetson at the entrance to the bridge aiming a handgun in his direction.

"What's going on back there?" said Strider over the walkie-talkie. "Over."

"This is Cardinal Two. We got ghouls on our tail," said Halverson. "Over."

"I heard gun reports. Are you firing on them? Over."

"It wasn't us. There's a guy on a horse at the bridge entrance. He's the one doing the shooting. Over."

"At what? Over."

"He's shooting at the ghouls, I think. A couple of his bullets hit our vehicle, though. Over."

"Who is he? Over."

"He looks like that guy Gatling we met before. Over."

"I don't trust that guy. Over."

"His gang is with him. They're all on horseback and heading this way. We cleared a path for them. Over."

"We need to get off this goddamn bridge ASAP," said Strider, plowing the pickup out of his way. "Over."

"There are ghouls all over the bridge behind us and making for us. Over."

"To hell with them. We don't need to get into a firefight with them. Over."

"What about Gatling? Over."

"We can't waste time with him. We got a mission to do. Let's go. We don't want to get trapped on this bridge. If that happens, their horses give them more maneuverability than us with our blocked cars. Over."

Halverson watched Gatling and his men gun down the ghouls that had shambled onto the bridge.

"Maybe they're coming to help us again," said Halverson. "Over."

"Do you really believe that? Over."

"Oh, hell."

"What? Repeat. Over."

"Rafferty's with them. Over."

"I blew that asshole away. Over."

"I see him clear as day. His leg irons are off. He's riding behind Gatling. Over."

"Why's Rafferty coming back to us? It makes no sense. Over."

"He also has a piece in his hand. Over."

"Once I plow this pickup out of the way, we'll have a free lane to the other side of the bridge. Over and out."

Halverson fired his Suburban's engine and drove after Strider.

Chapter 51

Strider plowed the pickup to the side, but he didn't have enough room to pass thanks to a Greyhound bus abandoned on the other side of the street. The bus extended a good yard into the opposite lane, blocking the Beast.

Strider knew he needed to plow the pickup farther into the chain-link fence, but the fence wasn't giving. The pickup's driver's-side front tire burst as Strider's plow creamed it. The steel plow scraped against the pickup's driver's-side door with a nerve-racking screech.

"Keep grinding," said Joon-ho, eagerly watching the pickup contort under the impact of the plow.

"Gatling's almost here," said Halverson over the walkie-talkie. "We got ghouls coming. Over."

"All right," said Strider. "We're gonna have to find out what he wants. We're not gonna get by this pickup soon enough. Over."

Strider threw the Beast's shifter into Reverse.

"What are you doing?" said Joon-ho.

"I can't open my door if we stay here," said Strider. "I don't want to be trapped in here when Gatling arrives."

Strider tried to pull free from the pickup, but his SUV plow had hooked onto the pickup's twisted door, preventing him from reversing.

"Shit," he said.

He could see Gatling approaching on horseback in his rearview mirror, blasting ghouls with his .50 Magnum.

"You're almost free," said Joon-ho, inspecting from his seat the section on the pickup's door where the plow had snagged. "Go forward and reverse again."

Strider did so, flooring the accelerator when he reversed to give the Beast as much momentum as possible to pull free.

The pickup's door groaned and creaked as the plow pulled free from it.

Strider backed up enough so he could open his door to find out what Gatling wanted. Strider climbed out of the driver's seat.

"Howdy," said Gatling, riding toward him, .50 Magnum in hand. "What say ye?"

"We meet again," said Strider, stone-faced.

"Long time no see."

"I don't have time for social visits."

"I understand. That's why I'm here."

"What do you mean?" said Strider, frowning in puzzlement.

"We want to join your mission."

Halverson climbed out of his SUV and walked over to them.

Meanwhile, Gatling's men used their AR-15 assault rifles to finish off the ghouls that had invaded the bridge.

Strider said nothing, searching Gatling's face.

"As you can see, we got a lot of firepower," said Gatling, indicating his armed men with a sweep of his hand. "Don't tell me you don't need firepower on your mission."

"It's TS/SCI," said Strider. "I'm not allowed to divulge its nature to anyone without the highest clearance."

Rafferty rode up, showing off his AR-15.

Strider glowered at him.

"We got a new member in our gang," said Gatling, eying Rafferty. "He's pretty good with that thing."

"He's had practice killing and raping people," said Strider. "All women."

"We saw him in action," muttered Gatling with disdain.

If Rafferty heard the comment, he ignored it.

"Not much difference between sluts and ghouls," said Rafferty, gloating at Strider. "I bet you never thought you'd see me again, *boss*."

Hiking his eyebrows Gatling feigned surprise. "What? You two know each other? It's a small world, ain't it?"

Chapter 52

"I'd appreciate it if you holstered your piece," Strider told Gatling.

"I was blasting zeds and saving your bacon again."

"We can make do without your help."

Gatling continued holding his .50 Magnum. "We came all the way here to join your mission. We want to help the president's men. Is that any way to thank us?"

"It's a secret mission. Like I said before, I'm not allowed to divulge its nature to anyone."

Gatling leaned down toward Strider from his black stallion. "Psst. It's not secret anymore. You're on your way to get the zombie plague vaccine from the doctor who invented it."

Strider widened his eyes. When he realized what had happened, he turned his head and locked his gaze on Rafferty's grinning face.

"Traitor," spat Strider.

"Who are you calling a traitor?" said Rafferty, outraged.

"You. There's only one way he could know where we're going. You told him. You're a traitor. You're going before a firing squad when we return to the president."

"I'm not going anywhere with you. I joined Gatling's gang."

Strider confronted Gatling. "He's one of ours."

"Not anymore," said Gatling. "He left you of his own free will." He turned to Rafferty. "Do you want to join his group or stay with us?"

"I wouldn't go back to that guy if he was the last man on earth," said Rafferty. "He tried to kill me."

"You don't have a choice," said Strider. "You're a convict under my supervision."

"The president pardoned me."

"You're only pardoned if we succeed in our mission. Until that time, you're a convict facing the death sentence."

Rafferty drew a bead on Strider's face with his AR-15. "What's to prevent me from blowing off your face here and now?"

"Hold it," said Gatling, snatching the AR-15 barrel and pointing it skyward. "We come in peace," he told Strider. "We didn't come here to do battle with you. We want to help you get the vaccine."

"Then prove it," said Strider.

"What more can we do? We helped you battle the zeds on the bridge. What more do you want?"

"Give me back Rafferty. He's my prisoner."

"No way," said Rafferty, bristling.

"Why is that so important to you?" said Gatling. "Your mission should take priority over everything."

"The prisoner was entrusted to me. I am responsible for him. I need to handcuff him."

"In your dreams," said Rafferty, leveling a baleful gaze at Strider.

"How can he fight the zeds if he's in handcuffs?" said Gatling.

Halverson stepped closer to Strider. "He's got a point. We need him without his cuffs so he can help us fight the ghouls surrounding Wheelhouse."

"That guy's a serial killer," Strider told Gatling. "Do you really feel safe with him free to do what he wants?"

"Under ordinary conditions, no, I wouldn't feel safe," said Gatling. "But these aren't ordinary conditions. We're trying to survive the apocalypse. We need his gun in our arsenal."

Steaming, Strider continued to resent Rafferty's escape. "We don't have time to dick around. We need to get moving. I'm telling you, you need to watch your back around that guy if he's got a gun in his hand."

"It may have escaped your notice, but I too have a gun in my hand," said Gatling, holding up his .50 Magnum.

"It's your life. You keep him with you. If he comes near me without cuffs on, I'll take him out."

Gatling reached over and wrested the AR-15 out of Rafferty's hands.

"Hey, what are you doing?" said Rafferty.

"We wasted all the zeds on the bridge," said Gatling. "You don't need this now. When the time comes, I'll give it back to you."

"You really think I'm gonna plug one of you?"

"You don't need the piece now. I'll decide when you need it. Got a problem with that?"

Rafferty shook his head. "Why's everyone so scared? You're scared of your own shadows. Bunch of pussies."

His face ashen, Joon-ho climbed out of his seat, staggered to the front of the vehicle, bent over, and threw up more blood.

"What the fuck?" said Gatling, steadying his horse, which was nervously shifting under him. "Did a zed bite him?" he asked, aiming his .50 Magnum at Joon-ho's head.

"No," said Strider, holding up his hand to prevent Gatling from firing.

"He's spitting up blood like he just chewed on someone's flesh."

"He's got pancreatic cancer," said Strider. "He's not turning."

"Are you sure?" said Gatling, keeping his gun trained on Joon-ho.

"I believe him. Nobody saw him get bit by a ghoul."

"I dunno. You better keep your eye on him. I wouldn't let him near me, if I was you. He gets too close to me, I'll whack him. I don't take chances with the infected."

Joon-ho took a couple of deep breaths, regained some color, and returned to his seat.

Gatling lowered his .50 Magnum.

"I need to push that pickup out of the way so we can get off this bridge," said Strider, setting off for his vehicle.

"I can give you a push," said Halverson.

"Yeah. OK. We got hung up on the pickup the last time we tried. A little extra horsepower should help."

Halverson returned to his vehicle.

He clambered into the driver's seat.

Gatling rode his stallion back to his gang and joined them battling the zeds pouring onto the bridge.

Chapter 53

"What was that all about?" said Marta in Cardinal Two's shotgun seat.

"Rafferty told Gatling about our mission," said Halverson, keying the ignition. "He knows about the vaccine."

"Is that a bad thing?"

"The less people who know about it, the better. Can you imagine if everyone knew about it? They'd be rioting to get it from us."

"I never thought about it."

"We can't let anyone know about it till the president's scientists find a way to mass-produce it."

"So what about Gatling?"

"He's coming with us," said Halverson, face glum. "We don't have much choice in the matter. Anyway, we can use all the firepower we can get. Wheelhouse is supposed to be surrounded by millions of ghouls."

"Maybe we should tell the president about Gatling."

"We're under radio silence. No comms. The president doesn't want any of our comms to be intercepted."

Halverson fired Cardinal Two's engine. He put the shifter in Drive and followed Strider, who plowed the Beast into the pickup and passed the Greyhound bus on his left side. Halverson drove his vehicle into the Beast's tailgate and shoved it, increasing the pressure that the Beast exerted on the pickup, crumpling the pickup and forcing it into the chain-link fence that bordered the bridge. The chain-link fence bellied out over the river under the pressure of the pickup being shoved into it.

With a final screech and clang of steel, the Beast broke free of the pickup.

"We're free," said Strider over his radio. "Over."

"I thought you said we're under radio silence," Marta told Halverson. "Why's he using the walkie-talkie?"

"These transmissions are burst transmissions that cover only a few feet. Nobody will intercept them. It's the transmissions over long distances that can be intercepted, like one to Mount Weather."

"So we're on our own," said Marta, a distant look in her eyes. "Nothing new for me."

"Me neither, I guess."

Halverson followed Strider's vehicle off the bridge.

"Cassavetes says we're almost there," said Strider via his radio. "Over."

"Now all we have to do is drive through a million zeds surrounding Wheelhouse," said Laci from the backseat. "Looking good."

"At least it stopped raining," said Marta, gazing out the windshield.

"I don't like the idea of having Rafferty behind us," said Strider. "Over."

"I don't either," said Halverson. "But there's not much he can do to us as long as we're in our vehicles. Over."

"I want you to take him out. Understand? Over."

Halverson exchanged looks with Marta.

"Do you think that's necessary," said Halverson. "Over."

"He's a threat to the success of our mission. Over."

"How so?"

"He's a serial killer for Chrissake. He wants us all dead. He's been a thorn in our side from the get-go. Over."

"Understood," said Halverson. "Over."

But he thought Strider was exaggerating Rafferty's danger to the mission and Rafferty didn't need to be wasted. Rafferty wanted the vaccine as much as everyone else. Why should the guy sabotage the mission?

Halverson believed it was personal between Strider and Rafferty. Strider had just missed killing Rafferty when Rafferty had escaped by jumping off the bridge. Strider didn't like unfinished business, decided Halverson. If Strider thought he had whacked someone, he wanted the victim to stay whacked. He didn't want the victim to come back and haunt him.

"I knew I could count on you," said Strider. "Over."

"I can't get to him while we're in our vehicles. Over."

"No problem. Do him when the time comes. Over and out."

"Are you really gonna kill Rafferty?" asked Marta.

"I'm not gonna think about it as long as we're in the vehicles," answered Halverson. "One thing at a time. We have to reach Wheelhouse."

Chapter 54

"How much farther do we have to go, Cassavetes?" Strider said at the wheel, driving down the rain-slick throughway beyond the bridge, glancing over his shoulder at Cassavetes in the backseat.

"Not more than ten miles from this bridge," said Cassavetes.

"When are we gonna run into the ghouls?"

"They're surrounding the hideout."

Strider lowered his voice and turned to Joon-ho. "Were you telling me the truth that you weren't bitten?"

"Of course, I was," said Joon-ho, resentful.

"Why are you still puking blood?" said Strider, suspiciously.

"How do I know? I'm not a doctor. He told me I had pancreatic cancer. I don't have much longer to live. Maybe three months at the most."

"Sorry to hear it."

"He's lying," cried Purl from the backseat. "He's turning."

"You're full of shit," said Joon-ho. "No ghouls bit me. Period."

Strider scrutinized Joon-ho's face, seeking tells that would indicate Joon-ho was lying. Strider didn't see any.

"If he got bit, he should've turned by now," Strider told Purl. "I never seen anybody turn this slow."

"Why would I lie?" said Joon-ho.

"To save your skin," said Purl. "You know we'd have to clip you if you got bit."

"I don't want to talk about this anymore. I get sick just thinking about the cancer eating away at me." Grimacing, Joon-ho clutched his forehead. "I might not last three months."

"I saw him get bit by a zed on the bridge when we were clearing cars away," burst Purl.

Strider eyeballed Joon-ho.

"He's lying through his teeth," said Joon-ho in white heat. "Nobody bit me. Examine my body if you want. I got nothing to hide."

"Where did he get bit, Purl?" said Strider.

"Uh, his leg."

"Whereabouts?"

"Uh, the thigh."

"Which one?"

"Uh, it happened so quick I can't remember."

"He's lying," said Joon-ho, staring in earnest at Strider.

"Why would I lie?" said Purl.

"I dunno. Maybe you believe I got bit, and the only way you can get anyone to believe you is by lying."

"The thing is, I'm not lying. You got bit, and you know it."

"You lying cop-killing asshole," said Joon-ho, his face flushing, fit to be tied.

He suffered a coughing fit.

"See," said Purl. "He's turning."

Strider watched Joon-ho carefully.

"It's the cancer, damnit," said Joon-ho between coughs.

"Joon-ho's not a crook facing a death sentence," said Strider over his shoulder to Purl. "I believe him."

"Then you're an idiot," said Purl. "Who cares anyway? Do you think I care if he bites you?"

"If you saw him get bit, why didn't you tell us sooner?"

Purl didn't answer right away.

"Because I didn't get bit," said Joon-ho.

"I didn't tell at first because I knew you'd kill him if I told you, Strider," said Purl.

"You want me to believe you care about him?" said Strider, incredulous. "You were just telling me to shoot him."

"I'm not a monster. I figured Joon-ho would confess eventually to being bit and I wouldn't have to rat him out. You have to understand, snitches are considered the lowest of the low in the joint. I'm not gonna reduce myself to being a snitch."

"How can you believe a word he says?" Joon-ho asked Strider.

"You know you got bit," said Purl. "Time to fess up."

"Stop," said Joon-ho.

"Time to come clean, Joon-ho."

"Stop." Joon-ho saw Purl was about to speak. "Stop."

"I know your game, Purl," said Strider. "You want to set us all at each other's throats. Then we kill each other so you can escape. It's the oldest trick in the book. Divide and conquer."

"Ah, you don't know nothing," said Purl, retreating into himself. "I don't give a shit what happens to any of you."

"Ghouls in the road dead ahead," said Joon-ho.

"There must be even more of them now," said Cassavetes, disconcerted. "They hadn't spread this far when I left Wheelhouse."

"Time to take these cuffs off me and give me a piece," said Purl.

"It's time when I say it's time," said Strider.

"What's the point of my being here if I'm cuffed all the time? It makes no sense."

Strider plowed the Beast into the ghouls huddled in the road, sweeping them out of the way and driving onward.

"You're not gonna be able to drive all the way to Wheelhouse's lair in this thing," said Cassavetes.

"Why not?" said Strider, turning his head to look at him.

"He's got the mountain pass barricaded with an eighteen-wheeler to keep the zeds out. You won't be able to plow it out of the way."

"Then we'll get out and fight our way through the ghouls to reach him. We're prepared for that. We've got thousands of rounds of ammo."

Strider encountered more and more ghouls milling on the road. He continued his journey plowing through them. There were fewer derelict motor vehicles on the road than on the bridge and Strider didn't have to stop thanks to gridlock. He made good time.

They were heading up a mountain on a winding road. Strider heard his ears popping as the air pressure changed the higher they climbed.

Chapter 55

Halverson followed Strider up the mountain pass until he didn't.

Halverson's Suburban started juddering.

"What's wrong?" said Marta.

Halverson checked out the dashboard gauges. The fuel gauge needle was pointing to the red Empty zone. The Suburban came to a halt.

"We're out of fuel," he said. He shook his head. "We had a quarter tank a short while ago. It doesn't make sense. Unless—"

She stared at him with inquisitive eyes.

"Unless one of Gatling's bullets hit our fuel tank," he said.

"Did he do it deliberately, you think?"

"Could be. It doesn't really matter. We're out of fuel."

"If he did it deliberately, he might be planning something."

Halverson chewed it over. "I wouldn't put it past him."

"But what?"

Halverson scoffed up his radio. "This is Cardinal Two. We got a situation. Over."

"Why are you falling back?" answered Strider. "I can't keep you in sight. Over."

"We're outa fuel. Gatling must've shot our fuel tank or fuel line. Over."

"The ghouls are swarming around us," said Marta, eyes wide.

"Your vehicle is armored," said Strider. "How could he hit the fuel tank? Over."

"Maybe his bullet ricocheted off the pavement or hit inside the wheel well," said Halverson. "Over."

"I'll stop," said Strider. "Can you at least drive up to me? Over."

"No can do," said Halverson, eying the Beast in the distance. "We came to a complete stop. Over."

"All right. I'll back up to your vehicle. Over."

"The ghouls are closing in. How can you get past them without a plow on your tailgate? These vehicles weren't built for going backward. Over."

"Never give up ground. Rules to live by in the SEALS. I know what you mean, but this is an emergency exception. Over."

"Roger. Over."

"They're closing behind us fast. I don't want their dead bodies getting trapped in my wheel wells when I back over them. Over."

The ghouls had now fully packed the road between Strider's and Halverson's vehicles.

Strider stopped backing up.

"There's not enough room for all of you to fit into my vehicle," he said. "Over."

"We have a spare five-gallon jerrican of fuel in the trunk. Over."

"It's just gonna leak out if you got a hole in your fuel tank like you said. Over."

"It might give us just enough gas to get us going for a ways. Ask Cassavetes how far we have to go to reach the entrance to Wheelhouse's hideout. Over."

"He thinks it's another mile or so from here. Over."

"It this doesn't work, we'll have to walk the rest of the distance and catch up to you. Over."

"Negative. We're not leaving you behind. If anyone's doing any walking, we're all walking. Over."

"That could jeopardize the mission. Over."

"We're not leaving you. We're coming back there to cover you when you refuel. Over."

"We're leaving the vehicle now to get the jerrican," said Halverson. "Over."

He watched the shambling, squirming ghouls approach with a cloud of flies hovering over them, his pulse accelerating.

"We need to go outside, get the jerrican in the trunk, and refuel," he said.

"Then it's time to give me a gun," said Laci in the backseat, eyeballing the ghouls pressing their mortifying faces against her window.

"I'll give you my MP9. I'll use my SIG P226 until we reach the trunk where I can get another MP9."

"There are too many of them," said Marta.

"When did that ever stop us? We need to refuel. We can't stay here."

Halverson heard gunshots up ahead.

His cue to leave his vehicle. MP9 in hand, he racked the slide and flung open the Suburban door.

Chapter 56

Kicking the ghouls away from his door, Halverson fired a burst into the advancing ghouls, turning their heads into bone fragments and oozing glops of brain matter.

He sprang out of the driver's seat, opened the back door with his key fob, and let Laci out. He handed her his MP9 and a handful of spare magazines, as Marta came up from behind him with her MP9 cutting down ghouls that were fixing to bite him.

He whipped out his SIG from his waist holster and plugged the nearest ghouls. He cut a path through the things to the rear trunk. Laci opened fire on grimacing ghouls that lurched toward her with outstretched arms, baring their broken teeth and growling.

Halverson saw Strider and his men approaching, firing their guns, blasting apart ghoul heads. Ghouls were dropping everywhere.

Halverson popped the trunk with his key fob and retrieved a fully loaded MP9 as well as a bunch of spare mags. He stuffed the mags into his cargo pockets, firing at ghouls to keep them at bay. He grabbed the jerrican of fuel. Gunning down nearby ghouls he made his way to the Suburban's fuel cap. He unscrewed the cap and commenced pouring diesel into the tank.

Strider, Purl, Cassavetes, and Joon-ho hosed the area with cover fire, downing scores of ravenous ghouls. A blonde female thirtyish ghoul wearing scrubs snagged Halverson's arm, opened her drooling mouth, and prepared to bite it, exhaling fetid breath at him. Marta blew a piece of skull out of the ghoul's head with a brief, well-aimed burst of her MP9, spoiling the ghoul's dinner plans.

Halverson emptied the diesel fuel into the tank, discarded the jerrican, and replaced the fuel cap. He signaled to Strider that he was done.

Firing continuous bursts, Strider retreated with his men to his vehicle.

Halverson was sick of the ghouls. They just kept coming. There was no end to them as far as the eye could see.

"Let's get back inside," he told Marta and Laci.

Gritting her teeth Laci emptied her magazine into a pack of six ghouls that were pressed together and reaching for her with waving arms like an octopus. The ghouls crumpled into a mound of putrescent corpses.

She swapped mags and retreated to the back door, picking off ghouls.

Marta blew apart ghoul heads and ducked into the Suburban's shotgun seat.

Halverson emptied his magazine into a one-eyed, one-armed sixtysomething ghoul with a long white beard, who grunted at him, slobbering maggot-riddled saliva. The creature jutted its jaw at Halverson and tried to bite his hand. Adrenaline shooting through him, Halverson withdrew his hand like a shot.

Strider, Joon-ho, and Purl formed a circle covering each other's backs as they retreated toward their vehicle, pelting ghouls with lead from their overheated MP9s, swapping mags as they went.

"Come and get it," cried Purl, wasting ghouls.

A tall black ghoul leaned forward and grasped Purl's ear. Purl screamed and pistol-whipped the ghoul's emaciated face with his empty machine pistol. The ghoul ripped Purl's ear off his head. Blood gushed out of the wound. Purl screamed in pain.

He swapped magazines and shot the tall ghoul in the forehead, cracking the ghoul's skull. The ghoul's knees buckled. It collapsed into a lifeless heap. Purl's spouting blood aroused nearby ghouls, triggering a feeding frenzy. Agitated by the proximity of fresh blood, they moved faster, charging Purl, growling and swiping their arms quickly.

Joon-ho helped Purl blast them, their MP9s chattering nonstop at the voracious ghouls.

Strider hadn't seen Purl lose his ear.

When he saw Purl bleeding, he yelled, "Did they bite you?"

"No," screamed Purl, fearing Strider would shoot him. "It ripped my ear off with its hand. I'm bleeding like a stuck pig."

Aiming his weapon at Purl, Strider weighed Purl's words.

"Ask Joon-ho, if you don't believe me," said Purl, his face sweaty, the tendons in his neck sticking out. "He saw the whole thing."

"Joon-ho?" said Strider.

Joon-ho didn't answer right away.

"What about it?" said Strider.

"Tell him, for Chrissake," said Purl, grimacing in pain.

"It tore his ear off," said Joon-ho. "His blood is driving the ghouls crazy."

"Did any of them bite him?" said Strider.

"I wasn't watching him the whole time."

"None of them bit me," said Purl, pressing his hand against the ragged ear stub on his head trying to stanch the bleeding. "I need my ear bandaged before I bleed out."

Strider fired a burst into a thickset middle-aged male ghoul with grizzled, shaggy black hair who lunged at him in jeans and a navy blue Yankees sweat shirt. The ghoul splayed on the tarmac.

"You better be telling me the truth," said Strider.

"I am," said Purl. "If I got bit, I would want you to ice me. I repeat, I didn't get bit."

"Everybody, get back into the vehicle," said Strider, walking backward to the driver's seat, firing his MP9 into the phalanx of ghouls that surged toward him in an implacable wave.

Joon-ho aimed his MP9 in Strider's direction.

Strider froze.

Joon-ho squeezed his MP9 trigger, clipping a twentysomething male skinhead ghoul with tattoo sleeves, stitching a dotted line of bullets across the ghoul's moldy cheeks. Skinhead collapsed in the road, his milky eyes gazing heavenward.

Strider gave Joon-ho a thumbs up.

Joon-ho retreated to his seat in the front of Cardinal One, mowing down ghouls that blocked his path.

Clutching his wounded ear Purl piled into the backseat with Cassavetes. Strider took out the ghouls following them, ducked into the driver's seat, and slammed the door shut behind him.

Strider pumped his fist in front of his rearview mirror hoping Halverson could see the signal for him to follow Strider's lead.

Strider fired the Beast's engine, put the shifter into Drive, and drove forward.

Chapter 57

"Cross your fingers," said Halverson, keying the ignition.

Sitting beside him Marta watched expectantly.

He fired his Suburban engine, shifted into Drive, and applied the accelerator. The vehicle moved forward after Strider.

"So far so good," said Halverson, accelerating.

"How far is it gonna go?" said Marta.

A half mile down the road, the Suburban commenced juddering again as it ran out of diesel. Halverson, Marta, and Laci jerked forward in their seats.

Halverson keyed his radio. "The only way we're gonna get this car going is by plugging the hole in the fuel tank. Over."

"The hell with it," said Strider. "We'll hoof it the rest of the way. Over."

"You can fit Marta in your vehicle. Me and Laci will walk the rest of the way. Over."

"Nothing doing. We're staying together. Over."

"There are too many ghouls out there. On foot, all of us aren't gonna make it to Wheelhouse's. Over."

"We're all gonna make it. Any sign of Gatling? Over."

Halverson consulted his rearview mirror. "No. Do you want to wait for him before we leave our vehicles? Over."

"No. I'd rather lose him if possible. Over."

"We could use his help. Over."

"If it's on the level. Why didn't he hand Rafferty over to us? I don't like it. Grab as many mags as you can stuff into your clothing, and let's go. Over."

"I'm taking the Browning M2. We need firepower to blast through these things. Over."

"Go for it. Time to move it. Over and out."

"Let's go," Halverson told Marta and Laci.

"Go where?" said Laci, sitting in the backseat taking in the ghouls surrounding them.

"We're walking the rest of the way to Wheelhouse's hideout."

"Good luck."

"You're coming with us. You have no chance alone."

"How far do we have to walk?"

"We're pretty close, according to Cassavetes."

"Forget it. 'Pretty close' could mean anything."

"You can't stay here by yourself, Laci," said Marta, torquing her back around in her seat to face Laci.

"You're going with him?"

"We're all going."

"Not me."

"You can't stay here forever."

Laci shivered. "I hate those things."

"Rafferty's coming this way. You don't want to deal with him alone, do you?"

Laci considered this. "No."

"Make sure you have a fresh magazine in your MP9," said Halverson. "We'll get more mags in the trunk."

Halverson popped a fresh mag into his MP9 and flung open his door, smashing two ghouls that were trying to get in. He blew their brains out, reached the trunk, and popped it.

With Marta behind him providing cover fire, he pulled out the Browning M2 and fed an ammo belt of three hundred rounds into it. The machine gun weighed over sixty pounds. He swung around and made mincemeat of a swarm of ghouls converging on him. Their heads exploded into dust and dollops of brains.

"Jesus," said Laci, watching him. "Rambo time."

"Stuff as many magazines into your clothing as possible," said Halverson, and blew apart more ghoul heads.

Marta and Laci jammed mags into their clothing, Marta into her jeans, Laci into her prison coveralls.

They opened fire on the ghouls with their MP9s.

Halverson used the time to grab a spare M2 ammo belt from the trunk and drape it around his neck. He whipped the heavy machine gun around and commenced drilling ghouls.

"Let's go," he said, his face sweaty from wielding the M2.

"Cut those suckers in half," said Laci, baring her teeth and disintegrating a hag's ghoul face with a burst from her MP9.

A crazed grin slashing his face, Halverson cut a swath through the ghouls that poured toward them until he, Marta, and Laci reached Strider and his crew. The air was thick with exploding brains and chunks of bright white skulls.

"That's what I'm talking about," said Purl, riveting his eyes on the grisly proceedings. "Let me have one of those babies," he added, eying the M2.

"Halverson, you take point," said Strider.

Halverson advanced to the front and opened fire, clearing a path through the tightly packed ghouls.

"The sound of that M2 is gonna attract more ghouls," said Joon-ho.

"Let 'em come," said Strider. "We'll turn their brains into sawdust."

Joon-ho bent forward and vomited blood.

Laci watched in horror. "Did a zed bite him?"

"Yeah," said Purl. "He's turning."

"He's lying, goddammit," said Joon-ho, straightening up, wiping streaks of vomit off his lips with the back of his wrist. "And I'm getting sick of hearing his lies. I didn't get bit."

Chapter 58

Rafferty rode up to Gatling, as the militia gang cantered down the road after the convoy of Suburbans. Horse hooves clop-clopped on the tarmac.

So far, the stretch of road they were on was clear of ghouls.

"We can't let the government get that vaccine," said Rafferty.

"Why do you say that?" said Gatling, riding beside Rafferty.

"Once they get it, we'll never see it again. They'll take it all for themselves."

"You may be right. Don't think I believe the government for one second, not after the president nuked our great country."

"We're gonna have to waste all of the feds and take the vaccine from them. They're not gonna give it to us willingly."

"We need their help fighting the zeds. We can't take out the feds now."

Rafferty narrowed his eyes. "Mark my words. Once they get their hands on that vaccine, we'll never get it."

"You ride that horse like a pro."

"Beginner's luck. Are you listening to what I'm saying?"

"Listen," said Gatling, cupping his ear with his hand. "I hear gunfire ahead of us in the distance. There must be zeds up ahead."

"We need to make the decision now to waste the feds the next time we see them."

"Loud gun reports," said Gatling, impressed. "They must have some heavy artillery on them. It's not the zeds. They can't shoot a piece if you handed it to them. Jesus. If my ears don't deceive me, it sounds like a Ma Deuce."

"Ma Deuce?" said Rafferty, puzzled.

"A Browning M2. Damn, I'd give my left nut for one of those babies."

"I know they got guns and plenty of ammo. I don't know about any Ma Deuce."

"It's a Ma Deuce, I tell you."

"All the more reason to whack out the feds, every last one of them. Then we confiscate their Ma Deuce whatever."

"If the feds need an M2, they're in a serious firefight. We need to give them a hand."

"Am I not getting through to you?"

Gatling spurred his horse's flanks and rode at a full gallop in the direction of the pitched battle.

"Follow me, everyone," he cried over his shoulder at his gang, raising his .50 Magnum over his head and pointing the barrel forward.

Shaking his head Rafferty galloped after Gatling.

Chapter 59

"More people are dying of hypoxia, Mr. President," said Dr. Morrow in the president's office at the Mount Weather bunker.

"How do we remedy the situation?" said President Mims, sitting behind his desk munching Fritos.

"We need to increase the amount of oxygen everyone is getting to 19.5 percent."

"That will shorten the number of days we are able to go on living in this bunker."

"True," said Morrow, his bald head shining under the fluorescent light mounted on the ceiling. "But more people will survive."

"For a shorter time," added Mims.

"Correct."

"Where are we supposed to get this extra oxygen to give everyone?"

Morrow hesitated. "We need to reduce your oxygen level, Mr. President, in order to increase theirs."

"If you reduce my oxygen intake, my health will deteriorate. Correct?"

"It's the only way, sir."

"Answer the question. Am I correct or not?"

"You are correct."

"I am the president of this great country. I need to be in peak condition to run it. Do you want a sickly, dying man as your leader?"

"Of course not."

"It would send a terrible message to other countries, wouldn't it? What about Russia and China? They might decide to attack us with a weakling at the helm. It's not a message we can afford to send."

"Are you saying you don't want me to increase the oxygen supply to the other residents of the bunker?" said Morrow, trying to understand the president's instructions.

"Not if it leads to the deterioration of my health. I am the president. My mind must be sharp at all times so I am able to deal with each crisis as it arises."

"Then more people in the bunker will be dying from hypoxia in the near future," said Morrow, puckering his brow with worry.

"Not if we can get our air ducts cleared of ghouls." Mims picked up the phone receiver from his desktop. "Henry, send out another patrol in hazmat uniforms to clear the ghouls out of the main air duct."

"Yes, Mr. President. But more ghouls keep filling the duct after we leave. It's never-ending." Henry sighed with frustration. "There are just too many of the things."

"Then we'll clear the duct again. And if they clog it up again, we'll clear it again. And again. And we'll keep clearing it."

"Yes, sir, Mr. President."

"Never give up."

Mims hung up.

"There are those who claim that the definition of insanity is doing the same thing over and over again expecting different results," said Morrow.

"Are you saying we should give up?" said Mims, his face stern.

"I would never say that, Mr. President."

"Then are you saying I'm insane?"

"Absolutely not, Mr. President."

"Let me remind you, my mental faculties are crystal clear. I'm getting plenty of oxygen, and I feel excellent."

Mims stood up and paced around his office, holding his arms behind his back. He was wearing a navy blue suit with a red tie, as was his wont. He believed in wearing a suit even if he was inhabiting a bunker. The presidency was all about image. He must at all times appear presidential.

"We're living in tough times," he said. "No other president had to endure the misery and suffering of his people to the extent that I have—with the possible exception of Abraham Lincoln. But the apocalypse is even worse than the Civil War. The Civil War split the country in half. The apocalypse has caused the deaths of most American citizens. Few of us remain." He stopped pacing and gazed at Morrow. "Do you know what that means?"

"It means, we're on our last legs, Mr. President. We need a miracle."

"I don't believe in miracles. A man makes his own luck in life. If you sit around and do nothing, you will go nowhere in life. If you take your chances, you could succeed. Not all the time, mind you. Quarterbacks rarely complete every pass they throw in a football game, but that doesn't stop the good quarterbacks from winning the game. The passes they *need* to complete, they *will* complete. That's what separates a good quarterback from a bad one. Do you understand what I'm saying, Doctor?"

Morrow cleared his throat, looking bemused. "I think so, Mr. President."

"The bad quarterback won't complete the passes they *need* to complete, which is why they don't win."

"I see," said Morrow, uncertainly.

"This is why I will go down as the greatest president who ever lived, even greater than the greats, like George Washington and Abraham Lincoln. Because I'm gonna save this country. Even though we're facing the most perilous era in the short history of our great country, we will survive because I will save America. Great men aren't born great. They become great in the crucible of life. Life is our great teacher. From the trials in our lives we either learn to endure or we fail. The apocalypse has been my crucible. It has annealed my will, and I promise you I will never give up."

"We need a great president during these trying times."

"And you got one. Cole, my predecessor, unfortunately, wasn't up to the task. He went mad and committed suicide by nuke. He made the wrong decisions. He nuked our own country, slaughtering millions of law-abiding Americans. Can you believe it?" said Mims, his voice fairly throbbing with outrage. "He did more harm than good. He was our worst president since Herbert Hoover and the Great Depression. A chicken in every pot and all that malarkey. In fact, he was worse than Hoover. Cole made my job harder by making such a mess."

"Yes, Mr. President."

"Have no fears. I'm not gonna drop any more nukes on this great country." Mims held his hand over his heart. "God bless America."

A solemn expression on his face, Morrow mimicked the gesture.

"I had a hardscrabble life as a child, Doctor. I grew up with hand-me-down clothes. My family ate at Burger Kings. That was our idea of a great supper. My dad worked in the coal mines of West Virginia, and, you know, I wouldn't swap my life with any person on earth. I didn't have an easy childhood. I lost my dad to lung cancer when I was only sixteen. I had to mature quickly to become the breadwinner in the family and take care of my younger brothers and sisters. The struggles I endured growing up strengthened my character and formed me as the man I am today— the greatest leader this country has ever known.

"In order to complete my great mission on this earth, I need to be in perfect health in order to be up to my monumental task. In other words, I need to continue to receive my rightful share of oxygen—19.5 percent—so I can continue to lead America to greatness."

Mims bowed as if reacting to a standing ovation.

"As president," he went on, "many times I am faced with the heavy task of making difficult decisions, as in the case of disseminating the oxygen, which, as you say, if left as it is, will cause deaths by hypoxia. I must think of the greater good. Some people must die that others may live. Thus it has always been, and forever will be. As our glorious leader, I cannot sacrifice my health. Above all others, I must remain in excellent health. Make no changes in distributing the oxygen, Doctor."

"As you wish, Mr. President."

Chapter 60

"Abandoned car up ahead," cried Cassavetes, standing behind Halverson, who was raking ghouls with slugs from his M2.

"Check it out," said Strider, standing ten feet behind Cassavetes. "Is there anybody inside?"

"I can't tell from here," said Cassavetes.

As he approached the Prius, he could see it had its windows shut and a thirtyish blonde's limp body was bowed over the steering wheel in the driver's seat.

"Anybody inside?" said Strider.

"Yeah," said Cassavetes. "A driver and two kids. The kids look like five or six years old, and they're in the backseat."

"Are they alive?" said Strider, walking up to the car, MP9 in hand.

"I dunno."

Cassavetes watched in revulsion as a middle-aged scrofulous ghoul in a nun's habit shambled toward him, gnawing the flesh off a human arm she was holding in her bony hand.

"The person who was sitting in the front passenger seat must've gone for help and didn't make it," said Strider, blowing away the nun ghoul who was noshing the arm.

Cassavetes inspected the driver. "She must be alive. Her breath is misting the inside of her window."

"What about the kids?"

"I can't tell."

"All right. Get them out of there."

Cassavetes tried to open the driver's-side door, but it was locked. He knocked on her window to get the attention of the slumped driver.

The driver didn't respond.

Cassavetes pressed his face against the window, peering inside. For the first time he noticed her right leg was mauled and she was sitting in a pool of blood.

"Aw Jesus," he said.

He picked up on movement of the boy's head in the back. The boy was bowed forward and greedily consuming something in his hands. It was a clump of bloody flesh from his mother's thigh. Fresh blood smeared his mouth. Cassavetes grimaced.

"What's wrong?" asked Strider

"It's too late," answered Cassavetes. "The driver's bleeding out. Most of her right leg's missing. Her—her kid's eating it."

The boy gulped down the rest of the flesh in his hands. Seeing Cassavetes, he opened the door and climbed out of the Prius. Growling, blood dripping from his lips, he plodded toward Cassavetes, fixating on his next meal.

Cassavetes blew the kid's head off with a brief burst from his MP9. He winced in disgust. The zeds had got the kid. Beside himself with fury and grief, Cassavetes fired another burst into the back of the fallen ghoul's head. He clutched his forehead.

"Are you OK?" said Strider.

"I'm all right," said Cassavetes, gathering himself. "He was just a kid."

"Is anyone else in the car?"

"There's a little girl." Cassavetes beckoned to the girl. Clad in a yellow dress, she was slumped forward with her head down between her legs. "You can come out now, honey."

He leaned into the backseat, holding his hand out toward her.

She sat up, munching on someone's finger, her face twisted with menace. Spotting Cassavetes's hand she attempted to bite it. The finger fell out of her mouth. Cassavetes pulled his hand back in the nick of time as the girl's jaws snapped shut on air.

"No," he said, distraught.

He took her out with a burst to her head.

"She was infected?" said Strider.

"Yeah. I don't know if I can stand doing this much longer. These things—they were children once," said Cassavetes, his torso still leaning inside the car.

"Not anymore, they're not."

Cassavetes felt rather than heard movement to his left in the direction of the dead blonde. He felt an ice-cold hand grabbing his head and pulling it toward the driver's seat. His heart racing, he struggled in terror to yank his head free. He heard gunfire and the shattering of glass behind him. The hand on his head released its grip. Sweating freely, he backed out of the car, stumbling in his haste.

"The driver was turning," said Strider, letting her have another bullet to her brain to make sure she was dead.

Cassavetes started laughing.

"Are you OK?" said Strider, incredulous. "Did she bite you?"

"I just remembered I'm vaccinated," said Cassavetes with relief. "Why am I so scared of getting bit?"

He continued laughing.

"You could still get tetanus from one of those things. They're filthy."

"Doc Wheelhouse told me they might try to bite me, but they can't actually do it because I'm vaccinated."

"I dunno. They came awfully close. I wouldn't push my luck if I was you."

"I'm not gonna worry about it."

"How long does that vaccine last? Do you have to get it every year like a flu shot? Or more often?"

"The doc didn't tell me."

"If it's brand new, he probably doesn't know yet."

"I just got it. It can't have worn off yet."

Cassavetes saw a ghoul standing in front of the Prius scooping brains out of a thirtyish male human head it was holding. The brains smeared the ghoul's hand like grey paste. The ghoul licked the paste off his hand and purred with ecstasy.

Strider followed Cassavetes's gaze. "The driver's husband no doubt."

Strider nailed the ghoul with a brief burst to the head.

Cassavetes looked farther up the road. "There's the eighteen-wheeler blocking the way."

Chapter 61

Halverson could see the eighteen-wheeler and he saw a lot more. The mountainside had been cleared of trees and replaced with five rows of barbed wire, including one row of concertina wire, that encircled the entrance to the mountain cave. Hundreds of ghouls were strung up in the wire and writhing like bugs caught in a spiderweb, trying in futility to escape their entrapment.

Situated between the rows of wire were scattered X-shaped crosses, aka St. Andrew's crosses, sticking out of the ground with ghouls crucified on them—a warning to ghouls to stay away.

The place looked like a death camp, decided Halverson, taking a brief respite from firing his Browning M2. Wheelhouse's lair, he decided.

Thousands of crows and buzzards wheeled in the sky, darkening it like thunderclouds. The crows cawed raucously, starving for food, getting ready to feast on corpses in the field of death below them.

Hordes of ghouls were surrounding the barbed wire, pressing against it, trying to get past it. Their clothes shredded by barbs, an odd ghoul here and there had passed through the first row of wire, only to be stymied by the second.

Halverson could see that some ghouls had gotten past four rows of wire and were trying to pick their way through the last remaining row, tearing their scathed bodies apart on the barbs. One ghoul in her late thirties had lost all of her clothing, leaving it hanging on the barbed wire behind her. The fact that her putrefying body was now lacerated meant nothing to her. She felt no pain. She kept trying to pick through more wire. Dying of hunger, she knew food lay beyond the last row of wire. She could smell the odor of living humans wafting on the breeze.

Shaking his head Cassavetes walked up to Halverson. "They don't care when the barbs stick in their flesh. They feel nothing."

"Their clothing gets hung up on the barbs, though. The wire ensnares them."

"We put those crucified zeds out there, sort of like scarecrows, but the attacking zeds don't feel fear. They're totally dead. They have all the feelings of a plank of wood. They ignore their comrades nailed to the crosses."

"We found that out ourselves. You can't scare them away."

"The only way to be rid of them is to kill them."

"Have a lot of the ghouls broken through the barbed wire?"

"Some," said Cassavetes, hangdog. "They keep the guards at the entrance to our hideout busy. That's why Wheelhouse sent me to get help from the government. He didn't know who else to turn to."

"How do we get past the semi blocking the road to your hideout?"

"We go through it. I can open the rear door to let us in. Then we walk through the trailer and exit through the front. That will put us past the barbed wire, and we can head directly to camp."

Halverson heard an abrupt increase in firepower behind him.

"Howdy," said Gatling, riding toward them, icing ghouls with his .50 Magnum.

His gang and Rafferty rode behind him, shooting ghouls.

"I was hoping we'd be inside before he showed up," Halverson told Cassavetes.

"Is he gonna be a problem?" said Cassavetes.

"Maybe. Rafferty is definitely a problem," said Halverson, watching Rafferty putting down ghouls with his AR-15.

"I knew I heard a Ma Deuce," said Gatling, grinning ear to ear, riding up to Halverson on his black stallion. "Do you have another one of those for us?"

"You're out of luck."

"I could make short work of a lot of zeds with that little piece."

Strider approached Gatling. "I told you, we don't need your help."

Gatling laughed. "You don't need my help? You're surrounded by flesh-eating zeds and you don't need my help?" He laughed again.

"This is a clandestine government mission. We're not asking for help."

"It *was* clandestine. We know all about it, and we know about the vaccine."

"Thanks to me," said Rafferty, smirking.

"Where is it?" said Gatling.

Halverson knew Strider wanted Rafferty dead. Halverson thought about training his M2 on Rafferty and blowing him away now. The problem was, the M2 at over sixty pounds was a heavy load. He wouldn't be able to wield it quick enough to blow away Rafferty without Rafferty preempting him and firing his lighter AR-15 at him. It was the age-old problem with heavy artillery in CQB.

"We're all on the same side here," said Gatling. "We all want that vaccine. The sooner we get it, the better."

"If you and your gang stay back here and provide cover fire for us, we will be grateful," said Strider.

"If we 'stay back here,' as you say, how will we get the vaccine?"

Strider didn't like negotiating with Gatling. "This is my mission. I make the rules. If you want to join us, you need to take orders from me."

"Let me remind you, I'm a self-made man. I don't take orders from no one," said Gatling, pointing his gun barrel at his black Stetson and tipping the brim upward with the muzzle.

Strider leveled his MP9 at two attacking ghouls who emitted an abhorrent stench and looked like they had just climbed out of their graves wearing linen shrouds. He fired a burst from his MP9 that sent them back to their graves for good, their heads destroyed.

"We don't have time to discuss this," said Strider.

"Why do you still think you're in charge?" said Rafferty.

Strider exchanged looks with Halverson. Halverson shook his head almost imperceptibly, signaling he couldn't take out Rafferty at this moment.

"Because I am," said Strider. "The president put me in charge. He is our commander in chief."

"We don't recognize him as our legitimate president," said Gatling. "He is, in fact, wanted for treason by our militia."

"You're the one committing treason by claiming Mims is illegitimate. You have no legal authority to declare him illegitimate."

"I have the authority of Mr. Smith and Mr. Wesson," said Gatling, brandishing his .50 Magnum.

"I agree that Mims is an illegitimate president," said Rafferty.

Halverson felt like shooting Rafferty here and now, but he didn't want a war to erupt between his forces and Gatling's.

"You're a convict, Rafferty," said Strider. "You don't even have the power to vote. In fact, as a convict on death row, you have no power whatsoever to decide who is president."

Rafferty trained his AR-15 on Strider. Strider returned the favor with his MP9.

Things were about to take a nasty turn, decided Halverson, preparing to use his M2 if needed on humans as well as on ghouls.

That was when he heard a whump-whump above him. He looked up and saw a chopper flying in his direction.

Chapter 62

The olive drab Boeing AH-64 Apache helo hovered above the convoy.

"This is the United States government," announced the gunner in the two-seat aircraft through a bullhorn. "You are ordered to disperse and shelter in place."

The gunship hovered lower. The whump-whump became louder.

Halverson knew the Apache was equipped with some serious firepower. Between its main landing gear it carried an M230 chain gun, a chain-driven autocannon, which fired armor-piercing projectiles. As well, the typical Apache carried AGM-114 Hellfire missiles and Hydra 70 rocket pods.

Halverson's team wouldn't stand a chance against the Apache once it started firing on them.

"You are not the United States government," hollered Strider up at the helo. "*We're* the United States government."

"Who are they?" Marta asked Halverson, eying the Apache.

"Another militia," he answered.

"We're ordering you to disperse and shelter in place to avoid being infected by the plague," said the gunner.

"You're not the United States government," cried Gatling. "We are. The former US leaders have been found guilty of crimes against humanity for nuking this great country and wiping out half the population."

"If you do not obey our orders, we will be forced to open fire on you."

"We can't let them shoot first," whispered Halverson to Strider. "They've got the firepower. They'll kill all of us before we can respond."

Halverson's face broke into a sweat. He felt his heartbeat racing, as adrenaline surged through him. He would have to use the M2 any moment, and he could not afford to miss the attack helicopter's gunner, who had to be taken out before he could initiate fire. A burst from the Apache chain gun would inflict casualties on a massive scale at this close range.

"Who is your leader?" Strider demanded of the helo.

"We are the United States government," said the gunner.

"Our leader is the president. You have no leader. You have no authority. By authority of the president I'm ordering you to leave this area now or face the consequences."

"By authority of the American Militia, I'm ordering you to surrender your chopper to me," Gatling told the gunner, pointing his .50 Magnum at him.

The gunner opened fire with his M230 chain gun on Gatling, tearing his body apart like it was a ragdoll, mottling it with red splotches.

Halverson fired a continuous burst from his M2 at the gunner and the pilot, taking them both out and sending the helo into a tailspin. The helo crashed into a mob of ghouls, exploded, and erupted into gouts of flames that shot skyward, accompanied by a pluming dense black column of smoke.

Halverson swiftly trained his M2 on Rafferty.

Seeing that Gatling was dead, Rafferty threw down his AR-15 and held one hand up and one on the reins of his horse.

"I surrender," he said. "I'm one of you."

Strider signaled to Halverson to hold his fire.

"Come over here," Strider told Rafferty.

Continuing to hold up his empty hand, Rafferty rode his horse to Strider.

"Give me one good reason I shouldn't blow you away," said Strider, leveling his MP9 on Rafferty.

"You need all the manpower you can get," said Rafferty, gnashing his teeth, uncertain what Strider would do.

Rafferty flinched when he heard another explosion emanating from the downed chopper behind him.

"I hope that Apache wasn't carrying nukes," Strider told Halverson.

"That militia obviously stole it from a military airport," said Halverson.

Seeing that their leader Gatling was dead, his gang commenced retreating.

"Gatling was a maniac," said Rafferty, glancing askance at Gatling's mutilated corpse on the ground.

"Then why'd you join his gang?" said Strider.

"I didn't have a choice. He said he was going to kill me if I didn't."

"Why'd you tell him about the vaccine?"

"He got it out of me at gunpoint. If I didn't tell him, I'd be dead by now."

Halverson noticed Rafferty had a sallow complexion and glazed eyes. "Did a ghoul bite you?"

"No way. Inspect my body if you want. Not a tooth mark on me."

"Are you running a fever?"

"I'm under a lot of stress. I'm not sick. Pieces pointed at me tend to stress me out."

"By rights I should clip you as a deserter," said Strider. "You deserted us in the line of duty."

As they were talking, ghouls kept closing in on them, having been distracted by the exploding chopper for a few moments but no longer interested as it burned out of control.

Halverson opened fire on the schlepping ghouls with his M2.

He stopped firing when he saw Diego, one of Gatling's men, approach on horseback. Diego wasn't holding a piece.

"What do you want?" said Strider, swinging his MP9 toward him.

"I want to join you guys," said Diego.

Halverson exchanged looks with Strider.

"We could use help," said Halverson. "And he already knows about the vaccine. It's better to have him with us than against us. Otherwise, he'll tell others about the vaccine. If people know we have it, they're gonna attack us to get it."

Ghouls yanked one of Gatling's gang off her horse and tore her arms out of her shoulder sockets. A young woman in her late teens wearing blue jeans and a flamingo pink T-shirt, she let out a nerve-racking scream, as blood fountained from her traumatic shoulder wounds. The ghouls lapped up her blood with their putrescent, leatherlike tongues and threw her to the ground.

In his thirties, wearing a silver hard hat, a construction worker ghoul with a beer belly, pounced on her head and fell to devouring her agonized face. He tore her cheeks off with relish like he was eating a chicken breast and chewed the raw meat with gusto. Tears and blood burst from the woman's face.

The hard hat's companion, laptop in hand, a white-collar guy pushing fifty wearing a mangled business suit with its sleeves ripped off and an askew aqua silk rep necktie, fell on her carotid and, consumed with bloodlust, ripped the artery out with his yellow teeth, spraying a fountain of bright red blood six feet high into the air.

Her life ebbing away, the woman stopped screaming and bled out.

Halverson fired a burst from his M2, transforming the two ghouls into ground meat, their demolished heads all but torn off their bodies.

He picked up on a gaggle of the bloodthirsty creatures converging on the Prius that had dead ghouls inside it. He turned his M2 on the Prius and fired at the fuel tank, which promptly burst into golden flames, tossing nearby ghouls every which way through the air. Flailing their arms uselessly as they catapulted through the sky, they landed on other ghouls, knocking them to the ground.

"Take us into your mountain hideout," Strider told Cassavetes. "We're running out of ammo, and the ghouls keep coming."

"What about me?" said Rafferty.

Strider spat on the ground. "I guess you're with us."

"Can I pick up my AR-15?"

"You're not of any use to us unarmed."

Rafferty dismounted from his horse and scooped up his AR-15. Rising, he swung it as a club to bash the head of a ghoul that lunged at him. The weapon's stock crashed into the ghoul's skull, crushing it. Brains leaked out of the fractured skull and oozed down the creature's bubo-infested neck.

Chapter 63

Rafferty looked sick to Halverson, who couldn't figure out why.

Strider cast a skeptical glance at Rafferty, as if wondering if he was doing the right thing by allowing Rafferty to live.

Diego dismounted and joined the team. "I'm a good fighter. I'll help you guys."

Halverson grunted. Covering the team's retreat to the semi, Halverson fired his M2 at approaching ghouls, splattering their brains.

Diego remained with Halverson and helped him waste ghouls with bursts from his AR-15.

"That guy's loco," said Diego, when Rafferty was out of earshot.

"Rafferty?" said Halverson.

"Yeah," said Diego, watching Rafferty depart and grimacing.

"He's a serial killer. He killed scores of women. He dressed up their corpses, put lipstick and makeup on them, and raped them."

"That explains it," said Diego, his face losing its color. "He blew away a stacked zed and fucked her."

Halverson did a double take. "I knew he was sick in the head, but I never thought he'd do something like that."

"I saw it with my own eyes."

"Maybe that's why he looks ill," said Halverson, glancing at Rafferty.

"Cuz he's loco?"

"Because he's infected."

"Can you get infected that way?"

"I dunno. I doubt anyone's done it before Rafferty. Only a sick wacko would try something as nauseating as that."

Halverson peppered more attacking ghouls with M2 slugs, his arms becoming sore from lugging the heavy weapon. He and Diego followed Strider's team.

Halverson wondered if Rafferty was turning. Maybe it took longer for someone to turn if they had sex with a ghoul than if a ghoul bit them. Or Maybe Rafferty wouldn't turn at all. It was uncharted territory, beyond Halverson's ken.

"I wish I had one of those," said Diego, eyeballing Halverson's M2 eagerly.

Halverson grunted.

He machine-gunned a dozen ghouls who were slogging toward him and getting too close.

"We need to catch up with Strider," he said.

The problem was he couldn't walk very fast hauling the heavy Browning.

"Want me to help you carry that thing?" said Diego.

"No," said Halverson.

He barely knew Diego and figured the guy might try to rip him off.

"It's getting dark," said Halverson. "We need to get moving. I don't want to get stuck out here in the middle of the zeds without being able to see them."

They reached the tail end of the big rig that was blocking the narrow road. Strider was already there with the rest of the team.

"I never seen so many," said Diego, dropping his jaw as he scanned the area down the mountainside.

Ghouls and more ghouls. No end to them. The air was fetid with their reek of death and putrefaction. Enormous clouds of flies hovered over them, darkening the sky with the help of thousands of crows and buzzards that swooped down on the prowl for carrion.

Nobody could get past the eighteen-wheeler, which blocked the narrow two-lane blacktop. Five rows of barbed wire reached all the way to the sides of the truck, preventing anyone from getting by. A row of concertina wire beneath the truck prevented anyone from crawling under the chassis into the hideout. The only way past the truck was through it, and Cassavetes had the key to the padlocked rear door.

He opened the lock and raised the heavy steel rear door. The trailer was empty. He climbed the tailgate into the trailer.

"Follow me," he said, striding through the entire length of the trailer.

The rest of the team piled into the trailer. Halverson brought up the rear, providing cover fire with the M2, whose ammo belt was all but spent, keeping the pursuing ghouls at bay.

When it was his turn to climb into the trailer, he handed the M2 up to Strider, relieving his sore arm and back muscles. He climbed inside.

Strider swept the M2 from side to side, taking out the nearest row of ghouls, who seemed to sense their prey was on the verge of escaping their clutches. The creatures growled louder, voicing their displeasure at the turn of events. Strider emptied the M2 feed belt into them.

"Shut the door," he said.

He handed the M2 back to Halverson.

Cassavetes slammed the steel door down and locked it from the inside.

"There's no way they can get in," he said. "Let's go meet the good doctor. He'll be eager to see us."

"Doesn't he post any sentries?" said Strider.

"They're near the mouth of the cave."

They exited from the front of the trailer and walked up the rest of the road to the entrance to the cave. A steel door blocked the entrance. Flanking the door were two ghouls shackled to ringbolts driven into the ground and held in place by concrete. One ghoul on each side of the door growled at them and tried to grab them.

There was something odd about these ghouls, noticed Halverson. One ghoul was a male ghoul in his late thirties who had arms and hands like a gorilla. The arms were covered with thick black fur. The hands looked like they were made of black leather. Halverson could see the hands weren't wearing gloves. The flesh of the ghoul's hands was black animal hide.

The other shackled ghoul, a female in her twenties, had horse hooves in lieu of her feet. She was shackled to the ringbolt by means of a leather belt fastened around her waist, since her hooves could slip out of constraints on her ankles.

"I've never seen ghouls like these before," said Halverson.

"They're spooky, aren't they?" said Cassavetes. "We keep them out here to scare away the zeds."

"What happened to them? They look like they're part animal."

"Ghouls," said Cassavetes, shrugging. "Who knows? Dead things. They give me the creeps."

"They're getting uglier and uglier," said Rafferty.

Cassavetes knocked on the steel door, using a special code.

The door rose and allowed the team to enter.

Chapter 64

They entered a large cave. A dozen armed men and women in a semicircle stood watching them.

Standing in front of the others a five-nine man wearing a white smock greeted Strider and his team. The man had hazel eyes with a half-mad glint to them and wore his white hair back in a ponytail, secured by a red rubber band. His lined forehead made him look older than his forty-six years. A Roman nose and undershot jaw dominated his large face. Belying his unsettling appearance he spoke in a low voice like your friendly family practitioner.

"Welcome," he said. "We need fresh faces."

"This is Dr. Wheelhouse," Cassavetes told Strider.

"Glad to meet you, Doctor," said Strider, extending his hand.

Strider had a strong grip. Wheelhouse didn't return the pressure and disengaged his hand quickly.

"Are you from the president?" said Wheelhouse.

"We are," said Strider.

"We need you to throw down your arms," said Wheelhouse, smiling amiably.

Strider stiffened. "Why?"

"I want to make sure you are who you say are."

"I don't like the idea of being unarmed."

"There's nothing to be frightened of in here. You're among friends. We're all on the same side. The zeds can't get in here. You don't need to be armed."

"I'm a professional soldier. A SEAL. We don't like being disarmed."

"I don't want you carrying guns here until I've checked you out."

"How do you plan on doing that?"

"I want to ask you certain questions. But first you have to put down your weapons."

Strider continued to bristle at the suggestion.

"I don't like it," said Halverson.

"I don't either, but . . . ," Strider trailed off.

"I don't want armed soldiers in here," said Wheelhouse.

"Unless they're yours," said Strider, nodding at Wheelhouse's armed contingent.

"If you don't like it, you can leave. But the president will be upset if you return without the vaccine."

"Do you have the vaccine?"

Wheelhouse hemmed and hawed. "Not yet."

Cassavetes looked puzzled, but held his tongue.

"Then how can we return to the president with the vaccine?" said Strider.

"I said not yet," said Wheelhouse. "We'll have it in a matter of days, or even hours. We're that close to finding it," said Wheelhouse, holding his forefinger and thumb close together as if pinching a dime.

Keeping his own counsel Strider weighed his options. He struggled to come to a decision.

"I can't agree to disarm," he said.

"Then you'll have to leave," said Wheelhouse, showing him the door.

"The president will be pissed," said Rafferty. "He'll put the lot of us back on death row."

"It's where you belong," said Strider, but made no move to leave.

"You'll be a failure if you don't return with the vaccine. You told us failure is not an option."

"If we hand over our weapons, do we get them back when we leave?" Strider asked Wheelhouse.

"Of course. You'll need to fight your way back past the zeds to reach the president."

"Put down your guns, team," said Strider, laying down his MP9 on the ground.

"I don't like this," said Halverson.

"I don't either, but we can't fail our mission. Lay down your arms."

Halverson complied. He also removed the M2 ammo belt draped over his neck and laid it on the ground.

"That includes you, Rafferty," said Strider.

"Of course." Rafferty put down his AR-15.

"All right," said Wheelhouse. "I want to ask you a few questions first."

"Shoot," said Strider.

"They're OK, Doctor," said Cassavetes. "The president sent them."

"I'll decide that," said Wheelhouse, holding up his hand for Cassavetes to be silent. Wheelhouse turned to Strider. "President Cole sent you?"

"President Mims sent us."

"Mims? What happened to President Cole?" said Wheelhouse, suspiciously.

"He's out of office."

Wheelhouse looked baffled.

"He committed suicide by nuke," explained Strider.

Wheelhouse quirked his eyebrows. "Do we still have a government?"

"We do, sir. The United States lives on with President Mims at the helm. We're in good hands." Strider paused for effect. "But as you know, our war with the zombie plague rages on, and we're losing it. Cassavetes told us you have a vaccine."

"He injected me with it," said Cassavetes, smiling proudly.

A somber expression clouded Wheelhouse's face. "We don't quite have it. We're almost there, but not quite."

"What do you mean?" said Cassavetes, dumbfounded. "You said you injected me with the vaccine before I left."

"I didn't think you would do your mission if you thought the zeds could infect you."

"Then why didn't they infect me? I feel fine."

"Because you didn't allow them to bite you."

"You mean, it was dumb luck?"

"And your survival skills."

"What did you inject me with?"

"Saline solution."

"Are you saying, we made this journey for nothing?" said Strider, seething.

"We're almost there," said Wheelhouse. "It's only a matter of days or even minutes till we have the vaccine. We've come very close. Let me show you around."

Chapter 65

Wheelhouse led the team through the cave, his armed contingent in tow.

"It's cold in here," said Rafferty, shivering in the dank cave.

"My apologies we don't have a nice bunker like you had at Mount Weather," said Wheelhouse, dryly.

He led them to a nook in the cave where a ghoul was shackled to a ringbolt set in concrete in the earth.

The ghoul had elephant trunks for arms. Growling, he waved in the direction of Wheelhouse with his trunks.

"What the hell?" said Rafferty, aghast. "I never seen anything uglier than that monster."

"This was one of my earlier experiments," said Wheelhouse. "I'm tweaking mRNA technology to get the right vaccine for the zombie plague. I've been combining human and animal mRNA with pretty good results."

"This is a good result?"

"This particular specimen grew elephant trunks to replace its arms."

"It belongs in a carnival of freaks, if you ask me."

"From each of my mistakes, I learn something. Science is a learning process. So is creating vaccines. It's trial and error. There's no magic involved."

"Why don't you kill that monstrosity? What's the point of keeping it alive?" said Rafferty in disgust.

"The vaccine might actually work in the end. This could be a temporary phase the test subject goes through before they are cured."

"No shit. That escapee from a zoo is gonna become human pretty soon?" said Rafferty, awestruck.

"I can't guarantee it. Nobody can. But it's possible. That's why I don't eliminate any of my experimental subjects."

"How do you get anyone to volunteer for this shit?"

"It's not easy. But then again, there are people willing to risk their lives in the name of science to save humanity."

"Like that poor sucker Dumbo," said Laci, who was standing behind Rafferty.

"You wouldn't call him that if he becomes cured in a couple of days," said Wheelhouse.

"I can't imagine him reverting back to human. How would he eat dinner with those elephant trunks for arms?"

"He can always eat peanuts," said Rafferty.

"If he reverts back to human, his arms will, too," said Wheelhouse, not appreciating Rafferty's joke.

To Wheelhouse's shock, Joon-ho threw up blood-streaked vomit beside him.

"Did a ghoul bite you?" asked Wheelhouse with concern.

"Yeah," said Purl. "I saw one bite him. He's gonna turn any minute. Somebody needs to take him out before he starts chowing down our flesh."

"He's lying," said Joon-ho. "No ghouls bit me."

"Why are you vomiting blood?" said Wheelhouse, inspecting Joon-ho's sickly face.

"I have pancreatic cancer. I'll be dead in the near future."

"You'll make a perfect test subject for me."

"I'm not gonna be no one's guinea pig. No ghoul bit me."

"We would be very grateful for your help in finding the cure."

"Gratitude will get you nowhere."

"But you're gonna die anyway. In the name of scientific progress why not let me test the vaccine on you?"

"I don't want elephant trunks for arms," said Joon-ho, looking at his arms with bulging eyes.

"He's gonna turn any minute, Doc," said Purl. "This isn't the first time he puked blood. He's been doing it a long time. Ever since he got bit."

Wheelhouse nodded. "This is a symptom of his being infected by the zombie plague."

"I wasn't bit," cried Joon-ho in apoplectic rage at Purl.

"I can understand your hiding it from everyone," said Wheelhouse. "You came to the right person. I'm the only one on earth who can cure you."

"No thanks, Doc. I'll pass."

"Take him," Wheelhouse told his men.

Two armed men seized Joon-ho's arms and used a black plastic zip tie to bind his wrists behind his back.

"Hey," said Joon-ho, trying to fight them off. "Let go of me."

"You'll thank me after this is over," said Wheelhouse. He faced his men. "Take him to my lab. I'll be along shortly."

"You should get his approval first," objected Strider. "Not everyone wants to be a test subject."

"He'll turn in a couple of days if I don't treat him. Do you want that on your conscience?"

"He says he wasn't bit."

"He's lying so you won't kill him," said Purl. "I already told you that."

"We're not killing anyone," said Wheelhouse. "We're curing him. I'm a doctor for Chrissake, not an executioner." To his men: "Take him away."

Two armed men frog-marched Joon-ho away.

"You call yourself a doctor?" cried Joon-ho. "You're a mad scientist. Didn't you take the Hippocratic oath? Help."

"He'll thank me when this is over," Wheelhouse told Strider.

"He'll shake your hand in gratitude with one of his elephant trunks," said Rafferty.

Glowering, Wheelhouse advanced on Rafferty. "Do you feel all right? Your eyes look glazed."

"I was joking, Doc. Can't you take a joke?"

Wheelhouse squinted at Rafferty. "I don't like that film on your eyes. Are you sure a ghoul didn't bite you?"

"Nobody bit me," said Rafferty, becoming apprehensive Wheelhouse would select him as his next guinea pig.

"Let's move on to the next phase in my experiments," said Wheelhouse, heading for another nook in the cave.

Chapter 66

In the next chamber stood a fortyish woman, though it was hard to tell her age because she had the head of a German shepherd on her body in place of her own head. With its milky eyes, it was obvious the German shepherd was infected with zombie plague. Shackled to a ringbolt like the other test victims, the woman/dog growled at Wheelhouse.

"Jesus," said Strider. "Don't you have a code of medical ethics you have to follow?"

"All my test subjects were volunteers," said Wheelhouse, steaming at Strider's insinuation.

"Like Joon-ho," chimed in Rafferty.

"And I don't approve of your calling into question my ethics," said Wheelhouse, glaring at Strider.

"He's calling a spade a spade, Doc," said Halverson. "It's hard to believe anyone would volunteer for experiments worthy of Josef Mengele."

"I resent your analogy. You obviously don't understand science, and you don't understand people. Some of them actually want to advance the medical profession by volunteering for hazardous work which could lead to their deaths. They are heroes, in my opinion, not victims. If it wasn't for test subjects, we wouldn't have any vaccines—even the one for polio. Comparing me to the Angel of Death is an insult."

Wheelhouse admired his handiwork. "This experiment nearly succeeded."

"Are you nuts? She's got the head of a dog," said Rafferty, sickened by the sight.

"But her entire body is perfectly intact. She's a perfect human specimen save for one thing."

"Oh yeah? Does she eat raw human flesh or milk bones?"

"She's infected. She's a zed. But this was a near miss. I am confident she will one day become human."

"With a craving for milk bones."

"You idiot," Wheelhouse snapped. "Do you feel no compassion?" Wheelhouse's voice became tinged with sadness. "This is Marilyn." His voice cracked. "She used to be my wife."

Rafferty's eyes bugged out. "Jesus. You injected your own wife with that rat poison?"

"She volunteered, knowing it was for a good cause. And it wasn't rat poison. It was a test vaccine."

Marilyn barked at him.

"I'm sure she recognizes me," said Wheelhouse, his eyes welling with tears. "And she knows she'll be well again soon."

"He's certifiable," Rafferty whispered to Halverson, appalled.

"Let's go to the next test area," said Wheelhouse, casting a final mournful glance at Marilyn and collecting himself.

"Do we have to?" said Rafferty.

"I want you to see the progress I've been making."

In the next chamber a black mutt with the head of a male human ghoul was fastened with a steel-chained leash around its neck to a ringbolt set in concrete in the ground.

"Holy shit," said Rafferty, and wretched.

Marta and Laci turned away in disgust from the horrid creature.

"This was one of my early experiments, and it shows, I'm afraid," said Wheelhouse, his face reflecting his displeasure. "I was feeling my way. I still have hope for him, though. When we finally find the vaccine, I will immediately inject him, and maybe he will return to normal," he said with a wistful smile.

"Who's this?" said Rafferty. "Your son?"

"Shut up, goddammit. What skid row did they drag you out of for this assignment?"

"He was in the brig," said Laci. "He's a serial killer."

"Is that some kind of sick joke?" said Wheelhouse, indignant.

"He figured it was better to visit your cave than the gas chamber. Maybe he was wrong, after all," said Laci, with a ghastly laugh.

"I thought the president sent me an elite team of commandos."

"He took only volunteers for this suicide mission. Most of the 'elite' commandos bowed out."

"So he sent me a bunch of convicts?" said Wheelhouse, widening his eyes in anger.

"Stop complaining, Doc," said Rafferty. "We made it here, didn't we?"

"What about you?" Wheelhouse asked Purl. "Are you a commando?"

"I'm a cop killer. What did you expect? James Bond?"

"I expected elite specimens."

"The elite specimens are over there," said Purl, chuckling, pointing at Strider and Halverson. "Experiment on them first."

"Nobody here is a specimen," said Strider. "Our mission is to take your zombie plague vaccine back to the president so he can begin distributing it to the rest of the country."

"All well and good," said Wheelhouse. "Except the vaccine needs a couple more tweaks before it will be ready for use."

Purl yawned, as did Laci and Marta.

"I'm sure you're all exhausted from your arduous journey here," said Wheelhouse. "I'll show you to your quarters now."

"How long will it be before you have the vaccine ready?" asked Strider.

"Any day now. Any minute now, I should say. I can speed up testing thanks to my new test subjects."

"You better not be referring to me," said Rafferty.

Wheelhouse ignored him. "Come with me."

Automatic rifles in their hands, his armed guards escorted Strider's team after the doctor.

Chapter 67

Wheelhouse led them to a wide nook with ringbolts embedded in concrete as in the other nooks.

"Here are your accommodations," he said. "I know it's not the Ritz, but what do you expect in a cave?"

The guards grabbed the team and shackled their legs to the ringbolts.

"What the hell are you doing?" demanded Strider, resisting the guards.

"It's for your own good," said Wheelhouse. "I don't want you wandering around the cave unescorted. You might hurt yourselves or get lost."

"You're making us your prisoners," said Strider, continuing to struggle with the guards who were trying to shackle his leg to a ringbolt.

The rest of the team resisted the guards, too.

Wheelhouse pulled a pistol out of his smock. "Stop resisting, or I'll shoot you. You should feel at home in leg irons. You're all prisoners in the first place."

"Let us outa here," said Strider.

"As long as you're my guests, you're staying here until I say so."

The guards finished locking everyone in shackles.

"I'll be back soon with the results from Joon-ho's tests," said Wheelhouse, leaving.

The guards followed him out.

"Doesn't he understand we came here to help him?" said Marta. "Why is he locking us up?"

"Because he's losing it," said Rafferty. "He lured us here to become guinea pigs in his twisted experiments. Cassavetes tricked us."

"Where is Cassavetes?" said Laci, looking around the cave for him.

"With Wheelhouse."

"I think Cassavetes believed what he told us about the vaccine," said Halverson. "Did you see how surprised he was when Wheelhouse told him he injected Cassavetes with saline solution?"

"It was an act," said Rafferty.

"I don't think so," said Strider. "Regardless, we have to figure out how to get out of here."

He scoped out the cave.

"I was better off in the joint," said Rafferty.

Strider yanked on his shackles, trying to pull the ringbolt out of the concrete without success.

"If we're his guests, why is he locking us up?" said Marta. "Hell, we came here to save him, and he locks us up. That's gratitude for you."

"Because he's an asshole," said Rafferty.

Marta thought about it. "It's not that simple. He injected his own wife with the vaccine. He must believe it will work eventually."

"Or he hated her and wanted to turn her into a freak."

"I watched him. He had tears in his eyes when he looked at her—what used to be her, anyway."

"So that makes it OK he's turning all of us guinea pigs into freaks?"

"I didn't say it was OK. I'm saying he really wants to find the vaccine to save humanity."

"I don't care what his motives are. The ends *don't* justify the means. He's a fucking psycho in my book."

"He's sicker than you, Rafferty," said Purl.

"No," said Diego, eying Rafferty with repugnance. "Nobody's sicker than that guy. I saw what he did with a zed."

"Shut up," said Rafferty. "You're not even part of the team. You're one of Gatling's running dogs. You don't know nothing."

"I know what I saw with my own two eyes," said Diego, pointing at his eyes with two forefingers.

"Instead of arguing, we need to find a way out of here," said Strider.

Marta yawned. "I'm beat. I'm getting some z's."

She lay on her back on the dirt.

"Sounds like a plan," said Purl, and followed her example.

"I say we kill Cassavetes for getting us into this mess," said Rafferty.

Halverson sat with his back against the cave wall and nodded off, ignoring the ache of his muscles from hauling the Browning M2 around for hours.

Chapter 68

The next day began with Wheelhouse sending a breakfast of flapjacks, scrambled eggs, and orange juice to the incarcerated team.

"Fattening up his victims, I guess," said Rafferty, tucking into his pancakes. "I could eat a horse."

"I guess they got chickens and pigs around here somewhere," said Strider, chewing on a rasher of bacon.

After the team was finished eating, Wheelhouse led Joon-ho to them. A four-foot-long metal pole for snake tongs had a noose at the end of it instead of the usual tongs. The noose was looped around Joon-ho's left neck, as Wheelhouse pushed him forward. Instead of one head, Joon-ho now had two heads, both of which were ferociously growling and dripping saliva. One of them was a cow's head.

Joon-ho had the milky eyes, putrescent face, and broken, jagged teeth of a ghoul on both of his heads. Much of the flesh on his cheeks had disintegrated, exposing portions of his skulls.

The rest of his body was unchanged by Wheelhouse's injection of his new vaccine.

"My newest vaccine didn't work with Joon-ho, I'm afraid," said Wheelhouse. "Do you want me to leave him with you?"

"Old MacDonald had a farm, Ee i ee i o, And on his farm he had some cows," sang Rafferty.

Laci choked on her pancakes at the stomach-churning sight.

"Do I sing that bad?" said Rafferty.

"What did you do to the poor guy?" said Strider, grimacing.

"I injected him with the vaccine to prevent him from turning," said Wheelhouse.

"They need to revoke your medical license. You're a menace."

"I'm getting closer to the proper vaccine. Notice the rest of his body is untouched. The only part that changed was his head."

"Yeah. Now he's got two of 'em," said Rafferty. "And they're not even his. One belongs to a cow."

"It proves a ghoul did bite him earlier, like I said," said Purl, nodding.

"Get it out of here," said Strider. "That's not Joon-ho. It's a monster."

Growling, Joon-ho flailed his arms.

Wheelhouse gave the snake tongs handle to one of his men, who led Joon-ho away.

"I need a new test subject," said Wheelhouse, gazing at Rafferty.

"No way," said Rafferty. "You can't punish me for singing off-key."

Wheelhouse approached him and scrutinized Rafferty's eyes. "That glaze over your eyes bothers me. You're not well."

"I'm as well as anybody else here," said Rafferty, extending his arms at his sides and inhaling a lungful of air. "I feel great."

"I want to save your life."

"You're a minority of one," said Laci.

"I don't want to have my life saved," said Rafferty.

"Don't worry," said Wheelhouse. "I tweaked the vaccine I used on your compatriot. You're not gonna end up like him."

"Take your vaccine and shove it, Dr. Frankenstein."

"This won't take long. The vaccine acts quickly."

Two armed guards approached Rafferty. One held Rafferty, while the other unlocked Rafferty's shackles. They grabbed his arms and bound his wrists behind his back with a black plastic zip tie. Rafferty struggled to escape—to no avail.

The guards hauled him away.

"Let go of me, assholes," cried Rafferty.

"I'll be back shortly with the results," Wheelhouse told the team.

"Let me get this straight," said Strider. "You're gonna take us out of here one at a time and poison us?"

"I'm going to save you. Let me be clear. I'm going to save the entire human race. In order to do that, I have to keep tweaking the vaccine till I get it right. The cliché is true: Rome wasn't built in a day."

"And we're supposed to be cheering you on, while you turn us into monsters?"

"I don't understand why you don't want to volunteer for such a momentous enterprise," said Wheelhouse, perplexed. "After all, you're preventing the extinction of mankind. Could anything be more monumental than that?"

"I don't care about the vaccine," said Laci, yanking at her leg irons. "I just want out."

"When we have the vaccine, you will be free to leave," said Wheelhouse. "I want you to take the vaccine to the president, as is your mission."

"Your experiments could turn us all into monsters by then," said Halverson.

"This is not open for debate."

"Your experiments are inhumane and banned by the Geneva Convention," said Strider.

"The Geneva Convention does not apply. You are *not* prisoners of war."

"How are we not prisoners?" said Strider, shaking his leg irons.

"You are my test subjects, not my prisoners. And I'm certainly not at war with you."

Wheelhouse slewed around and marched away, tugging at his ponytail as he departed.

Marta coughed on the musty odor of the cave.

"It smells moldy here," she said. "It smells worse than the bunker. And that place had less oxygen."

"We didn't have a mad scientist sharing the bunker with us either," said Laci.

"How do we get out of this mess?" said Purl, yanking at his leg irons fruitlessly.

"Maybe we're looking at this the wrong way," said Strider, becoming pensive.

"What other way is there to look at it?" said Purl, confused.

Chapter 69

"Let's look at it from the doctor's point of view," said Strider. "He's trying to find the vaccine to save humanity from the zombie plague."

"So? That trumps our right to go on living as humans?" said Purl.

"The object of our mission is to get the vaccine and bring it back to the president. If we give Wheelhouse enough time and whatever else he needs to find the vaccine, we can return to the president with the vaccine. We will have completed our mission," said Strider, full of pride.

"You want him to go on experimenting on us?" said Laci, gaping at him.

"Let me remind you, we have to take the vaccine back to the president. If we don't do it, we have failed the mission."

"Fuck the mission if I end up with two heads in the bargain."

"If you don't like our mission, you should never have volunteered in the first place."

"I didn't volunteer to grow another head."

"When it's your turn to get injected, Wheelhouse might have discovered the vaccine that will work without causing any side effects."

"I can't believe you're siding with the mad scientist."

"We must think of the greater good. If some people must die in order that Wheelhouse can find the vaccine, so be it."

"You're not gonna be so gung-ho when it's your turn to get inoculated."

Halverson couldn't believe his ears. He turned to Strider.

"You're saying we should stand here and wait our turns like lambs being led to the slaughter?" said Halverson.

"I'm in charge of the mission. The mission must succeed. It cannot succeed if we don't obtain the vaccine."

"What's so important about the almighty mission?" said Laci.

"The vaccine will save humanity," said Strider. "We're here to save humanity."

"I'm here to escape a death sentence."

"You're a narcissist. All you think about is yourself."

"I'm supposed to want to sacrifice myself for the greater glory of Wheelhouse? Give me a break."

Purl harrumphed and looked at Laci. "I want to make a confession, seeing that my time on this planet is almost over."

"I'm not a priest," said Laci. "Why tell me?"

"You're a fellow con. A fellow murderer."

"Thanks a lot, buddy."

"I—I didn't see Joon-ho get bit by a ghoul," said Purl, holding his head down. "I have no idea if a ghoul bit him."

"Why did you lie before and say you did?"

"I don't know. I guess, I was being disruptive. People have been blaming me all my life for things that weren't my fault. I— uh—I was getting back at the world, maybe. Hell, I'm not a shrink. I'm not into self-analysis. I just want to set the record straight before it's over for me."

"Poor Joon-ho," said Laci.

"Look at it this way. I bought us some time by lying about Joon-ho. Wheelhouse took him first, instead of you or me."

"There's no point in crying over spilt milk," said Strider. "We have to do our duty and wait our turn. Whoever is the last one standing must complete the mission and give the president the vaccine. Is that understood?" He searched everyone's face.

Laci stared at him with disbelief.

"What if Wheelhouse turns all of us into monsters before he finds a working vaccine that doesn't have obscene side effects?" said Halverson.

"Then we did our duty and have nothing to feel ashamed of."

"I'm not ashamed of anything right now," said Laci. "Hell, I used to be a stripper. I'm not ashamed to admit it. When you got a good body, men will pay to look at it. I needed money at the time, and I got some. Who the hell is ashamed?"

"Is this confession time?" said Diego. "I murdered my brother because he stole my girlfriend. I never felt shame for that. And I still don't. He deserved it."

"Let's clear this up," said Purl. "I don't feel any shame for lying about Joon-ho getting bit by a ghoul. The guy was a screw. I'm a convict. It's my duty to escape. If I have to lie to do it, I will."

"OK, I guess it's my turn," said Marta. "I was raped by a man and I stayed with him because I was scared of the ghouls getting me. I had nowhere else to go, so I stayed with him even though I hated him. He assaulted me for Chrissake. Do I feel shame about that? Hell no. Did I feel sorry for him when Halverson shot him dead? Are you kidding? Do I feel shame now for any of this? The answer is no."

"Just when did this turn into a group therapy session?" said Laci.

"I guess it's my turn," said Halverson. "The government tried to drone me in California. They thought I was a traitor. Do I feel shame because I survived? No way. The point is, the government makes mistakes," he said, turning his gaze on Strider. "Blindly obeying the government isn't always the right thing to do."

"The mission must succeed," said Strider. "I am in charge of the mission. I will do everything in my power to see that my mission succeeds."

"Even if it turns all of us into sideshow freaks?"

"We must help the doctor continue his experiments to find the vaccine."

"You're going around the bend, man," said Purl. "If you're so hot about the experiments, why don't you volunteer to go next?"

"I'm in charge of the mission," said Strider, his voice becoming strident. "I must see to it that the mission succeeds. It's on my head. I will go last to Wheelhouse's office, so I can oversee the mission to the very end."

"How convenient. You get to live longer than the rest of us because you're the boss. The way of the world, huh? No doubt about it."

Strider pulled himself together. "I guess it's my turn to confess. I lost a man to the Taliban on a mission near Kabul. A man named Hinson. A nice guy. Kind of naïve. An IED blew him up. As a SEAL, we never want to lose a single man on a mission. He went to pick up an AK-47 abandoned on the roadside. He wanted it for a souvenir. The AK was boobytrapped. I felt shame back then for having lost a man. His loss served no purpose. It was a total failure. At last I got over it. You can't live with shame eating away at your soul for the rest of your life."

"You lost one man, and you felt shame," said Purl. "Here you're in the process of losing your entire team, and you feel nothing. Where did you go off the rails?"

"There's no comparison. Hinson died for nothing. He wanted a souvenir of the war and paid for it with his life. It had no effect on the mission. Everyone here who is being vaccinated is serving a higher purpose—to find the vaccine against the apocalyptic plague wiping out the human race."

"I don't know who's worse. You or Wheelhouse."

Wheelhouse appeared, pushing something on the floor ahead of him with the snake tongs and a makeshift noose on the end of it.

Chapter 70

Secured in the noose was a ghoul head—Rafferty's. His eyes were completely white now, his cheeks putrescent, his flesh wizened. He squirmed on his belly on the ground. He couldn't walk because in place of his two legs were two anacondas.

"Jesus," said Purl in disgust. "Take it out of here."

"It couldn't happen to a more deserving guy," said Laci.

"Unfortunately, the new vaccine didn't work," said Wheelhouse. "As you can see, Rafferty completed his transition to an infected ghoul."

"How can you live with yourself?" said Marta. "You're dealing with human beings."

"I am advancing science. I must find the vaccine for the zombie plague in order to save humanity. Don't you understand? My wife understood. Sacrifices must be made. People must die that others may live," said Wheelhouse with a distant gaze.

"These creatures you're creating are worse than the ghouls," said Purl.

"The advancement of science is never easy."

"Go away," said Marta. "Leave us alone. How can you call yourself a doctor?"

Wheelhouse focused his eyes on the faces of the prisoners. "Who would like to go next?"

Nobody said anything. Everybody looked away.

Halverson felt like he was a kid back in school. When he didn't know the answer to a question the teacher asked, he would look away so they wouldn't call on him.

"If nobody volunteers, I will have to make the decision," said Wheelhouse. "Doesn't anybody here want to sacrifice their life for the sake of humanity?"

"You make us sound like creeps for not volunteering to become monsters in a carnival," said Purl. "You're the creep for creating monsters."

"You look like a good specimen. I approve of you."

"What?" said Purl, flabbergasted. "I didn't volunteer."

"Don't be alarmed. I'm convinced my new vaccine will work. We know mRNA technology can be tricky, but we're making great strides in our progress. If we keep tweaking here and there, we'll succeed."

"There's an old saying in the army—Never Volunteer. I'm not budging," said Purl, setting his jaw and crossing his arms.

"Unlock his shackles and take him out of here," Wheelhouse told his men.

"You're making no progress, Doctor," said Halverson, glancing at Rafferty.

Writhing, Rafferty growled at him, slavering on the ground as he opened his ghoul jaws.

"If anything," Halverson went on, "your experiments are regressing. Your abominations are becoming worse and worse."

"And you have a medical degree from where?"

"You don't need four years of medical school to know what a failed experiment looks like."

"Believe me, I'm getting closer. I know. I'm a doctor. I graduated with honors from the UCLA Medical School, one of the finest medical schools in the country."

Two of Wheelhouse's guards unlocked Purl's leg irons, bound his wrists behind his back with a black plastic zip tie, and took him away.

"No," said Purl, terrified, struggling to free himself. "I refuse. I'm not volunteering. Let me go."

"Take him," Wheelhouse told his men. "And him, too," he said, pointing at Diego.

"No, thanks," said Diego.

"It's not like you have a choice."

Two more guards unlocked Diego's shackles, bound his wrists like Purl's, and ushered him away.

"I don't want no stinking vaccine," said Diego, trying in futility to break away from his captors.

"We'll be back soon," said Wheelhouse, leaving the team and pushing Rafferty in front of him like he was pushing a broom.

Rafferty's anaconda legs squiggled on the ground before Wheelhouse.

"He's blind to his own faults," said Marta, shaking her head. "He doesn't realize he isn't making progress."

"It's pointless to argue with him," said Halverson. "We need to get out of here."

"On whose authority?" said Strider.

"I don't need anyone's authority to escape confinement."

"I'm still in charge of this mission. We can't leave until we have the vaccine in our possession."

"Can't you understand? Wheelhouse doesn't know what he's doing. His vaccines aren't getting any better. Look at the results."

"He knows what he's doing. It's taking longer than he thought. That's all. We can't lose faith in him. He's our last hope."

"I'd rather die than turn into one of those monsters he's making," said Laci, her face grim.

"Hold on a little longer," said Strider.

"What's the point of holding on? The end result is the same. He turns us all into flesh-eating freaks." Her face drawn, she ripped out a clump of her hair. "I can't stand the waiting. Will one of you kill me?"

"Just hang on. The doctor will find the vaccine any minute."

"Are you kidding? Look what he did to Rafferty." Laci wretched at the memory.

"We must complete the mission. Our lives have no meaning if we don't complete the mission," said Strider, absorbed in himself.

Laci shook her head at him. "You're a basket case." She turned to Marta. "Please kill me. I don't want to turn."

"I can't," said Marta. "It's murder."

"It's not murder if I want you to do it. It's—what do they call it—assisted suicide. I'd do it myself if I had a gun."

Marta screwed up her face. "I can't. Maybe he'll find the vaccine before he gets to you. We need to think positive."

"You're living in a dreamworld. He's gonna turn us all into ghouls."

"There's always hope," said Marta in a shaky voice.

"Listen to yourself. Even you don't believe what you're saying."

Marta clutched her face. "Stop. Stop."

Laci turned to Strider. "What about you? You're a professional killer. Will you kill me?"

"Absolutely not. You could be the test subject that saves all of our lives. The vaccine he uses on you could be the one that works."

"You don't actually believe that bullshit."

"We can't go back to the president without succeeding in our mission."

Laci turned to Halverson, who had been listening, stone-faced.

"You're my last hope," said Laci. "I beg you to kill me. There's no point in prolonging this misery. I want to die."

Chapter 71

Halverson chewed it over. He stood motionless looking quietly at Laci, studying her like a cobra fixing to attack. She was within his reach, he realized. Like Strider, he was a trained assassin. He could put her in a chokehold and strangle her. She would black out before dying and wouldn't feel too much pain.

"You're asking me to kill you in cold blood," he said at last.

"Please kill me. *Please*. I'm begging you," she said, clasping her hands together as if in prayer.

"I'm not a murderer."

"I'm asking you to help me commit suicide. Oh, forget it," she said in frustration. "What's wrong with you people? Wake up. He's not gonna find the vaccine before he turns every last one of us into a monster. I'd rather be dead."

She walked to the cave wall and commenced slamming her forehead into the rock.

"I'll kill my damn self," she said. "Thanks for nothing."

She smashed her face into a rock in the wall. Blood erupted from her forehead and spilled down her face. She yelped in pain, but continued butting her head into the wall.

"Make her stop," said Marta, weeping.

"I'm not gonna stop till I'm dead," said Laci in agony, blood gushing down her face and throat.

Halverson couldn't stand watching her. He grabbed her from behind, put her throat into a chokehold, and strangled her to death.

She slumped in his arms.

He felt miserable about taking her life. But it was what she had wanted. He doubted she could have killed herself by slamming her face into the cave wall. She would have passed out before she had the strength to finish herself off.

"Look what you've done," said Strider. "Wheelhouse has one less chance of finding the vaccine with her dead. All because of you."

Halverson didn't bother to answer him. Strider was gone, Halverson decided. Strider's obsession with the success of the mission had warped his mind, driving him over the edge.

Feeling sick inside, Halverson laid Laci's body on the ground. He noticed a bobby pin in her hair, as he released her. He removed the bobby pin.

"What's happening to us?" said Marta, dumbfounded.

Halverson took the bobby pin and inserted it into the lock on his leg irons, trying to pick the lock.

"You've sabotaged the mission," said Strider, beside himself with anger. "You're a traitor. I never thought you of all people, Halverson, would betray the mission."

Halverson doggedly attempted to pick the lock with the bobby pin.

"All traitors must be executed in front of a firing squad," said Strider.

"Shut up," said Marta.

"I cannot allow you to go on living and jeopardizing the mission," said Strider, as if in a trance.

Sweating, Halverson concentrated on picking the lock, knowing he needed to succeed before Wheelhouse returned to select another victim.

"I trusted you, Halverson," said Strider. "You were my wingman. What happened to you?"

"Wheelhouse is unhinged," said Halverson. "He's gonna add all of us to his menagerie of monsters."

"He's our last hope. We need the vaccine to save the country. The president is counting on us."

"Listen to yourself," said Marta. "Wheelhouse brainwashed you."

"What are you doing, Halverson? Are you trying to escape? Don't. I order you not to escape. We must get the vaccine before we return to the president."

Halverson knew Wheelhouse would return any minute. His pulse racing, Halverson forced himself to concentrate on picking the lock. This was the last chance he was going to get to escape. Either he or Marta would be Wheelhouse's next victim. Wheelhouse was probably saving Strider for last, since Strider was team leader and Wheelhouse wanted to put Strider through hell as Strider watched his team destroyed one at a time before his very eyes.

Halverson wondered if Wheelhouse had any intention of sending the vaccine to the president. Or was it all just a subterfuge to get test subjects for his experiments? Maybe Wheelhouse's constant failures testing the vaccine had unhinged him so he couldn't think straight anymore.

The apocalypse was driving everyone insane, decided Halverson.

He felt the lock give. He opened his shackles.

He bolted over to Marta and started working on hers.

"Don't leave, Halverson," said Strider, his voice monotonic. "It's your duty to stay and complete the mission."

Halverson continued picking the lock on Marta's shackles.

"I wish you could've thought of this before Laci died," said Marta, tears in her eyes.

"I didn't know she had a bobby pin in her hair," said Halverson.

"I just thought of something. What if Wheelhouse injects her corpse and brings her back to life as a ghoul?"

"If he does, Laci will never know. Ghouls have no memories."

"Do you think he can bring people back to life as ghouls?"

"I doubt it. But who knows?"

"He's the one who needs to be killed, not Laci."

"If you leave with him, you're a traitor like him," said Strider, watching them, unable to reach them because of his shackles.

"At least *he's* trying to escape this maniac," said Marta. "You're just giving up and letting the psycho transform you into one of his dreadful creatures."

"*I'm* not the one giving up," roared Strider. "You two are. You're betraying your country to save your puny lives."

Halverson knew he had to free Marta chop-chop. Strider's yelling could bring Wheelhouse's guards down on them any minute. He should be able to pick the lock on Marta's shackles faster than he had done his own, now that he knew how to do it. It was a matter of manipulating the pins in the Yale padlock to open it. He almost had it.

"Hurry," Marta whispered to Halverson. "He might start screaming for help any minute."

His heart in his mouth, he froze when he heard footfalls near the entrance to their chamber.

Marta widened her eyes in fear as she stared at the entrance, anticipating Wheelhouse's return.

Chapter 72

Cassavetes entered the chamber by himself.

Halverson had wondered what had happened to Cassavetes. Wheelhouse had not locked the guy up with the rest of the team, since Cassavetes worked for the doctor. Had Wheelhouse sent Cassavetes here to take one of them to get vaccinated?

Halverson eyed Cassavetes with uncertainty. However, as a trained CIA black ops agent he expected the worst. His heartbeat rattling his ribs, he prepared to launch himself at Cassavetes, hoping Cassavetes was alone. Halverson didn't see anyone behind Cassavetes.

"I want to help you," said Cassavetes in a low voice, glancing behind him to make sure no one was following him.

"Why should you want to help us?" said Halverson, unconvinced.

"Wheelhouse lied to me. He said he'd injected me with the vaccine, but the injection was useless. The zeds could have killed me any second. I was just lucky to make it to the Mount Weather bunker alive. He duped me into almost getting myself killed. I hate his guts."

It made sense, decided Halverson. Cassavetes sounded on the level.

Blowing out his cheeks with relief, Halverson resumed picking Marta's lock with renewed purpose and opened it.

"You're another traitor," Strider told Cassavetes. "I'm surrounded by traitors."

"What's wrong with him?" Cassavetes asked Halverson.

Halverson shook his head.

"Let's get out of here," said Marta, removing her leg from the unlocked shackles.

"The mission can't succeed without the vaccine," said Strider. "I order all of you to stay put until the vaccine is discovered."

"I don't have to take orders from you," said Cassavetes.

"You're part of the team. You're under my command. None of you leave this room. That's a direct order."

"Don't you understand? I'm helping you escape," said Cassavetes, frowning in bemusement.

"We don't want to escape. We want to complete the mission."

"Don't pay attention to him," said Marta. "He went nuts. Let's get out of here."

"I'll take you to the armory to get your weapons," said Cassavetes. "Doesn't he understand Wheelhouse is gonna inject him if he stays here? He'll turn."

"We cannot return to base without the vaccine," said Strider. "To do so is failure. Failure is not an option. Nobody move."

"He can't accept failure," Halverson told Cassavetes. "It drove him over the edge."

"Let him stay here, then," said Cassavetes. "I don't care. Let's go. Wheelhouse will be here any minute to grab another guinea pig." He noticed Laci's crumpled body. "What happened to her?"

Halverson paused before answering. "She tried to commit suicide."

"Tried? It looks like she succeeded."

Halverson didn't want to go into it. He felt sick about killing her. "She had help."

Cassavetes cast a questioning glance at him.

"He killed her," said Strider.

"I don't want to know anymore," said Cassavetes. "Let's get out of here."

He led Halverson and Marta to the entrance.

"You're all traitors and losers," said Strider.

"Good luck with your injection," said Cassavetes, knowing it wouldn't work.

In front of the entrance Halverson saw a guard's inert body with a knife stuck in his back and his shirt dappled with blood. Halverson bent over and pulled the knife out of the corpse's back. The blood-smeared knife dripped blood on the ground.

"I had no choice," said Cassavetes, glancing at the corpse. "I'll take you to the armory.

"You failed the mission, Halverson," Strider called after them. "This will haunt you for the rest of your traitorous life."

"There's no vaccine," said Halverson. "The mission can't succeed without a vaccine."

"We'll have the vaccine shortly if you wait your turn. We have to trust the doctor."

"Don't listen to him," said Marta. "Let's go."

"Follow me," said Cassavetes.

"I'm reporting you to the president, Halverson," said Strider. "You're going to death row for your heinous act of treachery."

"You're coming with us," said Halverson, approaching Strider, ready to pick the lock on Strider's shackles and free him.

"Get away from me. I'm not going anywhere with a traitor. I'm getting the vaccine and returning to the president with it. Until that time, I'm not budging. Bug off."

"Remember your SERE training as a SEAL in Warner Springs, California. Survival, evasion, resistance, and escape."

"What about it?"

"As part of your training you promised you would make every effort to escape and to aid others to escape."

"Only if I was being held by the enemy. Doctor Wheelhouse is *not* the enemy. He is our ally."

"How can you say that? He's turning all of our team into monsters."

"I will not fail my mission," said Strider in an all but robotic tone. "The mission is to get the vaccine. We can't get the vaccine until Wheelhouse invents it. I'm staying here until he does."

"Forget him," Marta told Halverson. "He's bonkers."

Halverson hung fire.

He didn't like the idea of leaving Strider behind. They had been friends before this mission. Halverson knew Wheelhouse would turn Strider into a freak like he had with the other members of the squad.

Halverson attempted to pick the lock on Strider's shackles. Strider collared Halverson's throat from behind with both of his hands and fell to throttling him.

Halverson elbowed Strider in the solar plexus. Gasping for breath Strider loosened his grip on Halverson. Halverson broke free. His neck red from Strider's attempt to strangle him, Halverson took a deep breath.

"I'm not going anywhere with traitors," said Strider.

"We don't have time for this," said Cassavetes. "We have to get out of here before Wheelhouse returns."

Marta snatched Halverson's arm and pulled him after her.

Halverson relented, leaving Strider behind to his miserable fate. Halverson felt bad about it, but Strider's mind had frozen. His thinking had gone rigid. The guy was unable to make a spontaneous decision in the field. He was trying to do everything by the book, even when the book didn't apply. The success of the mission had become more important to him than his life. Halverson knew it was fruitless to argue with him and get him to change his mind.

Halverson left with Marta and Cassavetes.

"Walk, don't run," Cassavetes told Halverson and Marta. "We don't want to attract attention by running. And put away that knife."

Halverson slipped the knife into his sock and covered it with his trouser leg.

"I can't get out of here fast enough," said Marta.

Chapter 73

In the Mount Weather emergency bunker, a clipboard in his hand, Dr. Morrow approached President Mims, who sat behind his desk in his office.

"Over 50 percent of our bunker's inhabitants have died from hypoxia, Mr. President," said Morrow, his head bowed, his voice low.

"This is not good news."

"We're running out of oxygen."

"We can't keep the ghouls out of the air vents. There are too many of them."

"I know."

"How are we supposed to get enough oxygen for everyone?" said Mims, standing up and pacing around, slapping his thigh.

"Lowering your oxygen ratio by three percentage points would help a little. It might let a few people live longer," offered Morrow, his tone deferential.

"You said I need 19.5 percent oxygen in the air I breathe to remain in good health."

"That is correct, sir."

"So what happens if you drop it to 16.5 percent?"

"Your health will suffer. Any physical exercise will tire you and your mental faculties will deteriorate."

"I am the president, Doctor. Can you imagine if we have a president whose mental faculties aren't 100 percent? The entire country will suffer if my intellect is impaired."

"We need a healthy president. This is true, sir."

Mims rubbed his forehead in anguish. "I certainly don't want more people to die in the bunker, but if my mental faculties are impaired, my decision-making powers will be affected. As president I have to make difficult decisions. I can't allow my intellect to deteriorate. It would be like killing the whole country if I made bad decisions.

"I am the anointed one. At an early age, I knew I was picked to achieve great things in my life. I knew one day I would become president of this great country. It was inevitable. As the greatest leader of the greatest country in the world, I cannot allow my health to deteriorate and hamper my intellect."

"I understand, sir."

"I can't knowingly reduce my intellectual abilities to possibly save a few other people in the bunker. Ultimately, more Americans would die, if I allow my intellect to deteriorate by cutting back on my oxygen to an unsafe level. With a deteriorating intellect I would make bad decisions, and the country would suffer as a result. As president, I must do what's best for the country, and, in this instance, my health is what's best for the country. I cannot allow a mentally incapacitated president rule the United States of America," said Mims, gesturing with his hands. "I must maintain my health at all costs. Do you understand?"

"Yes, sir. You don't want me to lower your oxygen level below 19.5 percent."

"Correct. My health and well-being are intrinsically tied to America's."

"What about the other inhabitants? Do we just let them die?"

"What?" said Mims, appalled. "Of course not. You're the medical professional. What's the best course of action?"

"Since they're not getting enough oxygen to continue normal activities, they need to reduce physical and mental exertion. Otherwise, they will perish sooner."

"All right, then. I'll announce over the PA system for them to stop exercising and stop—hmm—stop thinking? That doesn't sound right," said Mims, mulling it over. "What if we close the library so they can't read books and use their intellects."

Morrow shrugged, not thrilled with the idea. "I don't think they're gonna go for that idea. It sounds like the book burning carried out by Hitler's Nazis."

"I'm not talking about burning books. I just want to shut down the library for a while so they don't overexert their brains reading. You said they can't overexert their brains or their muscles or they'll burn too much oxygen and die." Mims paused in thought. "We probably should confiscate any books people own, also."

"That's not gonna fly, Mr. President," said Morrow, frowning with worry.

"Hmm. Maybe you're right. The idea of the government confiscating its citizens' books might be a little too much. It smacks of a banana republic. We don't want a rebellion on our hands, that's for sure."

"Maybe you could say you're closing the library for repairs and not tell them the real reason."

"Yeah, that might work. But I guess confiscating their books so they won't use their brains is going too far."

"I believe so, Mr. President."

"But it's for their own good, Doctor. I'm saving their lives by enforcing these measures. They'll live longer by not exerting too much energy. Maybe I should be more forthright with them and tell them the truth flat out."

"I dunno. Maybe . . ."

"This is tricky. This is why I need my brain in tiptop shape to make sure I make the correct decision."

"This may be a no-win situation. Whatever you decide could tick people off."

Mims riveted his gaze on Morrow. "Do they know I'm getting more oxygen than them?"

"I didn't tell them."

Mims stroked his chin in thought. "My dad worked in the coal mines of West Virginia, and the air down in the shafts was bad. He said it didn't bother him. He got used to it."

"Your dad was made of hickory. One tough customer."

"Granted, we don't have a bunch of rugged coal miners in the bunker with us. I take your point. Let's see. What if you give everyone sedatives? Wouldn't that slow down their metabolisms so they would need less oxygen?"

"They wouldn't burn as much energy, thus reducing their need for large amounts of oxygen. True."

Mims kept pacing. Being on his feet helped him think clearer, he decided.

"I'll tell them we need to cut down on their consumption of oxygen because we're running out of breathable air," he said. "We need to do away with exercising and reading."

"The people might become bored with so much time on their hands," said Morrow, switching his clipboard to his other hand in a nervous gesture.

"That's where the sedatives come in. You give them sedatives to zonk them out most of the time. They'll want to spend their days sleeping. They won't have enough energy to revolt."

"What if they refuse to take the sedatives?"

"Good question," said Mims, pointing at Morrow. "We could spike their drinks with Quaaludes."

"If they found out, there would be an uproar."

"Then don't let them find out. Do it on the sly." Mims returned to his desk. "Right now I'm gonna announce the temporary closure of the gym and the library. The idea is to keep them from using their brains and their muscles in order to lengthen their lives."

"They won't like hearing it."

"I'm just announcing the closures of the gym and the library for repairs. I'm not telling them anything else. Then you get to work spiking their water or whatever with ludes or Halcion."

"All right, Mr. President."

"We'll get through this, Doctor," Mims said cheerily. "You'll see."

"I just hope nobody finds out what's really going on. It's gonna remind people of spiked Kool-Aid at Jonestown if word gets out. You could have a purge on your hands. And we're the ones who would be getting purged."

"No worries, Doctor. You were following orders. Your ass is covered."

Morrow hawked. "That didn't work at Nuremberg, if I remember correctly."

Mims shot him a stern look. "Do you want to help me save the lives of Americans inside this bunker or not?"

"I do, sir," said Morrow, straightening.

Mims hesitated. "I had a thought. If everyone is sedated, it will leave the bunker defenseless against attack."

"There's that."

"Keep up the oxygen level of my Secret Service contingent to the requisite 19.5 percent and don't sedate them."

"I can make sure their living quarters get enough oxygen."

"We can't do the same for the rest of my military men, I'm afraid," said Mims, his face morose. "We have too many. Our oxygen would be depleted in no time."

"I was thinking the same thing, Mr. President."

"OK. Then let's do this for our great country," said Mims, his face beaming with pride. He lowered his voice. "And God help us if anyone finds out what we're really doing to save them. I didn't get to be top dog by not knowing people. I believe they would misunderstand my good intentions to save our country, if they learned the truth."

"The road to hell is paved with good intentions," muttered Morrow.

"What's that, Doctor?"

"I was quoting the Bible, sir."

"Ah, you're a religious man, Doctor." Mims's voice became more somber. "Then maybe you should pray for our immortal souls."

Mims snagged the PA system's microphone on his desktop.

"Attention. Attention. This is the president speaking," he declared. "I have an important public announcement to make that concerns all of us who reside inside this bunker. May I please have everyone's attention. The library and the gym are being closed for repairs. Please return the library books you have borrowed. The health of every American citizen is very important to me. Relax and make sure you get plenty of sleep. Soon we will have the vaccine for the zombie plague, and we'll be able to leave the bunker. Keep calm and take a nap. Everything is going to be fine. You are in good hands. I will safely steer our ship through these fraught and turbulent waters."

Compressing his thin lips Morrow watched Mims full of misgivings.

Chapter 74

Halverson and Marta strode after Cassavetes through Wheelhouse's cave lair, trying to avoid being noticed by anyone.

"We're almost at the armory," said Cassavetes. "We'll have to deal with the guards."

"I'll do anything it takes to get out of here," said Marta. "Poor Laci."

Halverson couldn't forget Laci either. The image of her dying by his hands stuck in his mind. He had to keep reminding himself that she wanted him to kill her. He would have nightmares about it for the rest of his life. Her smashing her face into the cave wall, cracking bones in her skull, soaking her face with blood, screaming in pain and desperation. Then, his finishing her off at her beseeching. The memory was stomach-turning.

Cassavetes ducked out of sight behind a jog in the cave.

"We better wait here for a bit," he said. "That guy we passed was giving me a suspicious look."

"Did he recognize me?" said Halverson.

"I dunno. He was giving me the fisheye for some reason."

"Are you under arrest like us?"

"No. Let's lie low for a couple minutes."

"Are you coming with us when we break out of here?"

"For sure. I can't believe Wheelhouse tricked me into believing he had vaccinated me against the plague. What a piece of work."

"And look at those monsters he's creating with his vaccine," said Marta. "You're better off that he *didn't* experiment on you as a test subject. At least you didn't turn into a freak—half human and half ghoul."

"True. But I could've easily been infected when I drove to your bunker. I had no idea the amount of danger I was in when I was riding my chopper. I thought I was protected from infection. Stupid me," said Cassavetes, slapping his head.

"You may be next on his list of guinea pigs," said Halverson.

"Another good reason to leave."

Halverson froze when he heard Wheelhouse's voice. Adrenaline shooting through him, he put his finger to his lips to silence Cassavetes and Marta.

"Where are they?" said Wheelhouse.

Halverson couldn't see him yet. He wondered if he should grab his knife now or wait to see how things played out. He had no idea how many people were with Wheelhouse. He could hear many footsteps approaching.

"What do we do now?" whispered Marta, her eyes huge with fear. "Don't let him take us back."

One knife against a bunch of antagonists wasn't going to do much good, decided Halverson. Maybe Wheelhouse and his guards would pass by them. As yet he couldn't see them.

"Oh there you are," said Wheelhouse, rounding the jog.

Halverson left his knife alone. Wheelhouse had armed guards with him. There were too many of them, including, to his shock, Strider, who Wheelhouse was guiding with a pole with a noose around Strider's throat.

Flummoxed, Halverson wondered what was going on.

It didn't take long to find out.

Chapter 75

"I've been looking for you," said Wheelhouse. "It was rude of you to try to leave us without saying good-bye. You are our guests here."

"What are you doing with Strider?" said Halverson.

"That's what I want to tell you. I've found the vaccine. You can take it back with you to the president."

"I don't believe it."

"See for yourself. I injected Strider with it. Look at him. He's fine."

To all appearances Strider looked normal.

"If he's fine, why do you have his head in a noose at the end of that pole?" said Halverson.

"I do this with all my test subjects. It's simply a precaution."

"I don't think so," said Halverson, suspicious. He turned to Strider. "How are you, Strider?"

Strider looked at him with vacant eyes and commenced shaking.

"Why's he shaking like that?" said Halverson.

"I want to inject you next so that when you go back to the president you won't become infected by the ghouls," said Wheelhouse.

Strider slewed around, breaking free of Wheelhouse's grasp on the pole. Halverson recoiled in horror. On the back of Strider's head was a growling ghoul face preparing to bite Halverson in the neck. Halverson bolted away as Strider lurched toward him, shambling backward on feet that were pointed in the opposite direction.

"What the hell did you do to him?" said Halverson.

"I vaccinated him," said Wheelhouse. "He can't become infected with the plague."

"He's already infected."

Marta screamed in terror as the thing that used to be Strider jerked toward her.

"I assure you, the ghouls will not bite him in his condition," said Wheelhouse, trying to grab the pole from the ground to gain control of Strider.

The pole kept skittering beyond Wheelhouse's grasp.

"They're not gonna bite him because he's one of them," said Halverson.

"If they're not gonna bite him, it means the vaccine works," said Wheelhouse.

"You're not injecting me with that crap. No way."

The Strider creature lunged at Halverson. Halverson dodged the awkward creature, who walked backward toward him, the ghoul face directing it.

Wheelhouse continued trying to fetch the pole off the ground in order to gain control of Strider.

Strider stumbled around, flailing his arms, trying to bite anyone he could get close to. The ghoul half of him had complete control of his body movements. Strider's face was devoid of emotion, a mask that saw nothing through blank eyes.

Unable to control herself, Marta vomited at the sight of the revolting creature.

"Be still," Wheelhouse told the creature, trying to retrieve the elusive pole.

Strider swiped his arms at him.

Trapped by the armed guards and the ungainly creature, Halverson couldn't escape.

"Shoot Strider for Chrissake," said Marta. "Put him out of his misery."

"No," cried Wheelhouse. "He's living proof my vaccine works."

Marta gaped at the doctor with disbelief.

At length Wheelhouse seized the pole handle and, straightening up, gained control of Strider.

"I want all of you to come with me to get your vaccine inoculations," said Wheelhouse, his face red from bending over.

He guided Strider ahead of him.

Wheelhouse's guards trained their AR-15s on Halverson, Marta, and Cassavetes.

"I'm one of you," said Cassavetes.

The guards didn't agree.

"I'm already vaccinated," said Cassavetes. "I don't need a booster."

The guards hustled him, Halverson, and Marta after Wheelhouse.

Chapter 76

At gunpoint Halverson entered Wheelhouse's lab.

In the center of the lab, a long black rubber-coated desktop had Bunsen burners and flasks arranged on it. At the end of the desk was a goose-necked faucet.

At the far end of the lab stood Wheelhouse's vaccinated monsters, including Joon-ho and Rafferty, shackled to ringbolts in the ground. Hissing, Rafferty squirmed on his snake legs. His wrist was shackled because the shackles couldn't secure his slimy anaconda legs.

Standing beside Rafferty was a new abomination with its human head perched on the neck of a giraffe. Except the head wasn't human anymore. It was a ghoul head. It was what used to be Purl's head with a necrotic face, milky eyes, and a drooling mouth. The creature craned its neck trying to locate fresh human flesh to sink its teeth into.

"Oh, no," said Marta, covering her mouth with her hand, realizing with revulsion that it was Purl.

"Another one of your success stories, Doc?" said Halverson, eying Purl with repugnance.

"Sacrifices are needed to be made in the name of science," said Wheelhouse.

"You're good at sacrificing other people."

Beside Purl stood a pig shackled to a ringbolt. Instead of its normal face the pig had Diego's ghoulish face growling/oinking on it.

"Can we please get out of here?" said Marta, her face wan.

"I don't know what the human race would do without you, Doc," said Halverson.

"I have your vaccine ready for you," said Wheelhouse. "Once vaccinated, you'll be able to return to the president in safety and give him the vaccine."

"With the body of a skunk or how about a porcupine? I don't think so."

Halverson bent forward, whipped his knife out of his sock, lunged at Wheelhouse, and held the blade at Wheelhouse's throat. Wheelhouse's eyes bulged in terror.

"Tell your slaves to drop their weapons," said Halverson between his teeth.

"They're not slaves. They follow me willingly."

Halverson pressed the knife tip into Wheelhouse's throat, drawing a trickle of blood.

"Tell them to throw down their guns," said Halverson. "Or I'll cut your throat."

"Throw down your guns," said Wheelhouse.

His soldiers obeyed.

"Let's go to your ordnance room," said Halverson.

Halverson headed out of the lab with Wheelhouse, Marta, and Cassavetes. As they left, Cassavetes and Marta picked up discarded AR-15s from the ground and aimed them at Wheelhouse's unarmed soldiers.

"Let us pass," said Wheelhouse to anyone they met on the way, terrified of the knife at his throat.

The ordnance room was well stocked, Halverson discovered. He picked up on his M2 lying in the corner.

"Cover Wheelhouse," he told Cassavetes.

Cassavetes trained his AR-15 on Wheelhouse.

Halverson slammed a full magazine into an MP9 and slung the MP9 around his neck. He stuffed fresh mags into his cargo pockets. He latched onto Wheelhouse's arm and put his knife to Wheelhouse's throat again.

"I'd like to take you with us, Doc," he said, "but you've lost your sense of values. I wouldn't want you to conduct any of your experiments at Mount Weather. Too many people would suffer at your hands."

"Let me remind you, you can't stop the progress of science. Another doctor will use similar methods and find the vaccine if I don't."

"I hope you're wrong about the similar methods and he won't leave behind a trail of freaks in his wake. Human life means nothing to you."

"How can you say that? I'm trying to save humanity with my vaccine."

"But you're destroying people in the process. Can't you see that?"

"Scientists can't be scared of failing. Otherwise nothing would get done. Sacrifices must be made in the name of scientific progress."

"You sound like Mengele. Human life meant nothing to him."

"You shut out the truth when it displeases you," said Wheelhouse, shaking his head with disapproval. "Typical of the herd mentality."

"I'm not taking you with us. Nobody at Mount Weather would be safe with you there."

"Nobody will ever be safe without my vaccine."

Halverson gave him a look. "Your so-called vaccines aren't safe for humans. They're worse than death sentences. They turn people into ghastly freaks."

"So far. But it's only a matter of time before I succeed," said Wheelhouse with a smug face.

"Should we take him with us?" Halverson asked Marta and Cassavetes.

"No," said Marta.

"No way," said Cassavetes. "He's a scam artist. He'll say anything to get his way."

He jammed spare AR-15 magazines into his cargo pants. Looking ill he hawked and spat blood-streaked spittle.

"You need my vaccine," said Wheelhouse.

"You try to inject me, I'll shoot you in the head," said Cassavetes.

"Looks like you're staying here, Doc," said Halverson.

"Fine," said Wheelhouse, arrogant as ever. "I can continue my research here."

Halverson released Wheelhouse. "Keep him covered."

"My pleasure," said Cassavetes.

He trained his AR-15 on Wheelhouse, while Halverson gathered incendiary grenades stocked in the armory. He clipped the grenades to his belt.

"Your research is over," said Halverson.

"What are you talking about?" said Wheelhouse, agitated. "I don't need you or the president giving me permission to carry on my research. I'm the one doing all the work."

"But you're not gonna do it here. I'm burning your chamber of horrors to the ground."

"You can't do that," cried Wheelhouse, indignant. "Mankind is lost without the progress of scientific discovery. You're consigning humanity back to the Middle Ages."

"If what you're doing is called progress, I want none of it."

"I'm done arguing. I know what I'm doing is right," said Wheelhouse, crossing his arms over his chest, supercilious as ever.

"I know what *I'm* doing is right."

"You're an ignorant fool."

"People mean nothing to you. You have to be stopped."

"I'm surrounded by ignoramuses," said Wheelhouse, incensed. He looked at Cassavetes. "And traitors. I'm a hero. You should be holding a parade for me. I'm the one trying to save the human race. You're the killers."

"Don't tempt me," said Cassavetes, gritting his teeth, jutting his AR-15 muzzle at Wheelhouse, and threatening to squeeze the trigger.

Wheelhouse swiped the automatic rifle barrel out of the way and hightailed it.

Cassavetes fumbled the gun, almost dropping it.

"We need to get out of here," said Halverson, draping the M2's ammo belt around his neck. "Without our hostage they're gonna start firing at us."

"I should've blown him away when I had the chance," said Cassavetes, gaining control of the AR-15. He watched in dismay as Wheelhouse bugged out and disappeared around the corner. "He moves fast for his age."

"Fear does that to you," said Halverson.

"He's gonna come back with his soldiers."

"Let's launch a preemptive strike."

Cassavetes looked puzzled.

"Let's go to his lab," said Halverson, clipping incendiary grenades onto his belt.

He lifted the heavy M2, his neck draped with an MP9 and the M2's ammo belt.

"Do you think that's wise?" said Cassavetes.

"Why don't we just get out of here?" said Marta.

"We have no choice," said Halverson. "Wheelhouse has to be stopped."

Marta completed shoving MP9 mags into her trouser pockets. MP9 in hand, she accompanied Halverson out of the ordnance room.

Cassavetes led the way, returning fire when a guard opened up on him. Shot in the chest, the guard crumpled. A bloodstain spread silently on his white button-down shirt.

Chapter 77

Stealing to the entrance of the lab, Halverson stood the M2 on its butt, snagged an incendiary grenade from his belt, and flung it inside.

The lab burst into flames. Screams of terror and pain resounded in the fire-engulfed lab. Howls from ungodly creatures punctuated the screams. The heat of the conflagration forced Halverson to back away from the entrance, grimacing, his face sweaty.

"How do we open the cave exit door?" he said, picking up the M2.

"I'll show you," said Cassavetes, and sprinted down the cave.

Halverson and Marta pelted after him.

The heartrending screams of both humans and creatures accompanied them.

The heavy M2 slowed Halverson down, but he managed to break into a fast trot nonetheless, adrenaline coursing through his body, the nerve-racking howls and screams motivating him to go faster.

Picking up on two guards training their AR-15s on him he opened fire on them. The bullets from his M2 tore them apart at close range. Their bodies flew backward, sprawled on the ground, and twitched.

When Cassavetes reached the steel exit door, he pressed the red plastic button that opened it. The door rose courtesy of the propane-fueled generator that provided power to the cave.

Halverson bolted out the door. Glimpsing the two chained creatures that flanked the entrance, he realized their mutant bodies were the products of Wheelhouse's obscene experiments.

Halverson scoped out his surroundings. There was no way he, Marta, and Cassavetes could escape through the rows of barbed wire—even if they were lucky enough to have bolt cutters. If they tried to crawl through the barbs, Wheelhouse's armed guards would pick them off.

"We have to go out the same way we came in," said Halverson. "Through the eighteen-wheeler's trailer."

"And then what?" said Cassavetes. "When we go out the back door, the ghouls will converge on us like nothing you've ever seen."

"You managed to do it when you came to the bunker."

"I was on a motorcycle. I drove that thing out of the trailer at sixty miles per hour. The ghouls couldn't stop me. And don't forget, Wheelhouse conned me into believing I was vaccinated so they couldn't infect me. I took risks I never would have taken if I knew the truth."

"Still, you made it to the bunker."

"Dumb luck."

"There must be a way we can escape the ghouls."

"I don't know how, especially without a hog."

"I got the M2," said Halverson, patting the Browning.

"Yeah, but it'll slow us down."

"We'll figure it out when we get inside the trailer. Outside, we're sitting ducks for Wheelhouse's gunmen. Let's go."

The three of them belted to the semi that blocked the entrance to the cave, just as soldiers appeared at the cave entrance, guns in hand. They opened fire on Halverson, Marta, and Cassavetes. Bullets strafed the ground near Halverson's feet, kicking up puffs of dust from the dirt.

Taking a bullet in the arm, Cassavetes yelped in pain.

The three of them ducked behind the semi's cab and climbed into the trailer. Holding his wounded arm, gritting his teeth in agony, Cassavetes pulled up the rear and shut the door behind him.

"We gotta stanch your wound," said Halverson, putting down his M2 and pressing his hand against Cassavetes's mauled shoulder to get it to stop bleeding. "What are those blisters on your face?"

"What? I dunno. My face hurts. It feels like it's on fire. I feel like shit."

The blisters reminded Halverson of pictures he had seen of victims of radiation poisoning. The results of the radioactive dust Cassavetes had breathed outside the Mount Weather bunker, Halverson decided.

At that moment, an explosion rang out, rocking the trailer.

Chapter 78

Charged with adrenaline and fear, Cassavetes sprang to the front door and flung it open to see what had happened.

Blasted bodies of guards minus some of their limbs lay strewn face down on the ground in front of the cave.

Jagged flames lunged out of the cave entrance, flicking at the sky with their coruscating yellow and orange tongues.

"The fire must have reached the ordnance room and touched off an explosion," Cassavetes said over his shoulder to Halverson, who stood behind him.

Flailing his arms, a man on fire fled out of the cave, screaming in pain, hysterical with fear. He ran straight into the barbed wire fence. His hair burning, the flesh on his face melting, he got hung up on the barbs that tore into his burning flesh. Struggling to free himself he left swatches of his smoking charred flesh on the barbs.

Marta appeared at the door trying to see what was happening.

Wincing at the pain in his wounded arm, Cassavetes pushed her back.

"You don't want to see this," he said, shutting the door. "The cave's blowing up."

Halverson nodded. "Thermite bombs. It's better that hellhole burns to the ground."

"Where does that leave us?" said Marta, wrapping a handkerchief around Cassavetes's wound, which had stopped bleeding.

"We have to tell the president what happened."

"How are we gonna get back?" said Cassavetes, coughing.

"Good question," said Halverson. "But we can't stay here. The supplies in the cave went up in flames. Nobody can live here anymore."

"We're surrounded by millions of zeds. How do we escape them?"

"There must be a way."

"They didn't call this a suicide mission for nothing," said Marta, eyes bleak.

Coughing, Cassavetes scratched his head. A clump of hair fell out in his hand.

"What the hell?" he said, staring at the clump.

"Are you sure Wheelhouse didn't vaccinate you?" said Marta, fretting.

"He said he injected me with saline solution. Do you think I'm turning? Christ, no."

Halverson lifted open the trailer's rear door and peered out.

Ghouls were everywhere, milling around, growling, shambling in search of food. They looked up at him when they heard the door slide open. Drooling at the sight of him they converged on the back of the trailer. Halverson slammed the door shut.

"I could wipe out hundreds of them with the M2," he said. "But then what? I'd run out of bullets, and we'd still be stuck here, and there would still be a million of those things out there champing at the bit to sink their teeth into our throats and feed on us to their hearts' content."

Cassavetes hung his head in despair. "We have no chance."

"Maybe we can make our way back to the Suburban," said Marta. "Then we could use it to drive out of here."

"There's only three of us left. I don't like our chances against millions of ghouls."

Halverson racked his brains for an idea.

"We're doomed," said Cassavetes.

He threw the clump of his hair onto the floor in disgust.

"How long can we hold out in this truck?" said Marta.

"Not long without food," said Cassavetes. "We're fucked. Don't let me turn. Promise you'll kill me first."

"Maybe you're not turning," said Marta. "Maybe you're just sick."

Halverson's eyes brightened as he got an idea.

"What if we use this semi to drive back to the bunker?" he said, stroking his jaw. "The ghouls can't get at us in here."

Cassavetes thought about it for a moment. "There's nothing in our way, except the zeds, and we can run them over with ease in this eighteen-ton behemoth."

"The only problem is, will it start?"

Despite his illness, Cassavetes's spirits lifted.

"We kept it in working condition," he said, becoming animated. "I forgot it was Wheelhouse's last resort of escape if the zeds breached the barbed wire fences and got into the cave."

"Then there's nothing to stop us from backing out. We can steamroll any ghouls that get in our way and find somewhere to turn the semi around and head back to the president."

"Sounds like a plan."

"How much diesel does the fuel tank have left?"

"We'll have to check. I'm sure there's something in it, because Wheelhouse wanted to be able to cut and run at a moment's notice."

His MP9 slung over his neck, Halverson hopped out of the trailer's front door with Cassavetes to inspect the cab. Halverson spotted two ghouls that had managed to climb through the first two rows of barbed wire. The barbs on the third row had stopped them. They writhed on the wire trying to escape, tearing their clothes and ripping their putrescent flesh.

Halverson climbed into the cab's driver's seat. Cassavetes claimed the passenger seat.

"Can you drive this thing?" said Cassavetes.

"I can drive anything. We have to be able to drive everything in the CIA black ops department. They train us well."

"I guess. I can drive anything, too. I was a car mechanic before the plague hit."

"You don't sound very proud of it."

"I've been wanting to get this off my chest for a long time. As long as I'm gonna die soon, now's as good a time as any. A couple months before the plague hit, I installed new brakes on a retired schoolteacher's Ford Focus. When she drove home, her brakes failed, and she got killed in a car accident. I don't know what went wrong. The new brakes I installed must have been defective. It's been bugging me ever since. I guess that's my deathbed confession."

"We're not dead yet."

"I'm not giving up. I can drive this thing. Let me do it."

"You can't shift gears with that wounded arm you got."

"True," said Cassavetes, wincing at the pain in his wound. "I feel like I might pass out any minute. You gotta promise me you'll kill me before I turn," he said, clutching Halverson's sleeve.

"I don't think you're turning." Halverson paused, wondering if he should tell Cassavetes the truth. He decided he should. "You've got radiation poisoning."

Taken aback, Cassavetes gawked at Halverson.

"Doc Morrow told me and Strider you had it," explained Halverson.

"How long do I got?"

"Two weeks at the most."

"So it really was a suicide mission, after all," said Cassavetes in a brown study. "For me, anyway."

"Hey, maybe he was wrong. Doctors don't know everything. Maybe you'll recover."

Cassavetes didn't say anything.

"Where's the key?" said Halverson.

Cassavetes said nothing, lost in a funk.

"If we don't get out of here soon, we're all gonna die for sure," said Halverson, regretting his decision to tell Cassavetes the truth about the guy's radiation poisoning. "Never give up."

"Can't you hotwire it with all your black ops training?" said Cassavetes, snapping out of it, sporting a half smile.

"I could. But don't you have a key stashed in here?"

Cassavetes reached under the passenger seat, felt around with his fingers, withdrew the key, and handed it to Halverson.

"Of course," said Cassavetes.

Peering out the windshield Halverson screwed up his face.

"What?" said Cassavetes.

Chapter 79

From the big rig driver's seat Halverson could see the entrance to the cave.

Lashing flames continued to thrust from the cave as grey smoke plumed out, billowing into the sky. With a start he saw a blonde in a frayed pinstripe pantsuit dash out of the fire-engulfed cave, her long hair ragged with flames. Screaming at the top of her lungs, exhaling a cloud of smoke, she darted toward the nearest row of barbed wire and tried to claw her way through it, becoming tangled in the barbs that tore her burning, blistering skin. The reek of her burning flesh and hair suffused the air.

Halverson felt like putting her out of her misery. He didn't have to. She was already in extremis. She died spread-eagled in the barbed wire, a gruesome warning to anyone who wanted to enter the cursed cave.

Even more shocking, and repellent as well, was the sight of the creature formerly known as Rafferty, who writhed out of the cave on his anaconda legs, his flesh rippling with flames. He emitted dire sounds from his burning throat, his ghoulish face scorched, his decaying flesh blackened, his eyebrows burned off.

Rafferty squirmed in the dirt, howling and screeching like a wounded animal.

The aberrant sound was sickening. Halverson wanted to wretch. The sight of Rafferty flopping around in the dirt like a beached seal was just as stomach-turning.

Why didn't the thing just die? wondered Halverson, transfixed by Rafferty. It had to perish eventually as the flames devoured its skull and melted its brain.

"Man, I hope I never see anything as godawful as that again," said Cassavetes, grimacing at the floundering Rafferty.

Halverson depressed the clutch, put the shifter into Neutral, and keyed the ignition.

The battery cranked, but the engine didn't turn over.

Cassavetes's face clouded with worry.

Halverson cranked the battery again. No dice.

He set his jaw with determination. His palms sweaty, he tried a third time, nudging the key clockwise just so.

The battery cranked. The engine revved to life.

"I told you they kept it serviced," said Cassavetes, pumping his fist eagerly then wincing, as he recalled his arm was sore from his recent gunshot wound. "Ow," he said, sweat beading on his face. "This is a diesel truck. You need to let it idle in neutral for ten minutes to warm up the engine before we go."

Another explosion rocked the cave.

Two boulders shaken loose from the mountain rolled down the incline into the barbed wire, bellying it.

"We better beat it," said Cassavetes, hiking his eyebrows at the sight of the boulders. "A boulder could slam into us next."

"We haven't idled ten minutes yet," said Halverson, glancing at his wristwatch.

"All right. Keep idling."

Halverson let the engine idle a little longer.

After checking his watch, he was about to put the big rig into reverse when he saw Wheelhouse stagger out of the cave, hacking, his smock on fire. Wheelhouse bent forward, clutched his knees, and vomited. He stood up, gasping for breath, his face contorted with pain. He stumbled away from the cave mouth that was spewing flames.

Purl shambled out of the cave following ten feet behind Wheelhouse, leaned forward on his giraffe neck, closed his jaws around the crown of Wheelhouse's skull, bit through the bone, and tore out half of Wheelhouse's brain. His jaws smeared with Wheelhouse's blood, Purl munched with relish Wheelhouse's brain and skull shards.

What remained of Wheelhouse's ragged brain swam in blood in his destroyed brainpan. His body dropped to the ground and spasmed.

"Our cue to leave," said Halverson, watching with revulsion.

Despite his pain, Rafferty slithered over to Wheelhouse to feed. Rafferty bit into Wheelhouse's arm, took out a large chunk of flesh, and gobbled it down. Rafferty's body continued to burn, and he screamed in agony as well as orgiastic joy as he feasted on Wheelhouse's flesh.

The blood drained from Cassavetes's face. "If this isn't hell, what is?"

Chapter 80

Halverson backed the big rig down the road. The axles made a loud cracking noise as they commenced to spin after an extensive period of disuse. Maybe they were suffering from rust, decided Halverson, studying the road behind him in his driver's-side mirror.

He was backing straight into the ghouls. So be it, he decided. The eighteen-ton truck would crush them to death, pancaking their skulls and killing their diseased brains.

As the truck cleared the outermost row of barbed wire, the ghouls converged on the stretch of road vacated by the truck and trudged toward the flaming cave entrance, drawn by the smell of human flesh roasting in the blazes.

When the ghouls spotted Wheelhouse's body on the ground, they hurried toward him dying to feast on his fresh flesh.

"There's nothing stopping the zeds now," said Cassavetes. "They have a clear path to the cave."

Halverson continued backing up the truck, running over ghouls that tried to block his way, causing a bumpy ride.

"I'll turn the truck around as soon as we reach a clearing where we'll have enough room," he said.

Ghouls swarmed around the truck as it backed down the road.

They stumbled and clawed the steel cab like drunkards trying to get inside.

The road was too narrow yet for Halverson to turn the truck around. He had to continue backing up, using the driver's-side mirror to see his way down the mountain pass.

Another explosion in the cave sent boulders rolling down the mountain. The rows of barbed wire caught them—for now.

"Can you drive faster?" said Cassavetes, worry lines creasing his forehead.

"If I go too fast, we could run off the road and jackknife," said Halverson, face sweaty, eyes glued to the mirror, steering carefully.

"All these curves in the road don't help matters."

"I was just gonna say that. On the other hand, by backing up we can use the trailer as a sort of plow to shove the ghouls out of the road or steamroller them."

Cassavetes nodded. "It flattens them better than if we were driving forward."

Halverson could see the sun was starting to set. Its dying light was turning the sky metallic salmon and pink.

"When it gets too dark, we're gonna have to stop," he said. "We don't have headlights in the back. Taillights aren't gonna give me enough light to see the way down."

"We should be OK even if we have to stop and grab some sleep. The ghouls can't get into the truck."

Chapter 81

"We're having problems in the bunker," said Dr. Morrow, entering President Mims's office in the Mount Weather bunker and shutting the door behind him, an agitated expression twisting his face.

"What kind of problems?" said Mims, sitting behind his desk, fiddling with a bronze paperweight in the shape of the Statue of Liberty.

"We just had a riot in the cafeteria."

Mims slammed down the paperweight on his desktop. "What's the problem? Don't we have enough food?"

"The problem is, people are strung out. They're irritable because they're not getting enough oxygen. They fly off the handle at the least provocation."

"I thought you gave them sedatives so they won't consume so much oxygen."

"I did. But they're still irritable because they're oxygen deprived. They refuse to spend all their time sleeping. They have short tempers because they're tired and aren't breathing enough oxygen."

"Was anyone hurt in the food riot?"

"A couple people lost teeth in the fistfights."

"We can't have riots. We have to keep up morale. How can we calm everyone down?"

"We can increase their supply of oxygen."

"We'll run out of breathable air sooner, if we do that," said Mims, ticked off.

"You asked me. I told you."

Mims gave Morrow a scathing look. "Are you criticizing my decisions, Doctor?"

"Not at all, Mr. President."

"Hmm. What about if we increase their intake of sedatives?"

"They're gonna feel exhausted all the time."

"Better than having them riot. They can't riot if they can't get out of bed."

"It would go a long way in helping them if we gave them more oxygen."

"We can't do that, Doctor," said Mims, standing up. "There's not enough oxygen to go around. We need to have enough so we're still alive when Strider returns with the vaccine."

"Not all of us will be alive at this rate," said Morrow, his face dour.

"We want as many to be alive as possible," said Mims, annoyed at Morrow for bringing up the obvious.

"When is Strider returning?"

"I'm keeping my fingers crossed he'll return any moment now. I don't know what the delay is, frankly. The mission is top secret and under radio silence. We can't contact him and vice versa."

Morrow heaved a sigh. "Fatigue and oxygen deprivation can lead to depression. The suicide rate is rising, as well, Mr. President."

"My mind is sharp. I'll see us through this ordeal—"

Mims stopped speaking and looked attentive when he heard yelling in the hallway outside his door.

"Is the door locked?" he said.

"I locked it when I came in. With all due respect, Mr. President, keeping your door locked is not the answer to our dilemma," said Morrow, gnashing his teeth with nervous tension, aware that he might be overstepping his rank in the bunker.

"When I need your advice on how to lead, I'll ask for it, Doctor," snapped Mims.

Morrow thought better of replying. He kept his own counsel.

Mims mulled it over. "Is there any way we can lower the oxygen intake of our citizens even further, in case Strider doesn't show up soon?"

"Their health is already at risk with the low level of oxygen they're receiving."

"The problem is, we don't have enough oxygen to go around, not with the goddamn ghouls blocking the air ducts," said Mims, eyes dark. He paused in thought. His eyes lit up. "What about the air outside the bunker? Is it breathable or is it still radioactive?"

"It's still radioactive, I'm afraid, Mr. President. We need the HEPA filters in the air ducts to purify it for us to breathe."

Mims hammered his fist on his desktop in frustration. "We need that vaccine."

"Even if we have the vaccine, it won't solve our oxygen problem."

"No, but we'll be able to leave the bunker and get far enough away from the radioactive dust to find breathable air without fear of getting infected by the ghouls that are surrounding us. You see, Doctor, as long as I can think clearly, our country is in good hands, and we will weather this storm," said Mims, pointing to his temple.

They heard more yelling in the corridor.

"Where's my Secret Service contingent?" said Mims, concerned. "Aren't they out there?"

"They were standing outside your door when I entered, sir."

The yelling became even louder.

Chapter 82

Halverson stopped the big rig.

"What are you stopping for?" said Cassavetes. "It's not night yet."

"I've been thinking," said Halverson. "This trailer is slowing us down. Do we really need it?"

"We can flatten the zeds with it so they don't block our way."

"We could go faster if we uncoupled the tractor from it. And I could turn around so we could drive in the dark with headlights."

Halverson heard the nerve-grating sound of ghouls scratching the cab's steel door trying to get in.

"If we go outside, the zeds will get us," said Cassavetes, staring out the windshield at the hordes of ghouls encompassing the truck.

"Can't we uncouple the trailer from inside the cab?"

Cassavetes shook his head no. "Somebody has to go out there and do it."

"I'll do it. You're wounded."

"You don't know what you're doing. I know how to do it. I can get it done faster than you."

"How can you do it with only one arm?"

Cassavetes closed his eyes and rubbed his eyelids. "Let's do it together. It takes several steps. We can do it faster together."

"All right. Tell me what to do."

"First, chock the wheels on the trailer so it doesn't roll down the slope after we uncouple it."

From the passenger seat Cassavetes set the emergency brake in the tractor.

"Let's do it," said Halverson.

He racked his MP9, flung open his door, and burst out of the tractor, peppering the ghouls with slugs. Ghouls fell high and low, their heads blown apart and spewing brains. Halverson jumped off the tractor's steel running board, located the chocks attached to the trailer, and chocked the trailer wheels.

Cassavetes blasted ghoul heads with his AR-15, jumped out of the tractor, dashed to the trailer, and, using a tire iron mounted near its front, attempted to lower the trailer's landing gear to stabilize the trailer. He found out he wasn't able to manipulate the tire iron with only one good hand.

"Halverson," he said. "Take over here."

Halverson took over for him and lowered the landing gear.

Cassavetes opened the steel jaws clamped around the trailer's kingpin. Then he bolted to the air and electrical lines attached to the trailer and released them.

Finishing lowering the landing gear Halverson wheeled around and fired a short burst at a fortyish bald male ghoul with a hawklike nose and a paunch who was getting ready to bite Halverson's arm. Two slugs crashed through the top of the ghoul's bald head, splintering the creature's skull.

Halverson breathed a sigh of relief. That was close, he decided.

"Let's get back in the tractor," said Cassavetes.

He fired his AR-15 at an attacking male mortician ghoul in his late sixties who stood over six feet tall, had a full head of white hair, and was holding his head canted to the right.

Nothing happened. The AR-15 magazine was empty.

"Shit," said Cassavetes.

The mortician ghoul closed its gaping jaws on Cassavetes's wounded shoulder.

Cassavetes screamed in pain.

Halverson whirled his MP9 around and double-tapped the ghoul's face, putting out both of its milky eyes. The mortician's knees buckled. The ghoul collapsed on the tarmac.

Halverson stood frozen, staring at Cassavetes. They both knew the worst had happened. The ghoul had bitten Cassavetes. Cassavetes's fate was sealed.

"This is when I need that damn vaccine," said Cassavetes, attempting a laugh, which died in his throat. "I was leading a charmed life when I drove my hog to your bunker, and I didn't even know it because Wheelhouse lied to me." He coughed out a laugh. "What a sick joke."

Halverson fired a long burst at two female ghouls, perhaps mother and daughter, wearing ragged dresses that bared their wasted shoulders, as they lunged at him. They ended up lunging into the tarmac, their foreheads stitched with bullets, dead before they hit the pavement.

A ten-year-old boy ghoul clad in powder blue shorts and a filthy white T-shirt bit Cassavetes in the hand. Screaming, Cassavetes ripped his hand out of the ghoul's mouth and swatted the thing's head with his AR-15 stock, fracturing the ghoul's skull. Even in death the boy ghoul wouldn't release the chunk of flesh it held between its rotten teeth.

"The trailer's uncoupled," said Cassavetes, face screwed up in agony. He gazed at Halverson with pleading eyes. "Kill me. Don't let me turn. And get out of here."

Halverson swapped mags and gunned down two male ghouls in jeans and long-sleeved plaid flannel shirts. He knew he had to get moving. He didn't know if he could bring himself to kill Cassavetes. Strangling Laci was still plaguing his thoughts. He could feel her neck in the crook of his arm, feel the pulse in her carotid artery slowly guttering out. It was something he would never forget.

Cassavetes was asking him to do it all over again. Maybe it wouldn't feel as bad if he shot Cassavetes instead of strangling him, decided Halverson. At least he wouldn't feel Cassavetes's life draining out of him in his arms. Still . . .

"Do it," cried Cassavetes, as a middle-aged Asian female ghoul wearing coveralls bit his stomach and tore out a hunk of bloody flesh, which she gobbled down.

Cassavetes was dying, Halverson knew. If he let the ghouls continue to take bites out of him, it would prolong Cassavetes's misery.

Taking a deep breath Halverson drew a bead on Cassavetes's head and fired two bullets.

Cassavetes crumpled. A dozen ghouls descended on his supine body, ripping apart his flesh like vultures. One of them, a young thickset male wearing a postal uniform and a straw coolie hat, gouged out Cassavetes's left eye and popped it into his mouth.

Sickened, Halverson sprang to the front of the trailer and knocked on the door.

Chapter 83

"It's me," said Halverson. "Open up, Marta."

Tentatively, she cracked the door and peeked out at his anguished face.

"What happened?" she said, terrified.

"We're leaving the trailer. Let's get into the tractor."

Halverson smoked a cross-eyed thirtyish male ghoul that was advancing on him, its arms extended in front of it. The ghoul head jerked back as the slug entered the creature's left, maggot-infested eyebrow.

"Where's Cassavetes gonna sit?" said Marta, puzzled.

With her MP9 she cut down a fortysomething black-gowned male minister ghoul who shambled toward her, its mouth open wide, exposing cracked, broken yellow teeth.

"He didn't make it," said Halverson. "Hurry. Get in the tractor."

"What about the trailer?"

"We're leaving it behind. We don't need it."

"What about your machine gun?"

"Oh, yeah."

Halverson leapt into the trailer and retrieved the M2 and its ammo belt. He handed the M2 down to her and jumped down from the trailer with the ammo belt draped around his neck. He took the M2 from her.

"Behind you," he said.

She wheeled around to confront a trio of ghouls who were trudging toward her from behind. They were half-dressed teens, two blacks and one white, wearing shoulder pads and white football pants with knee pads, like they had just left their locker room at a high school football game. Their arms had bite marks on them, where they had become infected with the plague.

She let loose a long burst and strafed their heads. They staggered and fell on top of each other the better part of two feet away from her, their brains minced, worms crawling out of their ears.

She and Halverson dashed to the tractor. Halverson unleashed the M2, cutting a path through the ghouls that converged on them. Marta swapped magazines and opened fire with her MP9, raking the ghouls with 9mm Parabellum slugs.

Out of the corner of her eye, Marta glimpsed a ring of ghouls tearing apart a male body in the middle of them with gore-smeared hands and devouring his bloody chunks of flesh.

She looked hurriedly away, knowing instinctively it was Cassavetes's body they were feasting on.

Halverson and Marta sprang into the tractor and, gasping for breath, slammed the doors shut behind them. He stood the M2 next to the door.

"And then there were two," Marta managed to say between gasps.

They exchanged looks.

Would he have to kill her, too? he wondered. Laci, Cassavetes, and Marta. Was he the designated killer of the infected? If he was, it was a job he could do without.

"A penny for them," said Marta.

He decided not to tell her what he was thinking.

An explosion sounded, jerking him out of his thoughts. It came from the cave, he decided. Seconds later a rock the size of a grapefruit crashed through the windshield and landed between him and Marta.

He cursed. Marta screamed, as glass shards spewed onto them, lacerating their faces and arms.

"Did the ghouls throw that rock?" said Marta, shell-shocked.

"It probably came from an explosion at the cave," said Halverson. "Those things don't know what they're doing. They haven't figured out how to use weapons."

A twentysomething male ghoul with a gymnast's body climbed onto the tractor hood and crawled over it to the open windshield, reaching its arms out toward Marta. She raised her MP9 and blew the ghoul's head apart with a spray of lead.

Halverson fired the engine and let it idle.

"What are you waiting for?" said Marta, shooting at an old grey-haired ghoul that was sticking his decaying hatchet face above the tractor hood, a worm squirming out of one of his nostrils.

The ghoul's forehead fractured under the impact of her bullet. Half of his skull fell away, revealing a bullet-chewed brain. The ghoul dropped out of sight.

"The cab engine is supposed to idle ten minutes after you start it," said Halverson, remembering what Cassavetes had told him.

"Are you kidding? Those things will be sitting in our laps in ten minutes," she said, squeezing off another burst at a ghoul trying to mount the hood.

She had a point, he decided. Maybe the tractor engine didn't need to warm up so long without having to tow the additional weight of the trailer anymore.

He depressed the clutch, put the tractor in gear, let up on the clutch, applied the accelerator, and pulled away from the uncoupled trailer, running over any ghouls in the way.

He hung a U-turn, drove into a ditch that bordered the road, and drove along it around the trailer, listening to dozens of ghoul bodies thud against the tractor grillwork as he ran over them. Driving the length of the trailer he was able to drive back onto the tarmac behind the trailer tailgate.

Marta raked any ghouls in the way with MP9 bursts out the shattered windshield.

"Did anyone ever tell you this is hopeless?" she said, her MP9 spitting out an arc of spent brass cartridges in the cab as she blasted ghouls. "Look at all those infected."

"It's called staying alive without a prayer."

When he reached the road, he kept running over ghouls that were milling on it.

"I'm gonna run out of bullets sooner or later," said Marta. "Sooner if those things don't thin out pretty soon."

"They're heading in the direction of the cave. Maybe they can smell burning human flesh coming from it."

"Do you really think we're gonna make it back to the bunker?"

"Do you really want to know?"

Halverson felt the tractor crush ghouls under its massive tires and heard bones crunching. The tractor felt like it was rolling over sandbags in the road as the vehicle rocked up and down over ghoul carcasses.

Halverson drove down the mountainside, which was studded with outcroppings.

"If we don't make it back to the bunker, would anybody give a damn?" said Marta.

"Not if they knew we don't have the vaccine."

"Then why do we even go back?"

"Where else do we have to go?"

Marta paused in thought. "Promise me one thing."

"OK," he said, facing her.

She stared into his eyes.

He slowed the tractor.

"If one of those things bites me, shoot me in the head before I turn," she said.

Designated killer, decided Halverson. His role in life foisted on him.

"Well?" she said, her eyes wide, concerned he might say no.

"OK," he said. "And do the same for me."

She nodded, her visage glum.

"We're gonna make it, though," he said, speeding up, smashing into ghouls and sending them flying in front of the tractor, driving like a wedge through them.

"Are you sure?"

"Sure."

They gazed with blank expressions out the shattered windshield. Ghouls pressed against each other in serried ranks, barely able to move because they were jammed so close together.

His and Marta's time on earth had probably run out, Halverson decided, but he wasn't going to give up. He would fight the infected flesh eaters to the bitter end.

Chapter 84

"The ghouls are slowing us down," said Halverson, as the tractor crushed ghouls under its wheels.

"Blow your air horn," said Marta. "Maybe it'll scare them out of the way."

"I doubt it. They're attracted to loud noises."

Halverson blew it anyway.

All of the ghouls within earshot looked attentive and made a beeline toward the tractor.

"Not the desired result," said Marta, watching them approach.

She emptied another magazine into the creatures assembled in front of them on the road, felling six of the noisome walking corpses.

A turkey vulture swooped down from the sky, tore a supine dead ghoul's stomach open with its red beak, bit the diseased entrails, and flew away with them uncoiling after it like the tail of a kite.

"I thought I'd seen everything," said Marta, watching the vulture fly away.

Halverson plowed forward with the tractor, crunching bodies and bouncing over them.

At last the hordes of ghouls began to thin out. As less ghouls converged in front of him, Halverson picked up speed and broke away from the slogging creatures.

"I can't believe they're gone," said Marta.

"Let's hope the road stays clear all the way to Mount Weather."

"Maybe we shouldn't go back. What's the point? We don't have the vaccine."

"I'm a CIA agent. I work for the president. I need to report to him."

"He's not gonna be happy."

The tractor CB radio barked to life, startling Halverson and Marta.

"This is the United States government," said the male voice. "Everyone is ordered to shelter in place. Watch the streets. Beware of people walking slowly or acting strangely. The zombie plague is everywhere. Stay home. Lock your doors. Do not invite your neighbors over. No one is safe."

"Is that the president?" said Marta.

Halverson shook his head no. "It's another militia. The militias are all claiming they're the government. They've hacked the airwaves."

"Shelter in place," said the voice. "You are ordered to stay in your homes until further notice. This is the United States government."

Halverson could discern movement in the distance. A knot of people in white hazmat uniforms were incinerating a stack of ghoul corpses with flame throwers. Other hazmat uniforms dragged ghoul corpses to a pile for future incineration.

"Who are they?" said Marta.

"They could be anyone," said Halverson. "There's a total breakdown in the government. People without authority are claiming it. Who's to say no to them? The real government is isolated in the Mount Weather bunker out of touch with the rest of the country."

"Should we join them?" said Marta, eying the hazmat uniforms wielding the flame throwers.

"I work for the president. We're going back to report to him."

"If the country continues to collapse, pretty soon there'll be civil war."

Halverson glanced at the tractor fuel gauge. "We're running low on fuel."

"Where are we gonna get gas around here?"

"We need diesel. Gas won't do us any good."

"Do we have enough to make it back to the bunker?"

"I don't know how much mileage this thing gets to a gallon. We might be able to make it without a refill. But I doubt it."

One of the hazmat uniforms had picked up on the tractor. He motioned for Halverson to stop.

"Now what?" said Marta.

"We're not stopping," said Halverson. "I don't know who those guys are."

The uniform aimed his flame thrower at the tractor.

Halverson floored the accelerator. He had a clear path on the stretch of road ahead, which was free of ghouls and derelict cars.

The uniform fired the flame thrower at him.

Marta fired her MP9 over the guy's head, not sure who he was. She emptied her magazine.

"We can't afford to waste bullets," said Halverson.

"They tried to kill us."

"Shoot to kill next time."

"They're not infected."

"If they're trying to kill us, we need to defend ourselves."

The unleashed flame fell short of the tractor by a few feet, scorching the grass that skirted the road.

"Do the idiots think we're infected?" said Marta.

"Who knows what anyone thinks anymore? Everyone's getting their information from different sources."

"Ghouls can't drive. Don't they even know that much?"

"It's not just about the ghouls versus us. It's us versus us."

"Then we have no chance. If the ghouls don't kill us, we'll kill each other."

"We need the president to unite the country. We have to tell him what's going on outside the bunker. He's too isolated to know."

Halverson sped the tractor down the road, willing it not to run out of fuel before they reached Mount Weather.

He could make out the bridge in the distance.

"We get past that bridge, we're almost there," he said, trying to sound optimistic.

The hazmat uniforms continued stacking dead ghouls to build a funeral pyre then ignited the infected bodies with their flame throwers. Six more hazmat uniforms stood beside a stake truck parked nearby and watched the fire. The mephitic odor of burning putrescent human flesh charged the air.

Chapter 85

The tractor barreled toward the bridge full tilt, Halverson at the wheel.

It was the same bridge they had so much difficulty crossing in the other direction when it had been blocked by abandoned motor vehicles, which the Beast's snowplow had shoved out of the way. This time they had a path through the cars. For a while anyway.

Halverson slammed the tractor brakes in the nick of time.

Someone had abandoned a metallic blue Fiat Abarth in the cleared path since Strider and his team had first crossed the bridge.

"Damn," said Halverson.

"Somebody else tried to cross after we did," said Marta.

"See if you can set the car in Neutral so we can push it out of the way. I don't see any ghouls around," said Halverson, scoping out the bridge. He checked the rearview mirror. "I don't see the uniforms following us."

Marta climbed out of the tractor onto the steel running board and hopped onto the tarmac, her MP9 in hand.

She tried to open the driver's-side door. It wouldn't give.

"The hell with it," she said, deciding to break in, knowing it would set off the car alarm and attract ghouls.

She pulled her short sleeve down over her elbow and smashed the driver's-side window with her elbow. The glass shattered, triggering the alarm. She flung open the door, sat in the driver's seat, put the shifter out of Park into Neutral, and released the emergency brake. She heard a noise behind her.

A seven-year-old girl in a white dress streaked with blood was standing on the backseat and staring at her with milky blue eyes, chewing on a human tongue, licking her lips. Her brother lay dead beside her with his throat ripped out and his mouth open minus its tongue and filled with blood. Marta knew the boy would rise soon as a ghoul, and she would have two ghouls to contend with.

The girl ghoul gulped down her brother's tongue and lunged at Marta's head. Marta jerked her head away. The ghoul reached forward and grabbed Marta's hair. Gritting her teeth Marta grabbed her hair and yanked it out of the ghoul's decrepit hand.

Her heartbeat racing, Marta scrambled out of the driver's seat and bolted back to the tractor. She gasped for breath in her seat.

"What happened?" said Halverson.

"A ghoul in the car attacked me."

"Did it bite you?"

"No."

"There's blood on your shirt," said Halverson, noticing a drop of blood on her shirt near her neck.

"It's not mine. It must be from the ghoul. It was feeding on a boy in the backseat."

Halverson inspected Marta's face and neck. He didn't see any cuts. He didn't want to have to kill her. He was going to be left alone in the world if he had to keep killing everyone. But he had to know the truth. Did the ghoul bite her?

He noticed a splotch of blood on her sleeve near her elbow, which was bleeding.

"What happened to your elbow?" he said.

Marta cut her eyes toward it. "I must've cut it when I broke open the window to get inside the car."

Halverson didn't know whether to believe her. If the infected girl had bitten her, Marta was now infected.

"Are you sure the ghoul didn't bite you?" he said.

"Positive," she said, trembling. "I would've felt it if it bit me. I'm not gonna turn. Don't get any ideas."

Why would she lie about it? he wondered. Unless she didn't want him to kill her. Could she be hoping against hope that even though the ghoul had bitten her, it hadn't infected her? When all is lost, hope is the only thing we're left with.

"I want to believe you," he said, searching her face.

"I'm telling you the truth. The ghoul didn't bite me," she said, not flinching from his gaze.

He didn't want to kill her. But the thought kept nagging at him—if she was infected, she would kill and eat him without a moment's hesitation. She had begged him earlier to kill her if a ghoul infected her. He had promised he would. He wasn't going to renege on his promise. He was sitting too close to her to use the bulky M2 with its long barrel. He would have to use his MP9. He didn't know if he could bring himself to do her. But if she was infected, he had to.

He scoped out the wound on her elbow again. The wound looked like a slash, not teeth marks, though it was difficult to tell thanks to the blood seeping out and covering it. He decided to believe her.

"OK," he said.

He drove the tractor into the Fiat Abarth, shoving it forward until the Fiat rear bumper got caught on another car parked on the bridge.

"Run over that car," said Marta. "And run over that ghoul inside it."

Halverson accelerated. The forty-inch diameter tractor tires drove onto the Fiat hood, crushing it and shattering the Fiat windshield. The tractor drove over the Fiat, leaving it a contorted, misshapen mass of steel, broken glass, and entombed cadavers.

The front tractor tires bounced and landed on the tarmac on the other side of the compressed Fiat followed by the back tires and kept going, the path clear to the opposite end of the bridge.

Three ghouls appeared at the farther sides of the derelict vehicles and made their way toward the tractor, groping with their arms.

Marta prepared to blast them with her MP9.

"Forget them," said Halverson. "They can't catch us. We have to watch our ammo."

"I hate those things," said Marta.

"We're gonna run into more of them when we reach the president. They've got the bunker surrounded."

"Waiting to tear us apart."

"They can tear my body apart, but never my spirit. I'll fight them to my dying breath."

Halverson accelerated.

Marta slumped in her seat with exhaustion.

"Too much stress," she said. "I need to rack out—even if I do have nightmares."

She shut her eyes and nodded off.

He didn't know how she could sleep with the wind constantly blowing in her face through the windshield broken by the rock catapulted from Wheelhouse's exploding cave earlier.

He glanced in the rearview mirror. He felt relieved not to see any hazmat uniforms in a stake truck driving after them.

He yawned. He could use some shuteye himself.

As he drove through the darkness, the wash of the tractor headlights shone on Cardinal Three, Joon-ho's Suburban that had been disabled by lightning.

Halverson pulled over. He had an idea.

Not seeing any ghouls in the area, he hopped down from the tractor and crossed the road to the Suburban. He tried to open the trunk. He was relieved to find Joon-ho hadn't bothered to lock it.

Halverson retrieved the two spare five-gallon fuel jerricans from the trunk and hauled them back to the tractor. He located the tractor fuel cap, unscrewed it, and poured the diesel from each jerrican into the fuel tank.

He heard a dry leaf crunch on the ground behind him. His pulse racing, he wheeled around and saw a bespectacled fortyish Asian ghoul wearing black trousers and a chambray shirt shambling toward him no more than three feet away.

Grabbing the MP9 hanging from his neck, Halverson slammed the gun butt into the ghoul's forehead, bashing the creature's skull. He didn't want to shoot the ghoul, knowing the sound of a gun report would alert other ghouls who might be in the vicinity.

The ghoul kept coming at him.

Halverson smashed his MP9 butt into the ghoul's skull again. He heard the skull crack, but the creature didn't drop dead. Halverson's blow must not have reached the ghoul's brain.

With all his might Halverson crashed the MP9 butt into the ghoul's forehead, pulverizing the skull and driving the stamped steel butt through the tough dura mater and into the tender brain tissue, rupturing it.

The ghoul crumpled.

Halverson sprang into the driver's seat. He didn't see any more ghouls in the darkness. Marta was sound asleep.

He drove ten miles. Overcome with exhaustion, he parked on the side of the road and fell asleep.

Chapter 86

When Halverson awoke, dawn was breaking. Marta was still asleep. He decided not to wake her.

He took State Route 601 to Bluemont, Virginia. He would reach Mount Weather in several hours, barring unforeseen circumstances, such as running out of fuel.

The wind was constantly blowing in his face through the shattered windshield.

The road was clear except for scattered derelict cars he had to circumvent.

The needle on the fuel gauge in the dash was bordering the red zone. He didn't know where he would be able to get diesel fuel around these parts if he ran out. The electricity at the surrounding gas stations had been knocked out by the EMP pulse that had hit the area after the self-annihilation of President Cole by nuke. The fuel pumps wouldn't work.

Halverson recognized the terrain. He was almost at the bunker. He spotted an odd ghoul now and then, but they were stragglers separated from the herd.

The tractor rolled over a pothole in the road, waking Marta.

She yawned. "I dreamed I was in a hurricane."

"Don't you ever dream about anything good?"

"Not anymore. When I'm awake, I'm in a nightmare. When I sleep, the only thing that changes is the nightmare." She took in the bosky surroundings of the Shenandoah Valley. "We're in the woods again. How's our fuel holding out?"

Halverson checked the fuel gauge. "The needle's in the red, but we're still going. We might have enough fuel in reserve to reach the bunker."

"I'll keep my fingers crossed. Pinch me if this nightmare ever ends."

"We should run into ghouls pretty soon. A lot of them. We need to be ready to fight."

"So what else is new? Every day a new battle."

She ejected her MP9 magazine, saw that it was empty, and slammed a fresh one into the receiver.

"You're getting good at that," said Halverson.

"Practice, practice, practice. I'm ready for bear." She paused. "Speaking of bear, I'm starving. Is there any way we could get something to eat?"

"I could go for a filet mignon right about now," said Halverson, wistfully.

They left the forest behind them and in the clearing saw thousands of ghouls milling. Beyond them Halverson could make out the Mount Weather bunker.

Halverson picked up on movement in the rearview mirror and checked it out.

Behind him a stake truck with white hazmat uniforms carrying flame throwers standing in it was trailing him.

"We got company," he said.

Marta saw he was looking at the rearview mirror. She turned around and spotted the stake truck approaching.

"Why have one problem when we can have two?" she said.

"How about a couple thousand standing in front of us?" said Halverson.

"How do we get past them? We don't have the snowplow like we had on our way out in the Suburbans."

"We got this," said Halverson, tapping the M2 at his side.

He hefted it up and trained it on the ghouls directly in front of the tractor and, driving into them, opened up on them, cutting them down like a scythe cutting bamboo stalks.

"Can you steady the steering wheel? I've only got two hands," he said.

Marta leaned over and latched onto the steering wheel.

They drove into the mob of voracious ghouls, mowing them down and crushing them under the tractor wheels.

He cut his wary eyes toward the rearview mirror, keeping track of the stake truck, which kept approaching. Wielding their flame throwers the hazmat uniforms laid down fire on the surrounding ghouls, torching them. The ghouls writhed in the flames, emitting ungodly screams, their blackening bodies trapped in the shimmering golden halo surrounding them.

As long as the uniforms were busy torching the ghouls, they would leave him and Marta alone, decided Halverson, concentrating on blasting the ghouls in front of him and running over them. He had to reach the bunker entrance the better part of a mile away. Marta kept steering toward it.

A thirtysomething ghoul in a dark blue firefighter uniform managed to clamber onto the hood of the tractor and inch toward Halverson. The ghoul was too close for Halverson to kill it with his M2. Marta let go of the steering wheel, snagged her MP9, and fired a burst into the firefighter's rotten face, riddling it with bullets. The firefighter opened his mouth, emitting a swarm of bluebottles. He slumped on the hood and lay motionless on his belly.

Marta waved the bluebottles away from her face and clutched the steering wheel again, as Halverson kept driving the tractor toward the bunker entrance.

It was slow going because they had to keep driving over clusters of ghoul corpses piled in the road ahead.

Five hundred yards behind the tractor, ghouls had swarmed around the stake truck, effectively blocking it from advancing on the road, while the hazmat uniforms continued incinerating the creatures with their flame throwers. Unlike the tractor's tires, the stake truck's weren't big enough to roll over the piles of corpses stacked on the tarmac in front of it. Ghoul stiffs got stuck in the wheel wells blocking the tires from turning.

Ghouls surrounding the stake truck burst into flames as the hazmat uniforms discharged their weapons at them, hosing them with streams of fire.

Halverson figured the uniforms had their hands full fighting the ghouls and would leave him and Marta alone for the time being, though he couldn't understand why they had tried to incinerate him in the first place.

"Who are those guys behind us?" said Marta.

"Some kind of shadow government?" said Halverson. "Who knows? There are so many militias fighting for control of the country, it's hard to tell who's who."

Clenching his teeth Halverson continued raining down bullets on the ghouls in front of him with the smoking hot M2 and stamping on the accelerator with his foot.

"We're almost there," he said with a clear view of the bunker entrance.

The tractor jerked to a stop.

Chapter 87

The tractor had run out of fuel.

"We'll have to walk the rest of the way," said Halverson, fixing to bail out of the driver's seat.

The ghouls shambled over their dead companions lying in front of them and moved in for the kill, growling in anticipation of fresh food.

Sweating, Halverson kicked open the tractor door and fired the M2 at the nearest ghouls.

Marta kicked open her door and unloaded on the ghouls with a long burst from her MP9.

Halverson and Marta met in front of the tractor.

Halverson cut a wide swath with a continuous burst from his M2, mowing down ghouls in front of them. He and Marta forged through the crumpled, stinking corpses to the bunker entrance, a cloud of flies floating over them.

"We can't do this much longer," he said. "My ammo belt's almost out. Let's step up the pace."

He and Marta walked faster toward the entrance, trampling the corpses that littered the road, taking care not to trip. If they tripped, ghouls would pounce on them.

"I'm out," said Marta.

She flung her empty MP9 at an approaching tall female redheaded ghoul in the face. Stunned, wearing a besmirched lime green pencil dress, the creature staggered around in a circle, disoriented.

Halverson scythed the M2 back and forth, clearing the way of attackers.

"There's a knife in my sock," he said.

Marta leaned over and whipped out the knife. She plunged it into the temple of a thirtyish male ghoul wearing jeans and a fluorescent aquamarine aloha shirt, impaling his brain. He collapsed at her feet.

Halverson reached the bunker entrance, wheeled around, and sprayed the nearest ghouls with bullets.

He made out the hazmat uniforms standing in the flatbed stake truck in the distance firing their flame throwers, torching ghouls.

He spun back toward the bunker door and pushed the code on the code pad.

The heavy bombproof steel door rose slowly.

Marta rolled under it into the bunker. Halverson emptied the M2 ammo belt into two ghouls and rolled after Marta.

Once inside, Halverson jumped to his feet, dropped the M2, bolted to the keypad for the door, and punched the button to shut the door. The door stopped rising and commenced lowering.

A rangy male ghoul pushing thirty rolled under the door into the bunker. Sporting three days' growth of stubble on his face, he was wearing mint green shorts and a mustard wife beater. He had a hairy back and hairy arms with green and navy blue tattoo sleeves. One of his forearms had bite marks in it where the ghoul that had infected and killed him had fed. His hairy face was half-eaten away by maggots, exposing broken teeth and blackened, rotting gums.

Lacking coordination he experienced difficulty getting to his feet.

Halverson kicked him in the head.

The ghoul reeled backward, unable to stand up.

Marta charged him and thrust her knife into the ghoul's temple, dispatching the creature. He sprawled on the floor.

The bunker steel door closed without admitting another ghoul inside.

Halverson looked around. "Where is everyone? Somebody should be guarding the door."

Marta yanked her knife out of the dead ghoul's temple and wiped his brains on his maggot-ridden face.

"Let's see the president," said Halverson, grabbing the MP9 that hung around his neck, unable to figure out why someone wasn't manning the bunker entrance.

"Were we poisoned by the radioactive air outside?"

"I'm hoping the radioactivity around here has died down since we left."

Marta coughed. "The air here smells worse than ever. How can anyone live in this place?"

"They continue to have a ventilation problem. You saw all the ghouls outside. They keep clogging the air ducts, cutting off oxygen to the bunker."

"I can't stay here much longer," said Marta, struggling to breathe, her face losing its color.

"Let's find out from the president what's going on."

Halverson led the way to the president's office.

"I hope he doesn't believe in shooting the messenger," said Marta.

Halverson knocked on the president's closed door.

Nobody answered.

Halverson looked around the hall and continued to see no one.

He knocked on the door again.

Nobody answered.

He tried the doorknob. It wasn't locked.

He opened the door and entered the office.

Taken aback, Halverson couldn't believe his eyes.

President Mims lay spread-eagled on his back on his desktop, his mouth agape, a square white cardboard sign two feet wide pinned to his blood-soaked chest with a knife buried to its hilt between his ribs into his heart. Scrawled in blood on the sign were the words:

The Purge Has Begun.

ABOUT THE AUTHOR

Award-winning author Bryan Cassiday writes thrillers and horror fiction. His postapocalyptic horror thriller *Horde (Zombie Apocalypse: The Chad Halverson Series Book 6)* won the Independent Press Award for Best Horror Novel 2022 and the American Fiction Award for Best Horror Novel 2021. He has won numerous other awards for his Scott Brody PI thrillers. He lives in Southern California.

www.ingramcontent.com/pod-product-compliance
Lightning Source LLC
Chambersburg PA
CBHW070659180626
46817CB00006B/2441